The Land of Four Seasons

Part 1 Innocence

D1501963

The Land of Four Seasons
By Sedric Horn and Amber Horn

This is book is a fictional account based on actual events. All names have been changed to protect the innocent. Places, businesses, and incidents are the product of the author's imagination or are used fictitiously.

Chapter 1 The Someday Ranch

They had just arrived in town. Jacklyn wanted to escape the intensities of living the Las Vegas fast life, and it seemed this quaint little town would provide that opportunity. It seemed an ideal place to raise children. A storybook setting nestled in a valley high atop the Sierra Nevada mountain range. A little-known place in California, a summit between the great central valley and the high deserts above Los Angeles. It was first settled by Native Americans, then ranchers moving west, and then later still by southerners in search of a promised land in the San Joaquin Valley. The southerners left the dust bowl of the South in search of greener pastures and promises of steady work, but instead they endured the grapes of wrath. There are many churches in this little town, of every Christian denomination, and it seems almost one on every street corner. In front of these little churches are signs proclaiming the word of God, a pointed finger

relying on guilt to beckon you in. The word of God is what they claim, but they are words that have been written by the hands of men. Sometimes words of encouragement are found upon these signs, but mostly it is a pointed finger warning of eternal damnation. It's a scapegoat philosophy by way of avoiding responsibility for our own actions. The only evil that truly exists in this world is the evil we perpetrate upon ourselves. There is no devil whispering in our ears.

It was an early spring morning in April of 1984. They came up the mountain pass, leaving the eastern shores of the desert behind them. The load-heavy Dodge truck was packed full of household furnishings. As they wound through the crevasses of the mountains and up into the clearing of the valley, they saw for the second time this sleepy little town. Along the eastern ridge of the valley, windmills stood as tall as trees and moved in synchronous motion. A beautiful sight in the early morning light. To the south were the tallest of all the mountains; they were green and covered in ponderosa pines. The surrounding mountains were sparsely covered in large golden

oaks. Through the center of town ran the railroad tracks of the old Southern Pacific rail lines. The train chugged its way up the mountainside early in the morning. Its whistle blew and echoed throughout the valley. A sound that softly entered your dreams, like the voice of an old friend nudging you up to start the day. Then the train raced down the mountainside, through the great loop, and off to the San Joaquin Valley.

They decided not to take the main roads through town, but instead decided to take Highline Road, which runs along the south rim of the valley. Over the rolling hills, they made their way until at last they came to Water Canyon Road. They turned onto Water Canyon and drove farther up the mountain until they came to a dirt road. Homes dotted the landscape, sitting on hillsides overlooking the valley below. The old western style is saturated in this place. It's a place that time forgot.

Up the oak-shaded road they drove until they came to the house that would become their home. It wasn't the largest house on the block and by no means the fanciest. It was a ranch-style single-family with three bedrooms. This meant the kids would

have to share rooms and bunk up together. The house needed some work. The front yard was overgrown, but with a little love this place could come to life. The house had a great view of the valley and tiny town below. All the stars at night shined brightly with a lucidity only seen in wide-open spaces, the Milky Way streaming prominently across the open sky like a river of cream running out into space. The truck came to a hissing halt, was put into park, and the ignition turned off.

"Unbuckle your seat belts, kids. We are finally home!" Jacky said excitedly. "Time to check out our new house!" The kids ran through the house like wild heathens. The boys went into one bedroom and the girls into the other, claiming official ownership of their new territory. The adults were in the living room, talking about how to situate the living room furnishings. Out the sliding glass door was the scent of pine, and oak-covered mountaintops could be seen. A bright-red barn with horses, pigs, and chickens grazed in fenced-in pens. The youngest boy, Michael, unlocked the slider and started to pull open the glass door when a voice shot out.

"You're not going anywhere until that truck is unloaded!" his stepfather said in an authoritative manner. "So, if you expect to go out and play, you better get started. And no horseplay, either, do you hear me?"

"Okay!" the kids said in sync. Although they had the sincerest intentions of adhering to their promise, they were kids, and within fifteen minutes the promise was forgotten. The boys were roughhousing within a few moments and the girls were bickering over how to decorate their room. Surprisingly nothing got broken as they unpacked and moved their lives into the empty house. The clouds were spraying a light mist over the valley as they unloaded the truck. The sun broke in and out of the cloud cover, casting a brilliant arc of colors across the eastern skies. The ground was covered in a patchwork of sunlight and shadows. The sun waxed and waned overhead. The rain-saturated clouds moved across the face of the higher elevations, caressing the titans with the wettest of kisses. The color displays in the air seemed a promise that a new life would now begin, a life away from the hustle and bustle of Las Vegas,

away from the fast lane of vices that come along with living in a place like Sin City. To Jacky it was not only an escape from the trappings of her personal choices in life, but a chance to raise her kids in an environment away from all those vices the fast lane was shackled to. To start all over again in a new place of hope. Of course, every decision holds an as-yet-unrealized future.

On the following morning the family awoke to the smell of a freshly cooked breakfast. Jacky had gotten up early to prepare what would be their first family meal in their new home, despite the fact that she had stayed up all night situating furniture and unpacking boxes. Everyone was in a happy state for the most part. It was as if they had finally made it and they were finally home. They sat there eating their breakfast among cardboard boxes and Styrofoam filling. The breakfast consisted of scrambled eggs, bacon, toast, and some orange juice to wash it down. The kids anxiously awaited the new frontier that beckoned them through the windows. Michael swallowed his food without really tasting it.

"Slow down. You're going to choke one day," his mother snapped. "Cut your food up into smaller bites. You don't want to choke like Mama Cass!" she said. He didn't know who Mama Cass was, but he knew he didn't want to end up like her. To a kid wanting to go out and play, cutting up food proportionately wasn't exactly on top of the agenda, but of course she was right, and he did what he was told. He grabbed up his dirty fork and empty plate. He grabbed the juice glass and slurped down the juicy pulp at the bottom. He was just about to depart the table when that all too familiar voice rang out.

"I didn't hear you ask to be excused from the table!" his stepfather said. The child sat there frozen like a deer caught in the headlights. "You need to sit down now!" Pete, his stepfather, commanded. The boy sat down slowly, afraid to make any wrong move.

"Can I be excused?" he said in a demur childish way.

"May you be excused? May you be excused, 'please'!" he corrected the child in a calm and all too controlled way. "I will have to think about it," he replied. He sat there for a few

minutes, which seemed to drag on for eons. Michael wondered when he would be able to get up and enjoy such an awesome day. Tick tock, tick tock…the clock went by, reminding Michael of every lost moment away from the outside world. After five minutes or so, his mother looked at her wristwatch, and then at her husband as he cut up his food and stared patiently into his plate.

Pete with a disgruntled look on his face looked at her, then at Michael, and said, "You can go out and play, but I want you to start minding your manners at the dinner table. I want you to wash off your plate and fork and rinse out your glass. Then you can go in there and make your bed." All the while he was pointing his fork at Michael like he was stabbing at a roasted pig.

Michael went through the checklist of obstacles holding him from the front door. He was finally outside in the great wide-open when he heard footsteps and his sister crying out, "Wait for me, wait for me!"

Dang! I wasn't quick enough, he thought to himself. "All right, I guess you can come," he said, slightly aggravated by the female presence on his first trip into this unexplored territory. They looked out into the expansive view of the whole valley around them. The rolling hills were beautiful and green from the April showers. The air was so pure and clean with a slight chill to it. There were dew drops upon the grass that caught the early morning light and glittered like diamonds along with the contours of the mountains. Wild orange California poppies and purple lupines bloomed in the fields. There were a few wispy clouds left over from the prior day's showers, but aside from that the sky was a perfect turquoise blue. They were children lost in wonder at the garden that lay at their feet; it was like heaven.

"Look, we have fruit trees!" she said as she bolted across the dirt driveway and into the little orchard. There was an assortment of apple, cherry, plum, apricot, and pear among the rows of trees. Although the pear tree never really produced any fully ripened fruit and the apples became infested with worms

before they ripened, the two cherry trees, as well as the plum and apricot, produced plenty of fruit. Unfortunately, it was still early spring, and nothing was ripened yet for eating. But the blossoms on the cherry and apple trees filled the air with a sweet aroma and held the promise of what was yet to come.

They walked the short distance that made up the small orchard. At the end was a fence that separated their property from the neighboring property. Beyond the fence was an enclosed chicken coop. They could hear voices of children, and around the corner of the coop appeared two boys. The older boy of the two was light-complected with cinnamon-brown hair. He had blue eyes and light brown freckles on his face. The younger boy was light complected as well but had hair of dark chocolate with matching brown eyes and matching dark freckles on his cheeks. The boys carried coffee cans full of chicken feed. The chickens knew full well what was in those cans and followed anxiously along the fence line. They waited for the boys to start throwing the feed into the open pens. As the feed rained down on them, the chickens scrambled around. They scratched and

pecked, bobbing their heads back and forth while eating the feed from off the ground.

"Hi!" Michael said with a smile and a wave of his hand. The boys looked up as if stunned, and with nervous anxiety raised their hands and softly said hello.

"I am Michelle, and this is my brother, Michael. We're twins!" Michelle interjected. "We just moved here yesterday from Las Vegas."

"My name is Raul, and this is my brother, Frankie," the older boy replied. A woman standing in front of the neighboring house called for the boys. She spoke in an unrecognizable language.

"Is that your mom calling you?" Michael asked.

"Yeah, we have to go and eat," the younger boy replied.

"Oh, okay," Michael said, slightly disappointed at having to say good-bye to their newfound friends. "If you're out later, maybe we can play?"

"Okay," the older boy said.

"That sounds like fun!" Michael responded. They said their good-byes and Michelle and Michael continued with the adventure of exploring their new surroundings.

Toward the end of the long driveway was a dilapidated old horse corral that Jacky and Pete had talked about fixing up and filling with horses, which in fact they would soon do. At the end of the driveway was the dirt road that connected the only three houses on the road. Frankie and Raul's house, Michael and Michelle's house, and then the house with the red barn at the end of the road. They followed the fence line as it descended the hill and passed the house with the red barn. At the bottom of this hill was a stream coming off the mountains, a stream that was fed from the winter's melt-off of snow. Frogs chirped, and tadpoles were swimming against the current of the small creek. Water spiders jetted across the surface of the stream as if they were dancing on ice. The sweet smell of rain and spring flowers was in the air. The kids were amazed at the beauty of this place. This new environment was bringing their senses alive in a way that living in the city could not.

"Look, there's holes in this rock," Michelle said. "My teacher told me that Indians mashed acorns in these holes and ate them." She sat on the granite slab under a large oak tree. Bore holes filled with rainwater, leaves, and debris were ground into the rock. "Wanna taste?" she asked as she waived the end of a stick full of debris in Michael's face.

"No thanks!" Michael said in disgust, pushing the stick away from himself. She was always trying to trick him into eating nasty things. Suddenly a fawn appeared from the bushes and started eating the grass in a clearing next to the creek.

"Gosh, these holes can get deep, and the bugs," she went on.

"Shush!" he said, cutting her off. "Look over there!" Her eyes shot up at the clearing. They both sat there as still and as quiet as they could, letting the animal graze in peace. Within a few minutes, the animal was joined by its adult family counterparts. The family of deer grazed there for a few more moments before a rustle in the bushes beyond the clearing broke the peace. Within a few leaps the deer were gone as quickly as

they'd come. Out into the clearing appeared a golden retriever, sniffing around at the scent the deer left behind. It paid no mind to the kids as it was caught up with the track of its prey. Within a few seconds, a girl appeared along aside the dog. She was a tall lanky girl with strawberry-blonde hair. She had two braids hanging off the side of her head. She reminded Michelle of Pippi Long stocking.

"Hi!" she said, loudly introducing herself. "Are you the people that just moved into the house up the hill?" she asked in a loud but friendly voice.

"Yeah, we just moved here from Las Vegas. I'm Michelle and this Michael. We're twins," Michelle responded in her usual outgoing manner.

"Wow! Las Vegas. I've never been there. I am Kimmy and I'm in the first grade!" she stated proudly.

"We're in first grade, too! But we haven't started school yet," Michelle said.

"Maybe we will have the same teacher. That would be cool!" Kimmy said.

"Yeah that would be cool, then we could all be friends," Michelle said in excitement. Michael was beginning to miss the boys from the orchard and started looking for the exit from the girls' club. He started to occupy himself with a stick and the silty mud along the banks of the creek. The girls got acquainted with each other while he slipped off his shoes and sock and rolled up his pant legs. He tried to catch the tadpoles that were swimming along the banks, but they seemed to keep slipping through his fingers. Next thing he knew, Kimmy and Michelle were bosom buddies, picking flowers in the clearing, and talking about whatever it is six-year-old girls talk about. Soon it was as if they had known each other for years. Kids can be that way, whereas adults cannot. Kids have not yet developed defenses. They have no guards to put up and no barriers to hold them back. Their world is wide-open. Before they knew it, the twins' mother's voice came charging down the hillside, calling them in for lunch.

"Shoot, we gotta go," Michelle said. Michael stood, up realizing the hunger their adventure was causing him. Michelle

suddenly gave him a triple shot of a glance. "Ohhhhh, Mom's going to be so mad at you!"

"Why?" he said defensively, not realizing the extent to which he had enjoyed his time on the muddy banks.

"Uh, because you're covered in mud," she said in disgust. He looked down at his mud-stained clothes.

"I don't care!" he said in bold defiance. "Let's go! I'm hungry!"

Michelle and Kimmy said good-bye and promised each other that they would meet up again later that afternoon. The twins made their way back up toward the house, Michelle in her clean dress with wildflowers in hand, Michael in his muddied overalls and new sneakers that were tied up and hanging around his neck. He wasn't exactly sure how he was going to explain this to his mother. Michelle went through the front door while Michael snuck around through the back. He ran into the bathroom and rinsed himself off. He took off all his muddy clothes and ran in his underwear into the bedroom.

Sonny lay on his bed with his headphones on, not paying any attention to the presence of his little brother. Mikey threw on some clean clothes and was in the dining room ready to eat in no time. As he sat down, Michelle kicked him under the table and muttered something as she pointed toward the kitchen. Jacky suddenly appeared from around the corner, carrying one plate in each hand. She looked at Michelle, catching the tail end of her little hand gestures.

"What was that?" she asked.

"Nothing!" Michelle said sweetly, then kicked Michael under the table for a second time.

"There you are!" Jacky said as she handed him the plate. "So, your sister said you met some friends today?" she asked, not really paying attention to Michael as she poured juice into their glasses.

"Yeah, the two boys next door, and Shelle met a girl that lives in the house with the red barn. And there's a creek over there by her house, too," he said excitedly. His mother suddenly stopped and looked at him with an inquisitive eye. "Weren't you

wearing your overalls when you left this morning?" she asked
with a puzzled look.

"Yeah, but I didn't like those," he answered with a
fumble and a lie.

"Oh, okay," she said, her eyebrows slightly furrowed.
His sister looked at him, then rolled her eyes. He sat there
looking down at his plate as he ate his bologna sandwich. He
hated bologna, but he didn't make a fuss at having to eat it. He
tried to avoid eye contact, hoping the thought would pass his
mother's mind. And within a few seconds she was on to
something else as he'd hoped. He gobbled up the sandwich and
chips and sucked down his juice.

"Are you in a hurry or something?" Jacky asked.

"Yeah, he's in a hurry, to go back to the creek!" Michelle
blurted out. He gave her a hard-cold stare.

"Well, there were a few things I wanted you to do before
you go back out, like unpack your clothes and put them away,"
Jacky said. He gave her a look of disappointment. "Well, I guess
it can wait until tomorrow," she said.

Woo, hoo! he thought. He was off the hook. Life was good. He finished off the meal, excused himself from the table, and rinsed off his dirty dishes. He threw on his flip-flops as he raced to the door. He turned the doorknob and winced as he heard his sister calling him.

"Wait for me, wait for me!" Michelle said in excitement from the dining room. He was about to walk out and close the door behind him when his mother called out.

"Now, Michael Thomas, you wait for your sister!" He knew by her using his middle name that she meant business. So, impatiently he waited for his sister on the front porch while she finished up her meal.

They made their way back down the long narrow driveway and toward the creek for a second time. This time he was ready for the creek. He had changed into shorts, a tank top, and his flip-flops. He didn't have to worry about getting his play clothes dirty.

As they walked past the orchard, a voice came called to them from the other side of the fence. It was Raul and Frankie. Michelle and Michael ran toward the chicken coop.

"Where are you going"? Raul asked.

"We are going to the creek. Wanna come?" Michael replied.

"Yeah!" Raul said. "Let me ask my mom!" The two boys ran to their house and returned quickly in shorts and sandals. All four kids raced toward the pool of water carved out by the creek. They were later joined by the tall, gangly girl who had introduced herself as Kimmy. They played into the early evening, muddy and wet from head to toe. Although the water was cold, they didn't let that stop them. They played until they could scarcely see one another in the twilight hours. Soon, with porch lights blazing, the adults beckoned them home. As the sun set, it seemed to seal their fate and the incredible adventures that they were about to have. In the beautiful nature around them, they would create their fondest memories of childhood and find a refuge in which to hide.

Chapter 2 Bright Lights, Big City

It was Las Vegas in the mid-1970s. Disco, cocaine, and bell bottoms were in, as flower power and tie-dye were on their way out. The Mob was coming into its height of power and Las Vegas was becoming a world-class destination. Driven by money, power, greed, and lust, the dusty valley of Las Vegas would flourish into a gaming metropolis. The promise of "All that Glitters" had money pouring into this once-sawdust town. The draw to this glitter gulch was like a magnetic vortex that was pulling people from all over the world and all walks of life. Drawing them in was the money that was running like a river through this town, and they were like moths drawn to a fire and burning into light. The lucky few were able to pull up in time to catch a little bit of gold, but most ended up a smoldering cinder on the other side. Las Vegas was an easy place to get caught up

in all that glitters, and yet seldom did it ever turn out to be gold.
It took a strong will to overcome all the vices that came with
living in this town. To do the hustling, and to avoid becoming
the hustled.

Jacklyn had moved here with her son and daughter, the
children she'd acquired through a failed and immature first
marriage. She was still very attractive and thin and came to
Vegas for the highly tipped service industry jobs. She made
incredible money as a cocktail waitress, enough money to pay
for her children, her apartment, and all the needed things that
come with living. She did this all on her own and still managed
to set a little extra money aside. She was no stranger to the
nightlife and soaked up the party atmosphere and the excitement
that Las Vegas had to offer.

Mike Biggs was a tall, attractive man with fair eyes and
light blond hair. He was recently discharged from the navy.
Having served a few tours in the South Pacific, he couldn't
imagine having to get back on another ship and set sail for
another six months to a year. He, like many men of the time, had

gotten up in the social revolt against the war effort. He had enlisted when he turned eighteen under pressure from his father, who had made a career out of the military. But he lacked the self-discipline that his father possessed. He had issues with figures of authority, and he despised anyone telling him what to do. After he had been given leave, he'd failed to report back for duty and was listed as going AWOL. He was let go through a dishonorable discharge, but his father, having some friends in high places, was able to get his discharge changed to an honorable discharge. His father not only did this to save his son embarrassment, but also to save himself the embarrassment. He didn't like where his son was headed, but now that he was an adult there really wasn't anything he could do about it.

The Biggs family had lived in Las Vegas for a while when Mike's father was stationed at Nellis air base, and later at the Nevada test site. Mike came back while on leave and it was a totally different town than what he remembered from his childhood. After he was free and clear of the military, he decided that that's where he wanted to return. He liked all the action, the

hustle and bustle of the place. All the money and all the beautiful women lured him back into this desert oasis.

He found a job working as a bouncer at a night club and that is where he met Jacky. He locked eyes with Jacky as soon as she walked into the club and he immediately made his presence known to her. Where she and her friends would dance, he would follow. She took notice of the tall and handsome man following her, but he was younger than the men she usually went for. After finally securing some confidence, he approached her.

"I guess I don't have to tell you that you are the most beautiful woman in the club tonight," he said to her. She stared at him for a second, looking over all the small details of his physique. Although she was very much attracted to him, she was a little cautious because she was a few years older than he was. She usually dated men who were older than herself because they were normally more confident, more mature, and secure in themselves.

"I've seen you in here before and I have been wanting to introduce myself for some time," he said. He looked her over,

his eyes moving up her long slender legs and then up to the rest of her beautiful body. As his eyes moved from her chest and fell onto her beautiful face, he knew he had to have her. She suddenly found herself caught in his gaze. She saw something in the blue of his eyes that stirred the woman inside of her. A quick flash, some connection to the future perhaps, or maybe it was the buzz from the Jack and Coke. She really didn't want to get caught up in somebody. She was in Vegas to work and focus on building a life for herself and her kids, but against her better judgement she decided to see where this would take her.

She stayed at the club that night until it closed and met with this strange beautiful young man whom she knew very little about. They sat at the bar as he lit up a menthol cigarette and inhaled the smoke with a sultry arrogance. It was a dirty habit he picked up in the Navy. "My name is Michael, Mike Biggs. My friends call me Biggs," he said proudly and without hesitation. She didn't know if he was another blowhard pretender like most of the men she'd met in Vegas or if his smile was genuine.

"And you would be…?" he asked her with a sly smile.

"My name is Jacklyn, but you can call me Jacky," she responded, drawn into his mesmerizing stare.

"Well, Jacklyn, you couldn't get any sexier than you are right now," he said.

"You haven't seen anything yet," she quipped as he melted in front of her.

"I may be young, but I'm wise beyond my years," he said as he raised his eyebrows at her.

"What exactly makes you think you'll get the opportunity to prove that to me?" she asked, trying to put him off.

"What if I just took the opportunity?" he said as he placed his hand behind her head and pressed his lips to hers, kissing her with an aggressive passion. They knew in that instant that there was something between them, something that neither one of them had ever felt before. In the moment a door opened and where it would lead neither of them knew. They laughed, drank, and talked as the late hours of the night escaped them and the early morning arrived.

"Oh shit! I have to get going! I have to get home and get my kids off to school!" she said.

"Kids!" he said, the words catching in his throat.

"Yeah, 'kids,' as in two! What? Can't handle that, playboy?" she said in defense.

"No, no! I love kids! What are their names?" he asked, stammering and trying to save face. "Sorry, I was just surprised; you don't look like you've had two kids."

"Flattery will get you nowhere, but nice comeback. This is Sonny, my son. He just turned seven. And this is my daughter, Faith, she will be three in a few months," she said, holding up her wallet proudly.

"It must be hard being a single working mom, trying to raise kids in this crazy town," he said, trying to sympathize.

"I'm just doing the best I can for my kids. So, are you going to walk me out to catch a cab before this carriage turns back into a pumpkin?" she asked.

They made their way toward the front of the casino, where the lights of the strip outshined the rising sun. He hailed a

taxi and watched as she pulled away. Lost in his thoughts and swept up in the moment he had forgotten to get her number.

I'll see her again, he thought as he looked out across the desert.

Jacky awoke to the racket of her alarm going off in her ears. It sent her head pounding to the beat of the little siren box. She lifted her head from her pillow. Her body felt the consequences of the late night she had had. "It was still worth it!" she whispered to herself. Thoughts of the man she had met the night before filled her mind.

She hit the alarm and made her way to the shower with a slight stumble. She turned on the water, making her shower hot and soothing. She washed the smell of perfume, cigarettes, and alcohol out of her hair and off her body. She stood there feeling the soothing nature of the warm water beating against her skin.

She was excited at the thoughts of the passionate kisses she had shared with her mystery man. Her heart was skeptical and leery of the prospect that meeting this person had brought

into her life. A part of her wanted to believe in love again, but another part of her was too tired to even want to think about it. *Men have let me down before in the past and why should this guy be any different*? she asked herself. But every time she blinked, there he was.

She got out of the shower and dried herself off. She put her wet hair up in a towel wrap and threw on her bathrobe. She walked into the kitchen and filled the coffee carafe with tap water. With a flip of the switch, the appliance came to life and began to hiss and a gurgle. She made her way to the refrigerator and started pulling eggs, milk, bacon, and orange juice out of the shelves. She put a pan on the stove and with a click, click, click fired up a circle of blue flames.

It was seven in the morning, and the noise coming from the kitchen awakened Faith, Jacky's young daughter. Her pouting sent her mother in to greet her and quiet her before she woke the neighbors sleeping behind the thinly insulated walls of the apartment.

"Shhh, be quiet," Jacky whispered in a soothing tone. She rapidly tried to cook breakfast and tend to the children at the same time. She saw Sonny standing in the doorway of his bedroom.

"Good morning, Sonny," she said with a smile. Sonny was seven and had attention deficit disorder or some such behavioral problem. She had taken him to many specialists, but they never seemed to give her a straight answer or offer up any solution to help her boy. Luckily, he was still waking up and hadn't stirred enough energy to start bouncing off the walls yet. He required a lot of Jacky's attention, and at times it was difficult and draining on her. She had to juggle two children, day care, school, and work, all the while paying the bills and rent by herself. Sometimes she felt stretched too thin, she would sit and quietly cry in her bedroom at night.

She wondered where she was going, wondered if she had made the right decisions. She sometimes wondered if she had enough strength to pull this single-mother thing off. She'd never been alone in ten years of her marriage, even though at the time

32

she'd felt more alone than she did right now. Her former husband wasn't much help to her during their marriage and hadn't been much help to her afterward, either. It was up to her alone to struggle to get things paid and to get things done. But when she looked at her kids and considered what she had accomplished so far, that normally was enough to get her up and out the door every day.

She got Sonny off to school just barely in time. He dragged his feet all the way there. She would get a phone call every day from the school about how he would be late to class, even though they lived right down the street from where he went to school. So, she had begun walking with him to the school and into his class.

She got dressed, cleaned up the mess from breakfast, took Faith over to the babysitters, and walked Sonny to school. She went home and tried to catch a few more hours of sleep. She then got up and got ready for her eight-hour shift slinging cocktails down on the strip. She started by blow-drying her hair in the fashion of Farrah Fawcett, which was the style of the time.

After blow-drying her feathered hair, she would then apply her makeup, carefully choosing her application of color. With experienced technique she would transform herself from a housewife to a smoldering sex goddess. Her cocktail uniform was skimpy and showed a lot of skin; the better she looked, the more money she made. What would gambling be without sexy girls walking around offering free cocktails to men as they bet their money away on table games? The sheer genius that was Las Vegas...

Jacky got to work and started her eight-hour song and dance. A couple twirls around the craps tables, glide through blackjack, and skirt the slots. They only gave a dollar at the slots, if she were lucky, but she might get a nickel at the tables. She walked passed Al, the shift security manager, who smiled with a smirk. "Hey, Jacky, how you are doing tonight?" he said excitedly.

"Hey, Al. How are you?" She smiled with a puzzled look on her face.

"I'm doing fantastic! Hey, I got a surprise for you!" he practically shouted.

"Oh yeah, what's that?" she asked with a sarcastic tone.

"Well, if you're not going to be nice, then I'm not going to give it to you!" he protested.

"All right, all right." She smiled. He reached down behind his countertop and pulled out a single long-stem rose in a fluted vase. Attached was a small white envelope.

"It arrived here about a half hour ago," the security guard said. She slowly opened the card with a slight anticipation beating in her heart. "To my Cinderella," it read, "thank you for the enchanted evening. Maybe we can cast one more spell. Will you see me tonight?" She smiled, slightly embarrassed that her romantic life had been exposed to the old security guard.

"Somebody's been burning the midnight oil!" he said, winking as she walked away. She walked down the long corridor that was the employee entrance into the belly of the casino and made her way to her locker.

How did he know where I worked? Did I tell him where I worked? she wondered.

She waltzed through her eight-hour shift in a dreamlike state as thoughts of Michael Biggs floated in and out of her head. She could feel the rhythm of her pulse quicken at the thought of another meeting with him, and her palms began to sweat a little. She made her last pass at the tables and was walking down the endless row of slot machines.

"Cocktails, cocktails," she said with a monotonous rhythm.

"Jack and Coke!" a voice shot out at her. A man turned in his slot chair with a startling jerk. She looked down and with a gasp stared dead into the eyes of her mystery man.

"Ha, I caught you!" he said, twirling her up in his arms as her empty cocktail tray fell to the ground. "So, what do you say? You want to cast a spell with me tonight?" he asked her, batting his pretty blue eyes at her, and smiling with a devilish grin.

"Um, all right, let me just call my babysitter and let her know that I will be home a little late. I'll meet you at the bar after I clock out," she said as she slowly slid his hand from around her waist, trying not to break eye contact with him. She didn't want her supervisor seeing her canoodling with one of the guests. She went to the locker room, changed, and called the babysitter.

They walked toward the front of the casino, where Biggs handed a ticket to the valet. The young kid raced off to retrieve the car. As they waited Biggs could not keep his eyes off her. Every time she glanced around, her eyes met his. Around the corner pulled up a white convertible Cadillac Eldorado.

Nice car for a bouncer! she thought. The car pulled up and Biggs immediately grabbed the passenger door for Jacky.

"After you," he said to her as he offered her his hand.

She sat down on the white leather upholstery. The top was down, and she looked up at the flashing lights over the canopy of the porte cochere in front of the casino.

So, this is what Vegas living is all about! she thought to herself. *I could get use to this!* Her companion sat down next to her in the driver's seat. The early summer air was sweet and soft to the touch. As they cruised down Las Vegas Boulevard, the glittering lights were sparkling in their eyes and the chemistry of attraction clouded their hearts with lust and passion. They drove out to the edge of town. A town that was burgeoning into a small city.

They drove up Charleston Boulevard, toward Red Rock State Park, through many miles of wide-open desert. Their hair was blowing in the wind as they held each other's hand. She was excited and scared to even be giving this guy a shot, but she thought, *What the hell! This is what starting over is all about.*

They made a turn, right or left she wasn't sure, onto a dirt road. She looked at him for a second before asking, "Where the hell are you taking me?"

"To the most romantic spot in all of Las Vegas," he replied, looking at her deeply.

"You're not some serial killer, are you?" she asked.

"No, you're perfectly safe with me? I would never hurt you." He said. They rounded up a curve in the road and came to a spot that had been flattened for the construction of new homes. All the lights of Vegas were shining below, and the stars were twinkling in the sky.

"Wow, you can see the whole town from up here!" she said in astonishment. He grabbed a paper bag from behind his seat and produced a bottle of champagne. He winked at her with a smile as he removed the metal cage from around the cork of the bottle. He pushed the cork up with his thumb and held the bottle over the side of the car. The cork shot off with a loud pop and flew across the desert, into the darkness. He opened the glove box and pulled out two champagne flutes wrapped in a clean towel. After he poured the two glasses, he raised his hand and proposed a toast to the future. They sipped their champagne, and he leaned in and planted a kiss on her lips. She opened her mouth to receive his kiss, tasting the fizz of the champagne upon his tongue.

"Would you like to dance?" he asked.

"What would you like to dance to?" she asked.

He pushed the play button on his eight-track player and a mixture of slow songs drifted into the open air. He got out and walked over to her side of the car, holding out his hand as he opened her door. They stood there dancing in the headlights of the Eldorado, dust flying through the beams of the headlights, streaming into the air and out into space. They danced in slow circles, kissing and running their hands over each other's bodies.

After a few songs they went back to the car. She lay next to him, looking out across the valley. The twinkling lights of the city superimposed against the twinkling stars made her feel as if she were dreaming. As she held him close, she shivered slightly.

"Are you cold?" he asked her. Before she could answer, he jumped out and came back from the trunk with a small blanket. They wrapped themselves in the blanket as they watched the sun come up. The sun rose as the darkness of night gave way to the colors of orange, pink, and purple that splashed upon the stark desert mountains. They drove back home early in

the morning. He dropped her off, and this time he got her number.

Jacky and Mike became close, and it was not long before they became lovers. She felt they were moving too fast, but she got caught up in the moment. Jacky began to suspect that Biggs was more than just a bouncer at a nightclub. He bought a house for them to live in together and moved her and her kids out of the apartment. They lived a decent life. He bought her nice jewelry and fine clothing from all the latest designers. He spoiled her in a way that she had never experienced. It was nightclub after nightclub, party after party. She didn't care for all the partying, but things were blissful, and they seemed happy together. She knew there was more going on than he was saying, and she knew that all the money he had been making wasn't coming from the him working as a bouncer. She wanted to know where all this extra money was coming from, but he would become very angry if she asked him about his work. As much as tried to tell herself

otherwise she knew what he was doing and where the money came from.

"Never mind all that! We have a roof over our heads, food on the table, and clothes on our back! What else do you need to know?" he'd said, not expecting her to answer. After a while she just tried to put it out of her mind. She stopped questioning where the extra money was coming in from. Everything seemed to be going well, and she figured she didn't want to stir things up. She knew he worked late and she knew he partied a lot. After a while she got tired of the partying, she got tired of the going out, and she got tired of the clubs, she just wanted to focus on being a family, but he wasn't there yet.

The drugs and the alcohol started to influence Biggs's mood and behavior. All the sleepless nights of club hopping, and entertainment began to wear on him. He became snappy and would go into unexplained fits of anger. She excused this and passed it off as him blowing off steam. She knew his job was stressful but for reasons he did not share with her. He had started

to spend more time away from the house than he spent there with her.

She was cooking dinner for the kids when Biggs walked in. He leaned into her, kissed her on the cheek, then stuffed his face in the refrigerator looking for cold water. He was acting out of sorts. He was acting agitated and on edge. She knew he was high again but didn't say anything.

"So where have you been. I been trying to get ahold of you?" she asked.

"What do you mean, where have I been? I've been fucking working," he screamed in a rapid way, spitting his words at her in automatic fire. His eyes were bugging and dilated, his pupils the size of pinheads. He could barely make eye contact with her. She looked at him in disgust, and he could read the reaction on her face.

"I thought you were going to try and not cuss around the kids anymore. I thought we were going to stop doing this shit and partying all the time!" she said, her voice getting slightly

louder with every syllable. "And you don't need to yell at me! I just asked a simple question!"

"I told you not to ask me about my business!" he shouted.

"What? So now doing shit is your business? What's your real fucking job? I mean where is all this extra money really coming from?" she finally shouted the questions that had been floating in her mind for quite some time. His blood started pumping and his pulse beat in his head. The massive amount of coke in his system sent his temper boiling over. He reached over and slapped her to the ground. The ladle she was holding flew out of her hand as tomato sauce sprayed red across the walls. Her body hit the tile floor with a thump and her head hit the floor with a crack. She saw white lights, then blackness.

He grabbed his keys and ran out the door. The white Eldorado spun its tires as it tore down the driveway. She lay there for a few seconds, blacked out. Slowly her eyes opened as she lifted her head off the tile floor. Her two kids stood next to her, wondering what was happening and crying. The side of her

head hurt where it had made contact with the hard tile, but it was nothing compared to the pain she felt as her eye swelled shut over the next few hours. She lay there on the couch, ice in a towel pressed against her eye socket. She reached over, grabbing the telephone. She dialed her dad's number, and after a few rings he picked up. He was delightedly surprised to hear from her.

"Hi, Dad. How are you?" she asked, trying not to sound out of sorts.

"I'm fine, and how are you? You don't sound so good!" he said.

"I'm okay. Um, would it be okay if I came and stayed with you for a few days? The kids and I?" she asked.

"Well, of course! Is everything all right, Jacky?" he asked in concern.

"Yes, everything is fine. Mike and I just got into a fight is all. We just need a break for a few days. I'll leave in the morning and should be there by the afternoon," Jacky said. Her dad lived in California, just outside of L.A. It was where Jacky grew up. Since her mother died, he was Jacky's only real refuge

left in the world. She didn't know exactly how she was going to explain the blackened eye to him. Jacky's father was a World War II veteran. He was very old-fashioned and didn't go for hitting women. She put the kids to sleep and packed their bags for the morning trek across the desert. *It would be nice to get out of town anyhow*, she thought to herself. She took a few painkillers and fell asleep.

When she woke up Biggs was not there, he hadn't come all night. The trip across the desert was long and painful. Her swollen eye still throbbed and made it difficult to drive. She kept having returning bouts of nausea. She tried the best she could to keep the swelling down but the purple bruise was unmistakable. She put some cover-up over it to try to conceal it, but it didn't help much. She stopped in Barstow to grab a bite to eat and to freshen up from the road. It was early evening when she got to her dad's house. She paused at the thought of explaining this hideous monster of an eye to him. Next thing she knew, he was standing on the front porch of the house with his hands at his

hips. He was an old southern boy with grass roots. He came out to greet her as the kids rushed up on him.

"Grandpa, Grandpa!" they squealed in excitement. He crouched down, so he could scoop them up into his arms.

"You kids are getting so big now. How old are you now? Forty?" he asked in his usual joking, lighthearted way.

"I'm eight," Sonny replied.

"Grampa, I'm only four," Faith said in a cute way. Jacky quickly ran to the back of the car, unloading the duffel bags from the trunk as she tried to avoid eye contact with her dad. She put on the largest pair of sunglasses she owned. He came around the other side. "What? Are you too old to give your dad a hug?" he paused and looked at her intently. "What the hell happened to your face? That son of bitch better not have—"

"Now, Dad!" she said, cutting him off. "It was an accident. He didn't mean to do it. Let me handle my own business," she said.

"Doesn't look like no fucking accident to me! I swear by god I'll kill that son of bitch. I'll kill him," he said, talking over her.

"It's over, Dad. Just drop it. I just want to relax. I am so tired. Okay?" she asked, looking at him with her one unbruised eye.

"I'll drop it for now, but don't think I'm going to forget it. I'm still your daddy. I may be getting old, but I still got enough fire in my belly to whip his ass," he said proudly as the kids snickered.

She unpacked her luggage in the kids' room as her dad prepared her a whiskey sour on the rocks. She sat in the dining room with her dad as the kids watched television in the living room. She told him only part of what had happened and only part of what had been going on. He accepted what she told him, even though he knew he wasn't getting the whole story. But he didn't press her for more.

She stayed up with her dad and chatted, letting the kids stay up a few hours past their normal bedtimes. She could see

pictures of her mother sitting on the mantel and hanging on the walls. She missed her mother and felt robbed of time and cheated by her death. They had found cancer in her spine and within a few months she was gone. They had no time to say good-bye, and no time to let go. It had been difficult for her father, and it had destroyed their family. Growing up with and witnessing the love that her parents had, had made Jacky want to find true love like that.

Jacky's generation was wild, rebellious, and unreliable. She left high school without graduating, a mistake she would always regret. It was 1965 when she met Sonny and Faith's father. Experimenting with everything from pot to LSD was the way that it was. Jacky was swept up in the social rebellion as most everyone was at the time. She was a true child of the flower power generation. Jacky gave her first marriage all that she could. But between Vietnam and all the changes society was going through, she couldn't make it work. Sonny Sr. was eventually drafted into the war. He did a few tours in Vietnam, but afterward he was not the same. The war had taken its toll. He

was not the same person when he came come. He became more distant from her and the kids. He became more despondent and he had eventually walked on out and didn't return.

When she awoke in the morning, she could feel that nausea again, only this time it was much worse. It woke her up early and she spent the first few hours of the morning hanging her head over the toilet. *I didn't have that much to drink!* she thought. But she knew it wasn't from drinking. She had felt this way before. Although she tried to tell herself different, in the back of her head she knew it was morning sickness.

When she felt somewhat better, she hopped into her car and drove to the local drugstore. When she returned home she sat on the toilet seat, waiting for the applicator to turn its designated color. Finally, there it was, blue and unmistakable. Absolutely "got to have a baby in the oven" blue. Her heart raced, and then she panicked.

Another child, another child! What perfect timing? she thought. *What am I going to do?* She looked in the mirror at the bruised reminder her man's rage left upon her face. *Well, here*

goes nothing! she thought. She walked into the living room and she picked up the receiver and dialed home. Biggs was asleep on the couch, his face sweating and stuck to the leather surface. The phone rang with a thunderous crash, collapsing in on his dreaming state. He peeled his cheek from the leather couch. His head rang in painful delirium. He had binged in excess, wrecked over feelings of guilt for what he had done, and for not being able to control himself. He rushed to the phone, hoping that it was her, hoping she might give him another chance.

"Hello!" His scratchy voice could barely muster the greeting. His heart raced as he braced for the barrage of words that he expected to assault his ears.

"Michael," she said, trying to stay calm. "What's going on with you? What's happening here?" she asked, her voice quickening its pace.

"I don't know!" he replied. "I've just been overworked and stressed, and—"

"And fucking high and drunk! Let's not forget that, Michael! Let's not leave that out!" she said as she began to cry.

"You said you would never hurt me. You promised you wouldn't do this. And now here I am, sitting in front of the mirror at my dad's house, staring at a black eye."

"I'm sorry. I don't know what to say. I was out of control and my temper just got the best of me," he said.

"You fucking hit me, Michael! You slapped me to the ground! I can't do this, and I won't. I've raised two children by myself, I can raise one more!" she blurted out.

"What are you talking about?" he asked as the air seemed to seep of out his lungs. His hands began to tremble.

"Yeah, Michael, I'm fucking pregnant. Your timing, as usual, is impeccable," she sneered. Mr. Biggs was, for what seemed like the first time in his life, completely lost for words.

"I…I…I'm so sorry. I didn't know! I promise if you come home this will not happen again," he pleaded with her. His voice was timid and terrified. "So, what are we going to do about this?"

"What do you mean, what are we going to do?" she asked him, unsure of what he meant.

"I mean how are we going to take care of this?"

"What are you saying here?" she asked.

"I mean, are you sure we are ready for this?" he asked.

"Are you asking me to have an abortion?" she asked, getting furious with him.

"No. I mean, I don't know! I just don't know if I'm ready for this!"

"Well, you better get ready because I'm not having an abortion!" she told him. "And this baby is coming whether you are ready for it or not!"

"Okay. Look, just come home and give me a chance to do the right thing!" he said.

"And what would that be Mike? What? What exactly would that be?"

"You know, marriage, do the family thing, settle down!" he said in desperation.

"What is that, some kind of proposal? Yeah, you have really fulfilled my childhood fantasies with that one, Biggs," she said. "You really are my fucking knight in shining armor!"

"Look, we can make this work. God, I feel like I'm shitting all over my self here. Why don't we just take a step back. I'm sorry I really am. I want to find a way to make this work." He said as he tried to calm her down. They stayed on the phone until finally he was able to persuade her that they needed to try to make it work. They now had a new life to think about and consider. A life that was part of both of them. A life that both of them knew would forever change the path of their future. The future that was once written had been wiped clean and a new slate started.

She stayed with her father for a few more days to let Mike stew for a while. Then she drove back through the Mojave Desert heading toward Las Vegas. She wondered if she was making the right choice. A part of her wanted to turn right back around, but she knew she couldn't do that. As angry and upset as she was, she still loved him. Purple and reddish peaks jutted from the desert floor. Little islands of green brush huddling around springs bubbling up from deep within the ground, life clinging to existence in the barren and stark landscape. She tried

not to think of the pain of her eye and in her heart as she drove,

but instead looked toward the future with hope and forgiveness.

Chapter 3 The Rise of Gemini

A few weeks went by and her morning sickness seemed to intensify. She had never had such extreme nausea and sickness in her previous pregnancies. She began to worry and decided to make an appointment with her doctor. He was a young, handsome physician by the name of Dr. Christiansen. She had gone to see him many times and didn't mind making an appointment with him anytime, for any minor ailment. He had kindness in his eyes and she felt relaxed in his presence. Her stomach had started to grow, and she had begun to show a lot sooner than she had with Sonny or Faith. She sat in the waiting room for the admitting nurse to call her in. After about twenty minutes or so, with clipboard in hand, the nurse called her name at the door. She was escorted into the examination room, where she waited for the doctor to come in. She was nervous as to how

he would react to the news of her pregnancy. He seemed to have an attraction to her and she didn't mind entertaining the fantasy of Mr. Doctor man sweeping her off her feet. Although that seemed a little far-fetched at this point.

"Good morning, Jacky. How are you feeling today?" he said with a bright smile of perfectly white teeth. She could tell by his nature that he was raised in an upper-class family, in an upper-class neighborhood. He was polite, well-spoken, and educated, the type of man that not only was she attracted to, but also the kind of man that intimidated her.

"I am good," she said as she drifted into his eyes.

"What can I help you with?" he asked, snapping her out of her little trance.

"Oh," she said. "Well, I have been feeling sickness in the morning, nausea, vomiting, head and body aches. I took a pregnancy test a few weeks back, so I think I am about six to eight weeks along." He took the flashlight out of his pocket and looked into her eyes. Her pupil dilated, and he could see broken

blood vessels in the whites of her eye and light yellowish bruised skin tissue around her temple and eye lids.

"What happened to your eye?" he asked her, taking the light away.

"I, uh, fell on some toys left on the stairs and smacked my head against the railing," she quickly said. He gave her a look of disbelief, having heard that story many times from many women over the years. "I have been experiencing severe morning sickness like I never had in my previous pregnancies, and I am beginning to show a lot quicker," she said, changing the subject. He told her to lean back after checking her breathing and heartbeat with his stethoscope. As she lay back, he felt her tummy, gently pressing his hand into her stomach. He noticed the firmness and roundness of her belly, signs that there was, indeed, something growing inside her.

"Well, you definitely seem to have all the signs. I will do a blood test to confirm your home results. You might be farther along than you think," he said. She looked at him. She tried to think back on when she'd last had her period. She left the

doctor's office with a bagful of prenatal vitamins and brochures on prenatal care.

As the weeks went by, her pregnancy ailments continued to worsen, and her stomach continued to get bigger. As her stomach seemed to grow, so, too, did the distance between her and Biggs. He seemed to try to occupy his time away from home, stating that he was just overly busy with work, that he was just trying to save money for when the baby would come. Soon talk of wedding bells and churches seemed a memory of the distant past, and Jacky was beginning to feel alone in her pregnancy. She was alone to take care of the pregnancy and she was alone to care for her two young children.

When she was a few months into her pregnancy she found herself in the waiting room alone reeling things over. She had begun to suspect that Biggs was starting to fall into old habits again. He was antsy all the time and somewhat paranoid. He would come in late at night, waking her up as he lay down next to her. He breathed deeply and slept restlessly, tossing back and forth, sweating profusely as he muttered nonsense in his

sleep. He normally wouldn't sleep but a few hours before stirring awake again. He always had large sums of cash on him, which he grudgingly gave to her. The days of jewelry and fine clothing were gone. She never knew what he was doing with the money, where it was coming from, or where it was going, and she dared not ask.

The nurse called her forward. She again made her way to an examination room, this time with a slight waddle to her walk. It was time for the ultrasound and a checkup. She felt extremely large and couldn't imagine another six months of pregnancy, at the rate at which she was growing. She felt like eating everything in sight, and her normal buck-twenty-five body frame was beginning to take on very large proportions. Dr. Christianson took one look at her and couldn't believe the difference in her. He welcomed her with a hug and his charismatic bright smile. She lay down on the table as he performed his medical examination once again.

"Today we will find out the sex of your baby," he said with a twinkle in his eye. "Any preferences?" he asked.

"Well, I already have a son and a daughter, so not really," she responded. A technician squirted cold jelly out of a tube and onto her stomach. With gloved hands, she spread the jelly onto her stomach, covering the entire center of her bulging belly. She rolled the ultrasound device around her belly. He looked to the screen and peered into the fuzzy gray static. The doctor let out a strange sigh.

"Hmmm...Well, it looks like the babies are doing fine!" he said in a sly manner.

"Babies!" she said. "What do you mean, 'babies'?" she asked, slightly frantic.

"Babies as in two?" the doctor said.

"As in two babies?" she repeated. "As in babies?"

"And if I'm not mistaken, I'd be safe to say a boy and a girl." Her head spun and reeled. Noticing her getting nauseous, he grabbed a paper basket for her to spill into.

She began to feel like things were growing beyond her control. She felt the news would drive Biggs further from her and that it would drive him further into a downward spiral. On

her drive home, she was caught up in the thought of how she was going to tell him. She couldn't judge how he would react these days and didn't trust him much since he'd laid his hands on her. As she pulled into the driveway, she saw that there were three or four cars parked in the carport next to the house. She entered the living room to find strange men standing in her living room. Her would-be husband sat on the couch. Tightly packed bricks, wrapped in black plastic, lay on the coffee table. One of the black bricks was cut upon. Razors and rolled-up dollar bills covered in powder were laid out on one of her sterling-silver holiday serving trays. A tray that had belonged to her mother. A small pile of cocaine sat in the corner of the trey with neatly cut lines waiting for a willing nostril. The men grabbed for their guns as she stumbled into this uncomfortable situation.

"What the hell is this?" she said to Biggs.

"It's all right. It's just my wife," he said in reassurance.

"First of all, I, am not your wife. And secondly, what the hell is going on in here?"

He grabbed her by the arm and dragged her into the bedroom.

"Don't ever fucking embarrass me in front of my business partners like that ever again, you hear me! Stay in here and be quiet until they leave, or I swear by god you will regret it!" His eyes popped, and his veins bulged as he got up in her face. He forced her to back up until she sat on the bed. "Do not move!" he said as he slammed the door shut.

About twenty or thirty minutes passed before she heard the cars pull out of the carport. She looked out the window as the four sedans pulled out of the driveway. She heard the bedroom door open behind her, and before she could turn around he was on her. He tossed her onto her back and slapped her back and forth across the face.

"You fucking want to embarrass me? You fucking want to embarrass me?" he screamed. He hit her, purposely avoiding her stomach. He struck her arms and legs, then struck her in the face a few more times before he let up on her.

She lay in bed crying, reeling in pain. Confusion clouded her mind. She wondered how she had gotten into this situation. She had become the poster child for domestic violence. A little bruised and battered, she stayed in bed for a few days. She only got out of bed to care for her kids, to feed them, and to get them off to school. Biggs was gone for most of the next few days, coming and going while avoiding contact with her. After about a week and a half of little to no contact, he sent her flowers and a card. An apology on the card claimed that he was sorry, that he was stressed from work, and that he was just doing this for them and the future of their family. She did not tell him about the twins for a few weeks. After some time and some major sucking up, he finally made it off her shit list. She told him that he would be a father twice over. He would not only be having a son, but a daughter as well. He made promises of change and renewed his talk of marriage once again. He promised he was going to get out of the business and get a more respectable job. He swore off drinking and drugs. But of course, she had heard it all before, and the more he talked, the more skeptical she became of him.

She grew big as a house. In her seventh month of pregnancy, she had to be hospitalized because she was breaking into hives. She arranged for Sonny and Faith to be care for while she stayed in the hospital. She knew Michael wasn't capable of caring for them. She couldn't get out of bed and needed a nurse's help to cleanse and care for herself. During her stay in the hospital, her pregnancy grew ever more difficult. She was given medications continuously to keep her from going into premature labor. The nursing staff would come in and check in on her, flipping her over to avoid her getting bedsores. After a month of medically prolonged labor, the doctors decided that it would be safe to deliver the twins, even though they were still a month premature.

Michelle was born with much labor but no complications. The pain from the first birth was excruciating as the anesthesia had not kicked in. At the start of the second delivery, Jacky asked for more medications and the medical team provided an epidural. She started going into labor with Michael a few minutes after Michelle was born. The doctors

realized Michael had turned in the birth canal and was in breech. Jacky's body suddenly went into shock. The pain medications and the epidural hit her simultaneously. Her heart gave out with a long bleep coming from the support systems attached to her body.

She suddenly felt as if she was floating near the ceiling looking down at herself. She couldn't feel the pain of her labor, or her body at all for that matter. She saw the doctors working over her as they tried to save and deliver her unborn child, while simultaneously trying to save her in the process. She then felt a sudden pull, something pulling her back down from the ceiling, and back into her body. She awoke later when Dr. Christiansen came in to check on her. A flood of memories from the delivery came back to her.

"What happened to me in there?" she said in a panic.

"Now, Jacky, you're all right," he told her. "You're okay. Everything is fine!"

"I died, didn't I, Chris? I saw it! I was floating, and I looked down and I could see myself on the delivery table! And

you, you were working over me, over my body!" she said as she looked him directly in the eyes.

"You had a difficult time but you're doing all right. The babies are fine, and you're fine. That's all that is important now," he said, trying to comfort her. She looked around but did not see Biggs. She knew he had not even bothered to show up for the birth of his children. Later she looked at her medical records. There in black and white she found where her she had flat lined and had to be revived. With all the small details, the records showed the complications of her pregnancy. It showed the turning of the male child, and the problems with the epidural and anesthesia. It showed how she had flatlined and lost consciousness. It showed that after a few moments they had been able to resuscitate her. She had confirmation that she had experienced what she thought she had. And that it was not a figment of her medically induced imagination.

Michelle was born at 3:58 p.m., Pacific Standard Time. She weighed five pounds and three ounces. She had blue eyes and dark blonde hair. Michael was born at 4:23 p.m. and

weighed three pounds and three ounces. He had no fingernails or eyebrows, and very little hair on his head. His premature weight made him susceptible to sickness, and he was kept in an incubation chamber until he was in the clear.

The babies quickly grew into toddlers, first crawling, then walking all over place. At night Jacky would lie awake and listen for the babies. Any cry or whimper and she would be up. She could hear Michelle sucking the air out of her bottle as its contents disappeared into her stomach. The empty bottle hit the floor as baby Michelle threw it over the side of the crib. Jacky heard as she crawled across the crib over to where Michael was sleeping, nursing away on his rubber nipple. With a popping noise, Michelle yanked the bottle from his mouth, and scurried back to the other side of the crib. Michael would start to wail like a siren in the night. Running into the nursery, Jacky would find the crime scene untouched and the perpetrator asleep in the corner of the crib with her stolen bottle of freshly pumped breast milk.

"You naughty little thing!" she'd say, as she picked up the empty bottle to refill it.

Biggs was trying to fly it straight. He got a job as a blackjack dealer on Fremont Street. This was a time before the strip was built up into mega-resorts, and downtown could still draw a strong crowd. He made decent money dealing cards, but nothing near what he had made working for himself. They soon began to realize that Jacky would have to go back to work to help support the family. She went back to cocktail serving and made a fair income. This, in addition to the tips Biggs made dealing cards, afforded them a comfortable life. They weren't getting rich, but all their needs were met. And things were peaceful between them.

Even though Biggs enjoyed his family life, his ego yearned for the streets and lusted for the money he made slinging dope on the side. It wasn't long before he succumbed to his ego and fell back into old habits. At first it started off as a way to make a little extra cash, but it soon became a larger and larger operation. At first, he wasn't using. He would try the

product just to make sure he was getting his money's worth. Then it became a weekend thing while he tinkered around in the garage. Soon after, he ended up right where he had left off before the twins were born. Biggs started getting restless and edgy again. He became impatient with the kids and with Jacky. She knew something was amiss, but fear and denial kept her from confronting him about it.

It was late one night as Jacky was sleeping. She could hear someone making noises downstairs like they were riffling through their belongings. She heard Biggs come stomping up the stairs and go into Sonny's room. He was almost a teenager now and had started to go through puberty. He had started to try to take pride in his appearance. He was at the age where he wanted to try to start to attract the attention of girls at school. *What now?* she thought as she got up. She heard screaming come from Sonny's room and she ran down the hall.

"Where the hell is my comb, you little son of a bitch!" Biggs yelled at the top of his voice as he pummeled the young boy with full force. "I know you stole it!"

The boy cowered in the corner, crying uncontrollably as Biggs continued hitting him repeatedly. Jacky sprang on Biggs, jumping onto his back, pulling his hair, and hitting him in the face.

"Get off my son!" she screamed. He grabbed her by the hair and threw her to the ground, then got on top of her and began punching her in the face as a man would punch another man. The twins woke up from the yelling and the screaming. They climbed down from their crib to see their father pounding on their mother like a boxer hitting a punching bag. The twins cried out as they saw the terrified look in their mother's eyes. Faith ran to the toddlers and swooped them up. She ran into the bathroom, locking herself, Sonny, and the twins inside. Jacky somehow got out from underneath Biggs. She ran outside the house, and down the sidewalk.

He grabbed a sawed-off dowel rod that he had sitting by the sliding glass door used to secure the door at night, and he tore off after her. She made it about a lot and half down the street when she could feel Biggs behind her. He grabbed her by

71

the hair and yanked her to the ground. He pulled her so hard that her legs flew out in front of her, and her body dropped to the ground like a sack of rice. He began wailing on her with the club. He took his fistful of her hair and began dragging her across the neighbor's front lawn, and back toward the house. Biggs was in such a state of alcohol and drug-induced rage that he didn't see the man come up behind him. Biggs suddenly felt a cold hard metal object hit him in the back of the head. He turned to realize that a man that lived a few houses down the street now had a loaded pistol pointed at the back of his head. "Let her go!" he demanded.

"What the fuck are you going to do, shoot me?" he asked in defiance. He heard the clicking of the trigger hammer being pulled back.

"Don't even try me!" the man said. "Now let her go! Now!"

Biggs let the wad of her hair go and Jacky hit the ground.

"Don't think I'm going to forget about this, buddy!" Biggs told the man.

"I won't be forgetting about this, either," the man said as he held up a badge. A police cruiser showed up within a few minutes, but Biggs convinced Jacky not to press charges. He once again got on his knees and groveled, he begged and pleaded with her. He had beaten her black and blue, nearly broke her wrist, and he was still able to convince her not to press charges. And the police stood back and shook their heads. They had saw this scenario hundreds of times over the course of the years. Things were different back then. The police didn't interfere with domestic affairs the way they do these days.

With promises of couples counseling and therapy, he begged and pleaded with her. She stayed with him not so much because she believed that he would change, but because the thought of being a single mother again with four children scared the hell out of her.

Although the abuse didn't stop, it happened with less frequency and less ferocity for a short time thereafter. From time to time, she would have to go to work with a slight black eye from when he'd slapped her, or small fingerprint-size bruises

where he'd grabbed her arm or legs. She would get looks and whispers when her bruises appeared, but as is often the case no one wanted to get involved and no body intervened. No one would step up and say anything to her about it. She went on pretending that it would eventually stop, and she went on pretending that there wasn't a problem. She didn't understand where the rage in him came from, but she knew that it was always there under the surface. And she knew that the drugs and alcohol only awoke the beast that lay dormant and sleeping within him. She suspected it came from his childhood, and she suspected that he was a victim of this abuse when he was a child. It had come full circle and that he was acting out the only thing he had ever known.

Chapter 4 The Fall of the Father Figure

Biggs was growing more and more impatient with life, with Jacklyn, with the kids, and with his job. Dealing cards wasn't pulling in the kind of cash he was used to. It never takes long for old habits to take hold again, and soon he was back to in the mix of it, running full steam. It wasn't long before he stopped dealing cards altogether. He had slipped down that hole again, secretly becoming more addicted to the drugs and alcohol, the money, and the power. It was a thirst he could not quench. He wanted out; he was too young to be a father. *That cunt probably planned it*, he thought. He stared at himself, half-naked, shaving in the bathroom mirror. Paranoia set in and it started to eat at his mind.

"They probably aren't even mine," he muttered to himself even though he knew otherwise. The drugs had changed him. It had destroyed the person he once was, the person he'd

once wanted to be, and changed him into something altogether different. The chemicals he was using had the power to turn a man back into a beast.

Jacky threw herself into work like she always did. That was her way of avoiding the issues in her life and escaping the problems she didn't want to deal with. Faith was too young to care for the twins but that was a responsibility that was placed upon. And she took up that responsibility and handled it well for such a young girl. This allowed Jacky to be available to pick up extra shifts at work, which in turn left Faith to pick up the twins from the sitter after school. She would cook for them, bathe them, and put them to bed. And after she put them to bed she would go into her room and finish her homework. She took on huge responsibilities at a young age and for the most part handled it all with grace. She had taken the place of a mother to the twins while Jacky poured herself into work. They'd shared a lot of good memories while living with Biggs, but now the bad outweighed the good. The darkness blotted out the light, and the more time that passed, the harder it was for them to remember

the good times they had had. Jacky couldn't remember the last she had laughed with Biggs, she couldn't remember the last time they had loved. She sometimes would look through photographs. She saw them all together with smiles on their faces. She saw Biggs holding the twins and she no longer recognized that man. She wondered if he had ever existed outside of her mind.

Faith put the twins in the bath, trying to keep the young toddlers quiet so as not to disturb Biggs. Every day she became more and more afraid of him. He seemed to get angrier, impatient, and violent as time passed by. One moment he would be nice to her; other times he would treat her as if she didn't belong there. He just started to become mean and cruel. They had to be exceptionally quiet while he was home. Most of the time, he was sleeping, and any slight noise would send him bursting out of his bedroom, face red, and screaming like a demon. Sonny became more withdrawn and spent most of his time in his bedroom trying to avoid Biggs at all costs.

Faith was sitting lost in her own thoughts when she heard Michelle start to wine and wail. Michael had taken the rubber

ducky she was playing with and started slamming it against his toy boat.

Biggs came flying into the bathroom, screaming, "Shut those fucking kids up! What the hell are they crying for?" His face was bright red.

"I-I-I think Mikey took Shelle's toy!" Faith stammered as she quietly tried to give the kids a bath.

"If you kids don't learn to be quiet it, you're going to regret it. Do you get me?" he shouted as he stared at them in coldly. He moved his gaze from Faith to Michelle, then to Michael. He made eye contact with the blue-eyed boy, who looked at him cockeyed and frustrated at the bath-time interruption. A chemical reaction welled up in Biggs. He once again lost his self-control. Biggs backhanded the little child, belting him across the face. Blood began spilling from the small boy's nose. The water turned red as the blood fell into the bath. The boy let out a silent cry as he was unable to catch his breath. His voice finally caught up with his pain, and in between gasps he began screaming. He let out a wailing cry that would have

deafened a choir of angels. Seeing the blood and terrorized by the curdling screams of her younger brother, Michelle began crying and soon matched her own pitch to her brother's cry. Faith immediately ran and grabbed towels off the bathroom rack, holding them to the boy's face. She applied ice and tried soaking up the blood, but nothing was working. She couldn't get Michael's nose to stop bleeding. She began to worry and panic set in.

As Jacky pulled into the driveway after getting off of work. She was tired, and her feet throbbed from eight hours of slinging cocktails all over the casino floor. She had just slid the key into the lock when she heard the crying. She quickly unbolted the door and rushed into the bathroom, where Faith was coddling Michael in her arms. Faith was crying in confusion, trying to get the bleeding to stop.

"What the hell happened?" Jacky yelled as she rushed to the toilet, where they were seated. "What the fuck's going on?" she said as she knelt beside them.

"He got angry and hit Mikey," Faith said, trying to explain what had happened. Jacky ran into the bedroom, where Biggs was lying in bed.

"Did you hit your son?" she screamed at him.

"Huh…what?" he said, waking back up. "It was an accident; I didn't mean to," Biggs said, shaking his head.

"Those kids need to learn to shut up while I'm trying sleep! Every night they're waking me up!" he said.

"What the fuck is wrong with you?" she screamed at him. "He's bleeding all over the place in there!"

"Mom, it's still bleeding!" Faith shouted from down the hall. Jacky ran toward the bathroom, leaving Biggs by himself. She grabbed ahold of Michael and took a closer look.

"Shit, he's going to have to see a doctor," she said. From the front of the house, she could hear the door slam and Biggs's car start up. "That figures," she said. She ran into the kitchen and dialed Dr. Christiansen's number. It was late, and his office was getting ready to close, but he agreed to wait for her. He could hear the distress and urgency in her voice. She directed Faith to

tilt Michael's head back and squeeze his nose as they made their way to the car.

Jacklyn could barely drive as her entire body was shaking in fear and anger. *How could he hit his own child?* she thought as her mind reeled over the events that had taken place. *He's just a baby! He is so fucking out of control. What happened to him? He used to be so different.* Her mind raced as thoughts filled her head. *No more broken promises of counseling, no more broken promises of a better future! No more black eyes! No more bruises!*

Dr. Christianson was waiting in the lobby when she pulled in front of his office. The young doctor tilted the child's head back and cleaned his nasal cavity.

"What happened to you, little fellow?" he asked as he shined a light up the boy's nose to see any obstruction.

"He fell down the front steps and smacked his face," Jacky said, nervously trying to cover for Biggs. The doctor looked at her in disbelief and shook his head.

"When is enough going to be enough, Jacky? What? Maybe when he accidently kills someone?" he implored her with reason, trying to get her to open up. "If this were anyone else, I would have already reported this!" he said to her in a stern voice. "By law I'm supposed to report this!"

"Please, Chris! I don't need any more problems right now! I'm taking care of it! I'm going to leave him!" she pleaded.

"Do you know how many women I have heard that same thing from over the years? How many times I've heard you say this say thing? I'm not trying to lecture you, but this has got to end!"

"I know. I know." she said solemnly. "It's over. I promise you, it's over. I just can't take this anymore." There was a long silence and unspoken tension in the air.

"You know that I care for you. You know I love your kids like they were my own. I've watched them grow and have been there when they have been sick. I was the one who brought them into this world," he said, trying to catch her eye. She sat on the chair, trying to avoid direct contact. She tried to avoid the

fact that her life was a mess and tried to avoid the honesty and sincerity with which he spoke.

"You know that you don't have to put up with this. You can leave anytime you want," he said to her as she finally looked up at him. "Not all men hit, Jacky. You deserve better than this. There are a lot of decent men out there who would be more than happy to have a woman like you in their lives," he said

"It's not that easy. I wish it was, but it just isn't." she tried to explain.

She felt attracted to him but had always felt insecure around him. She'd never felt she was good enough to attract a man like him. She felt that a man of his education and pedigree was out of her reach. He saw a radiantly beautiful woman with a kind and sincere personality. Someone who would stop to give to someone in need the clothes on her back and the cash in her purse. He, being a shy mid-westerner, had never pursued his attraction to Jacky. He felt nervous around her and the beauty she possessed.

"He would never let me leave, Chris. He would try to stop me. He would follow me wherever I went," she said, the desperation in her voice starting to grow. "He would probably kill me before he let me leave."

"Well, you can't continue to live this way! Eventually you are going to make a choice. Either it is going to be you and your kids, or it's going to be him. But you can't have it both ways," he said. She sat in silence, trying not to stir the conversation. She wasn't ready to confront the obvious aspects of her life that he had pointed out. Tears streamed down her face. He finished cleaning up the child's face, stuffing two tampons up his nose to stop the bleeding. Michelle and Faith started laughing at the silly look of the boy with the tampons sticking out of his face. "He looks like a walrus!" Faith said. The laughter eased the tension in the room.

The doctor took a pair of scissors and clipped the tampons short. Jacky thanked him for seeing Michael on such short notice. She gave him a hug and a kiss on the cheek.

"If you ever need anything, I'm always here for you," he told her.

It was late as she pulled in the driveway. She noticed Biggs's car was nowhere to be seen. She sighed in relief that the night might be peaceful without his presence and hoped that he wouldn't be returning anytime soon. She fell asleep with thoughts of what had happened, and the thoughts of what Chris had said to her, churning in her mind. She started thinking of a way out; she now started planning on how she would leave Biggs. She dreamed of escape that night.

She dreamed of being free from him and the painful chaos their lives had become. She began to work heavily to save up money, which she hid from Biggs. Money, she planned to use to make her move and leave him. She would be gone all day and would creep in at night, trying to avoid any contact with him. She was afraid to leave him with the kids, but that was the only way she could make the money she would need to leave him and start over.

One evening not long after, Faith walked out into the living room after she had put the twins to sleep. She cleaned up the mess the twins had created, putting away their toys and crayons. It was late, and she heard the key turn in the door; her eyes shot across the room to the clock. *She's finally home! It's only twelve thirty at night!* she thought. Faith immediately caught the strong stench of liquor. Her mother was drunk as she came stumbling in from behind the door. She was followed by a tall dark man in a large cowboy hat.

Faith had become more bitter every day over having to assume more and more responsibility for the care of the twins. She was tired of changing diapers and filling bottles while the rest of her friends got to go out and play. She was tired of cooking for the twins, bathing the twins, and putting them to bed. She was tired of staying up late to finish her homework. Biggs was hardly ever home, and Jacky knew he would probably be gone that night. Jacky hugged Faith and the smell of liquor was almost too strong for Faith.

"You smell funny, Mom," Faith said, irritated that her mother had come home drunk. "And you're acting funny!"

"I want you to meet someone," Jacky said, ignoring her daughter's comment. "This is Pete; Pete, this is my daughter Faith," she said with a smile. Faith looked at the tall man in the large cowboy hat. He had a long dark beard that was bushy and hid his face from plain sight. Faith looked at him uneasily and with a sense of precaution.

"Howdy!" he said as he bent down to shake her little hand. "Glad to meet you," he said with a slurred tongue. He smelled of liquor just as her mother did. *What is she doing? Biggs could walk through the door at any moment, and he will kill them if he finds this guy in his house!* Faith thought.

"Go wake up the twins and Sonny. I want them to meet their new dad," said Jacky.

Our new dad? Faith thought. *What does she mean by that?* It seemed a little soon to be calling this guy "dad." She didn't even call Biggs dad.

"Go on now," Jacky commanded. Faith did as she was told with a little reluctance. As she brought the twins into the den, she found Jacky and Pete were sitting on the carpet in the middle of the room kissing. Sonny walked in behind them, rubbing his eyes.

"Come and sit down. I have something I want to tell you," Jacky said. "This is Pete. We are going to be moving in with him soon."

Michelle looked at the man whom her mother was appointing to take over in her father's place. Even though she was a young child, she felt uneasy and distrusted the bearded man with the cowboy hat. Even though he was nice to her and smiled at her, there was something she did not like about this man. She wouldn't give him the time of day. Michael just sat there poking his belly button, not paying attention to what was going on. He was still lost between the waking and sleeping worlds. The night ended with Jacky kissing the stranger good-bye at the front door. She went to bed with high hopes that this was the man of her prayers and that he would come and save her

from her disastrous relationship with Biggs. That he would be able to sweep her away from all her problems and that she finally might find her happily ever after. She kept her affair with the man discreet and moved with extreme caution.

A couple of weeks had gone by since the encounter in the middle of the night with the strange man in the cowboy hat. The negative energy in the house had continued to grow. Jacky already had one foot out the door and was making plans on leaving. Faith had a feeling her mother was up to something; she just didn't know what. All she knew was the cowboy had something to do with it. And Faith and Sonny didn't speak a word of it. They were happy to be leaving that broken home. Living with Biggs was like walking on pins and needles, and if he were ever to find out what their mother was up to, he would go ballistic. Jacky feared that one day he would lose control and that he might one day accidently kill one of them. He was irate most of the time, and she was never sure what type of mood he would come home in.

She had a plan to get away from Biggs. After saving up a little money from her tips at work, she rented a small apartment on the west side of Vegas. She had talked to a coworker of hers and arranged to borrow his truck for a night. She was ready to move out of the house on Bearden Drive for good. She decided to call the police department and explain to them the situation that she was in with Biggs. She asked them to escort her while she moved her children and her belongings out of the house.

Her heart ached for the twins. Despite how erratic he behaved most of the time, the twins loved their father, and he loved them. But he was falling apart due to the drugs and alcohol. He chose that life over her and over his family. He was like a runaway train waiting to collide with life, and Jacky knew that his choices would catch up to him one day. But she could no longer allow his decisions to continue to impact her life or the lives of her kids. She could no longer be dragged along with him on his path of self-destruction. He was a sinking stone. What she knew was that this man in the cowboy hat promised her a good life. A life away from all the violence, drugs, and chaos she had

known with Biggs. What she saw in him was not the potential of true love, but her only way out.

As the time drew near to the day she had set to put this plan into action, she was constantly looking over her shoulder. She was scared about being caught. She was careful not to draw too much attention to herself. She knew that if Biggs were to catch on to her plan he would stop her. She packed a suitcase of clothes for herself and the kids, preparing for the night that she would make her escape.

She was nervous when the night finally came. She arranged for the truck she'd borrowed to be parked inside the garage at the casino. She left there after work and headed to the police station. Her body was trembling, and her heart was beating out of control as she made her way to the police station.

Come on Jacky, you can do this, you have to stay strong! Pull yourself together! she told herself as tears welled up in her eyes. She felt as if she were caught up in whirlwind of energy that she couldn't control. She turned the headlights off and quietly parked the truck in front of the police station. She spilled

her guts to them and told them of her living nightmare and they agreed to help her. They escorted her to the home on Bearden Drive while she removed her kids and belongings. Biggs wouldn't be home for hours, which gave her time to grab the kids and anything else she could fit in the truck. She could get the kids and their clothes and be out of there hours before he would get home.

She pulled up to the house as her police escorts followed closely behind. She looked up the driveway and didn't see Biggs's car. This put her at ease, and she felt more relaxed. The shaking of her hands eased a little. She jumped out of the car and told the waiting officers that she would grab the kids and her clothes, and that she would be out in fifteen minutes. She ran toward the front door; she could barely get the key into the lock as her hands began shaking again. The lock turned, and she entered.

The house was pitch-black, and she couldn't see anything as she walked through the threshold. She closed the door behind her.

"You think you can take my kids away from me, you fucking cunt bitch," Biggs's voice came quietly in the darkness. A hand seemed to come out of thin air and pull her down onto his lap. She gasped as the air in her lungs escaped. In the darkness seated in the corner near the front door, he had been waiting for her. He held her close and tight as she squirmed in shock.

"If you think you can just leave with that fucking loser, you're wrong." His voice still in a quiet near whisper. "What do you think, he's going to raise my children, fuck my woman, and that I'm just going to sit by like a chump and let it fucking happen?" His temper began to rise. Jacky squirmed as she tried to get away from his tight grip on her. He raised his other hand and she could feel the cold metal of a revolver pressed against the side of her head. "Don't fucking even try it, bitch!" he told her.

"Michael, there are two police officers waiting for me outside. They will come in to find me if you don't let me go,"

she said, trying to reason with the drug-crazed monster he had become.

"You think I don't fucking know they're out there? Those fucking pigs! You think I didn't know what you were up to? That I wouldn't find out, you conniving little cunt?" His hot sticky breath was against her neck. The clammy stench of air that came from his mouth was making her nauseous. It was the kind of breath that only a chemical addict possesses. It was as if the chemical had started to rot him from the inside out.

It seemed like an eternity, sitting there held hostage against her will. Her clothes were starting to stick to her skin. Her ass was numb from being forced to sit on his lap. He sweated profusely, his body reeked like onion and ammonia. The recliner in which they sat became warm and moist from the contact with their bodies. He peaked through the blinds of the window next to where they sat. He could see the two police cruisers sitting curbside in the street.

"So, what? Are you going to kill me, Michael? Is that what you're planning on doing?" she asked. "Is this how it's

going to end?" she wasn't sure how long she had been sitting there, but she was sure that it had to be past the fifteen minutes she had told the officers. In fact, it was over a half an hour before the officers got suspicious of Jacky's whereabouts. The two officers got out of the police cruiser and approached the front door of the Bearden Drive residence.

"Jacklyn, this is Officer Petty. Are you okay in there?" the officer asked through the closed heavy wooden door. He rapped on the door with his heavy mag light. Biggs grabbed Jacky's face, cupping his hand over her mouth.

"Don't you say a fucking word!" he whispered as he could hear the officers standing just on the other side of the door. The officers continued rapping on the door with no response. "Tell them you're okay and that you will be out in a minute!" he commanded her to say. She did as she was told, but the officers were not convinced, and were not buying it.

"Well, can we come in, so that we know you are all right?" the officer replied through the door.

"I'm almost done. I will be out in a moment," she said as prompted by Biggs.

"Sounds like she is just on the other side of the door," Officer Thompson said to Officer Petty.

"Yeah, I think you're right!" Petty replied. Officer Thompson retreated to the cruiser to report the incident to dispatch and to request an additional cruiser out to the location. Officer Petty remained at the door, trying to convince Jacky to open the door. He could hear stress in her voice, and knew she wasn't alone with the children. Within a few minutes, two more cruisers came to the residence, their red and blue lights flashing through the front window of the living room where Biggs and Jacky were sitting. It had started to sprinkle and soon it became a steady drizzle. The rain was a rare occurrence in the dry desert and made the night all the more ominous.

"Look outside, Biggs, we are starting to attract the attention of the neighborhood!" she said. He didn't say a word. He looked delirious.

"Michael Biggs, if you're in there you need to let her go!" shouted Officer Petty. No response. "If you're in there, Biggs, you need to let her go and come out with your arms up!" the officer repeated. Still no response. By this time the neighborhood had been closed off. There were five police cars and about ten officers surrounding the front of the house. "This is the last time I am going to repeat this! You either let her go and come out with your arms up, or we will come in there and get you!" With no response the police busted open the heavy oak front door using a battering ram. As the door broke through its locks, another loud bang came from the rear of the house.

They had busted in with guns drawn and came into the house from three entrances. They zeroed in on Biggs as he held Jacky, the gun to her head, on the recliner behind the front door. They officers locked in a battle of wills with Biggs. After some coaxing and reasoning, they were able to convince him to drop the gun and let her go. As soon as he dropped the revolver to the floor, Jacky sprang up off his lap and the officers rushed in on him. They dragged him to the ground, quickly overcoming him,

and placed him under arrest. Jacky cried out, tears streaming down her face.

"Where are my kids?" she screamed.

She ran into the back bedroom where the beds were empty. She opened the closet. Sitting in the dark, the faces of Sonny, Faith, Michael, and Michelle stared back at her. She put her arms around her children, sobbing.

"It's all over now, she cried. It's finally over."

Jacky put the kids in the truck and went back into the house to grab their necessities. Michael and Michelle sat in the truck looking out the back window as a police officer escorted their handcuffed father and put him into one of the awaiting cruisers. Biggs, face streaked with tears and eyes full of regret, looked at his two young children looking back at him.

Maybe he didn't realize the effects his behavior had on the people around him. Any joy or happiness that they might have experienced together as a family would forever be overshadowed by the poor choices he had made and would ultimately be forgotten and lost to time. Red and blue lights

brightly flashed onto the walls of the Bearden Drive home. Rain vividly streaked down the windows of the truck in which they sat. Although the twins could not understand the magnitude of what was happening, they could feel the fear and the stress in the air. It was like some kind of nightmare they could not wake up from. They sat in their pajamas as they waited and watched as the only life they knew shattered like glass all around them. It was a night that would be forever burned into their minds. This was their last memory of the only family they had known, a family where their father was an everyday part of their lives, albeit an unstable part. It was a memory that would haunt their dreams. Jacky made the decision to leave Biggs in the past and with that decision an uncertain future had arrived.

Chapter 5 The Dark Stranger

It was late morning as the twins sat in front of the apartment

complex, waiting for their mother to get ready. They were going

to spend the weekend with their father. It was their third visit

with him since Jacky had left him. She was hesitant at first about

allowing Biggs to see the kids unsupervised, but in the months

that had passed he seemed to be really trying to make an effort to

change. He had even applied for and been accepted to join the

police academy.

A group of older boys rode past on bicycles and

skateboards, teasing the twins as they passed by, and taunting

their young ears with derogatory terms and foul language. The

young toddlers stared at them, seemingly unfazed by their

teasing. The complex bordered with another adjacent apartment

complex, a Lucky's shopping center, and an undeveloped plot of

land. The desert lot was scattered with windblown debris and trash dumped off by Las Vegans too lazy to dispose of it properly. Plastic grocery bags were tethered to chaparral bushes and blew in the wind. The leader of the pack of boys was a one-legged kid named Dennis. He would pedal around town on his skateboard, sitting on the stub of right leg, his right hand resting on the front of his skate deck. With his left hand and left leg, he pushed himself along the sidewalks. It was known to the neighborhood kids that this was their turf and that these boys were in charge of this neighborhood. Or so they thought.

There was a rumor among the neighborhood kids that Dennis's stepfather was a raging alcoholic and that he would periodically beat on Dennis and his siblings. One day, as punishment for messing with his tools, he took an ax to Dennis's leg and cut it off just above the cap of his knee. From that day forward, he was known as the three-legged kid. How true this rumor was only one can guess. It was probably a story invented by the overactive imaginations of the neighborhood kids.

After the pack of boys rode by, the twins, feeling it safe, walked over to the desert lot to play while they waited. Lying in the desert sand, broken pieces of colorful plastic were strewn about. Pieces of red, yellow, and blue lay scattered across the ground. Michelle bent forward, pulling on what seemed to be strands of blonde hair sticking from the dirt. She pulled until the object was released from the grip of the earth. It was the head of a doll with a face that seemed familiar to the little girl.

As Michelle rubbed the caked-on dirt from the doll's face, she realized that the head belonged to that of her favorite Barbie doll. With panic-stricken eyes, she searched around the ground, looking for the body of her decapitated toy. Small pieces of flesh-colored plastic, and two rubber legs sticking from the sand, was all that she could find. Michael and Michelle realized somebody had gotten into their toy chest, which sat on the porch of their apartment. They had taken them out to the desert lot and smashed them up. She didn't cry as her face turned beet red.

With the head of her blonde Barbie doll in hand, she raced to the apartment to tell her mother of the crime scene she

had found in the desert. Michael followed shortly behind her. She ran into the master bedroom, where Jacky was getting ready for work. Pete, her new husband, hadn't been able to find a job and sat in the living room watching a small black-and- white television. They had quickly eloped shortly after she had moved out of the house on Bearden drive. They got married at a little chapel that dotted the Las Vegas strip. A chapel that specialized in fly by night weddings.

"Mommy!" she screamed as Jacky's hair dryer was going full blast. "Mommy!" she said again, this time tugging on her mother's cocktail skirt. Jacky flipped off the hair dryer.

"What do you kids want? You know I am trying to get ready for work!" she said, irritated.

"Somebody stole our toys. They broke them into little pieces. Look what they did to Barbie!" Michelle said as she held up the dirty head of her decapitated doll. Jacky didn't remove her gaze from the mirror as she put on her lipstick and fluffed up her hair to give it more body.

"Mom, look!" Michelle said, still holding up the rubber head.

"Well, I told you kids not to leave your toys in the front yard. There is a lot of kids in the complex who like to steal," she said as she continued to apply her makeup. "If you took better care of your stuff, this sort of thing wouldn't happen," she tried to reason.

"I think it was the three-legged kid, he's always teasing us, Mom!" Michelle said, hoping that her mother would go out there and do something about it.

"Well, after what you and Michael did to your sister's baton and her records, you probably deserved it! Now go into the living room. I am almost ready! We have to meet your father in twenty minutes!"

Michelle suddenly had a flashback of Faiths brand-new baton and her collection of black vinyl records. In her head she could see Michael smashing the black records on the rim of the toilet as she tried to flush the pieces down. Soon another memory entered into her young mind. It was of her walking

along a low-lying cinder block wall with a shiny new baton in hand. The metal baton was capped off with pink rubber ends, and pink and white tassels streamed out of the rubber caps. She had gotten frustrated that she couldn't twirl it around like her older sister. As she walked along the cinder blocks, she hit the baton along the corners of the block wall, putting dents, divots, and scratches into it.

Faith was angry when she got home from school only to find her baton beat up and her records missing. The twins were always getting into something. If mischief could be found, then they were in the mix of it. Michelle felt defeated as she made her way into the living room where Michael was seated. She wondered why her mother hadn't gone out there and done something to right the toy situation.

Pete sat across from them on the other couch. He watched them for a few moments, staring at the toddlers. He stared at Michelle's flower print dress and her little shiny shoes. He put his eyes on Michael and his little overalls. He watched

them for a moment, then turned back to the television, and took a sip of beer.

"Why don't you kids wait outside until your mother is done? Go play, or something!" he told them. They did as he said and went back out to wait for their mother.

A little while later, they sat in front of the 7-Eleven as they waited for their father to arrive. "Don't be going and telling your father where we are living now, or you'll be in trouble!" Jacky said to them. "I don't want him knowing where we are living."

"Okay!" they said. She figured they were still too young to remember how to get back to the apartment, but just in case she warned them against it. She didn't want Biggs to know to know where they were living in fear that he would show up unexpectedly to cause trouble for her and her new husband. They didn't wait long before Biggs appeared, pulling up in his Eldorado. With a few words spoken between them, she handed off the twins to their father for the weekend visit. He was still angry that Jacky had left him, and she still feared his anger.

The weekend flew by, and on Sunday morning, toward the end of their weekend visit, they all sat in the empty living room of the house on Bearden Drive. They watched cartoons while eating their breakfast, which consisted of milk and cereal. Their father sat with them on the folded-out futon, laughing at the Tom and Jerry cartoons with their slapstick comedy. After getting the kids ready, he loaded them up in the Eldorado to take them back to their mother. On the car ride back to the 7-Eleven gas station the kids recited with their father

"M-I-S-S-I-S-S-I-P-P-I." Biggs turned to the twins. "I-P-P? I didn't pee pee! Did you pee pee?" he said as the kids giggled with laughter. "Yeah, you pee peed." He laughed with them. "So where do you live? Would you know how to get back home?" he asked them.

"Mommy told us not to say anything or we will get in trouble!" Mikey said.

"Michael, I am your father and I say you won't be in trouble," Biggs told him. "Okay! So, you can tell me!"

With stunning accuracy, the small toddlers gave him turn-by- turn directions, and soon they were pulling into the apartment complex where Jacky was now living Pete.

Biggs got out and unloaded the kids. He stormed up to the front door of the apartment. He knocked loudly on the door as the kids stayed behind him. Pete opened the door with shock and fear in his eyes. He was stunned to see Biggs standing at the threshold. With a thrust he pushed Pete onto the living room floor. Biggs made his way into the apartment as Pete scrambled up to regain his footing. Biggs nailed him across the Jaw as Pete came toward him. Jacky was in the back of the apartment, and hearing the commotion, came flying into the living room.

"What the hell are you doing here, Biggs? How the fuck did you find us?" Jacky screamed. Biggs turned to face her as Pete came up behind him. He grabbed a wooden hat rack and hit Biggs across the back. Biggs turned around to face Pete.

"What? You can't fight me man to man, you fucking pussy?" Biggs grabbed the hat rack from Pete and snapped it over his leg. He threw the pieces to the ground and charged

toward Pete. Pete put up his fists in defense. Biggs gave him a right hook and then a quick jab, knocking him back to the ground. Biggs had been a boxer in the navy and was no stranger to fist fighting. Jacky stood in front of Pete, protecting her husband as he lay on the ground.

"Leave my husband alone! Go to the phone and call the police!" Jacky screamed to Sonny, who was now awake and watching the fight unfold. He ran to the phone and picked up the receiver.

"Your husband?" he asked in shock. "So, what? You two are married now?"

"Yes, we're married now?" she said. He felt like he had been hit by a ton of bricks. He felt a sense of defeat. "It's over between us, Michael! I will never go back to you! Never!" He stood there for a moment as reality set in. He looked around at the small apartment, and he realized he had caused all of it. By his actions he had allowed all of this to happen. "You need to leave!" she told him.

"All right, all right! I will go! Just remember those are my kids!" Biggs said. "And no matter what, I will always be a part of their lives."

"Get the hell out of here, or you won't ever see your kids again! Do you understand me, Biggs!" Jacky yelled. "I am with Pete now. And if I have to we will get a restraining order against you!" she warned him.

He left in anger. Peeling out in his usual way.

"You kids just had to go and tell your father, huh?" Jacky said, holding an ice pack up to Pete's face to keep the swelling down.

The twins couldn't believe what had just happened. They felt a sense of guilt. They didn't really like Pete. Although they pretended to like him, because that's what Jacky wanted from them, there was something about him they just didn't trust, and they were glad their dad had beat him up.

Biggs never came to the apartment again and kept his promise only to meet Jacky when and where she chose. He feared that she would leave and that he would never see his

children again. Biggs was now playing the game by her rules. The thought that this stranger was going to be a part of his kids' life irked him to no end. The thought that this man was now in bed with Jacky every night, when he came home alone, was like a needle through his mind. To Biggs, Pete was a well-oiled snake slithering through his garden. A snake that had entered when his back was turned. Pete was the weed, and as much as Biggs wanted to pull this intruder from his garden, he knew that it was all his own doing. And as much as he might pull, he couldn't grab this weed by the roots. So, there it would remain in his garden. It would grow and fester, and it would root out in all directions. This stranger was now a permanent part of Biggs's life and the future of his children.

Chapter 6 The Savior

Jacky was still working hard to make ends meet. Although she was still working hard she was seemingly happier now. The dark days of violence were behind her. Pete had finally found a job as a security guard after months of drinking and lying about on the couch. He drove around empty shopping centers and banks that were closed after hours. He drove away local teenage vandals looking for a clean wall as a slate to spray paint their names across. He would shuffle along the homeless looking for a warm shelter out of the cold desert winds. Both Jacky and Pete worked the evening shifts and did not come home until the early morning.

Faith continued taking on more than her fair share of responsibilities. She continued to watch over the twins. She made friends with the girls her age that lived near the apartment

complex, girls she went to school with. On the weekends, when Jacky and Pete were working, she invited her girlfriends for sleepovers. They watched movies and ate pizza, popcorn, and candy. VHS and cable were new phenomena at the time, and HBO was just making its debut. Faith's and her friends' favorite movie was *Grease*, and Olivia Newton John was their queen. They emulated the main character Sandy and the Pink Ladies club. Faith wanted to be just like her and asked Jacky if she would buy her a Pink Ladies jacket for her birthday.

Jacky was making decent money but felt guilty for having to spend so much time away from her kids. She was grateful for all of Faith's help. She wanted to do something to show her gratitude, so, after months of begging from Faith, she went out and bought her a pink jacket and had "Pink Ladies" embroidered on the back.

Faith screamed with excitement as she opened her birthday present. Her friends looked on with envy as she put it on. She was Sandy for the day and no one could take that away from her. Her friends soon followed suit, and it wasn't long

before they were doing dance routines and reciting songs from the musical on the front lawn of the apartment complex. "We're cool. We're hot!" they would say with a synchronous snap of their fingers.

Meanwhile Sonny got his first taste of freedom. He had always been controlled by Biggs. How he dressed, how he brushed his hair, everything was controlled by Biggs. Sonny was a teenager now and was beginning to experience the growing pains as rebellion boiled in his blood. MTV had just begun to air and was causing headaches for parents across the nation. Atari arrived on the scene with Pac-Man and Asteroids, and a "New Wave" was sweeping across the country, changing the styles and attitudes of America's youth. When Jacky and Pete were at work, Sonny danced and screamed in front of the television, imagining that he was a rock star playing his air guitar to a vast audience of screaming girls and head-banging guys. He would rock the living room like no one had rocked the living room before. He would run around with his imaginary guitar, jumping of the sofa as he went into his musical solo.

Sonny was like a wild animal let out of his cage. Since he had little to no supervision, he would ditch school all the time, and he would stay out late into the evening, knowing that Pete and his mother would be gone. He was going through puberty, and he and his hormones were raging. He was wild and rambunctious, and his hyperactivity didn't help the changes he was going through. Pete was no father figure to Sonny, and his real father showed no interest in him or Faith. With little guidance, it was not long before he fell into the wrong crowd and discovered drugs and alcohol. Las Vegas is a wild town, and for a wild child he was soon swept up in the never-ending party atmosphere that Las Vegas built its reputation on. He came home drunk a lot of the time, stumbling into his room and crashing into a deep sleep. Choosing to stay out, whether partying with his friends or hanging out at the arcades, he pushed his share of caring for the twins onto Faith. He left her home at night to care for the young kids as he roamed the streets of Las Vegas.

It was the middle of May as the desert heat had started to rise. Jacky purchased the twins matching bikes on their fifth birthday. The metallic blue bikes were the shiniest things the twins had ever laid eyes on. Michelle was the first to learn how to ride without the need of training wheels. She always seemed a little quicker to pick up on things than Michael was. He was jealous that his sister had got the best of him. Every time he saw her riding around without her training wheels, it made him green with envy. The other kids would taunt him for having to use them. He hated his training wheels, but he just couldn't seem to find his balance. Finally, he had had it. He looked for his bid brother. He walked into the bedroom they shared, but Sonny wasn't there. He walked around the complex outside and finally found Sonny hiding in the laundry room. He quickly stubbed out a cigarette, startled by the sudden appearance of his little brother. "Sonny can you take my training wheels off for me?" the little boy asked.

"Are you sure you're ready for that?" Sonny asked.

"Yeah!" Mikey said with uncertainty and fear.

"Okay!" he said. "I'll do it but don't tell Mom about me smoking. Okay?"

"Okay Sonny." He agreed. Sonny grabbed a wrench from the closet in the apartment and removed the little rubber wheels. Mikey hopped on his bike as Sonny held on to the back of the seat to hold him steady. He was nervous but excited. He started pedaling and rode about ten feet before losing his balance and falling over. He scraped up his and the palm of his hand. He sat on the ground feeling the sting of his scrapes. He rubbed the gravel of his palm.

"Are you all right?" Sonny asked him.

"I hurt my knee!" Mikey said with a little tear in his eye.

"Oh, you're okay!" Sonny told him. "You just got to get back on and try again."

"What if I get hurt again?" Mikey asked.

"How are you ever going to learn to ride your bike if you're afraid to get hurt?" Sonny told him. "When you fall down, you just got to get up, and try again, little brother."

Mikey got up and got back on his bike. He was a little afraid, but he started pedaling. He made it a little way and fell over a second time.

"How about I hold on to your seat and help you balance while you pedal?" Sonny suggested.

"Okay, but don't let go!" Mikey told him.

"I won't, I promise." Sonny said.

Mikey got on his bike and began pedaling while his brother followed behind him. Mikey pedaled faster. "Don't let go!" he said to his big brother as he continued pedaling.

"Okay, stop!" Sonny yelled. Mikey hit the brakes and came to a stop. He turned to find his brother, only to see him standing a good distance from him.

"I told you not to let go!" Mikey said in anger.

"But you rode by yourself. You did it without falling!" Sonny said to him. Mikey looked at the distance between them and couldn't believe he had made it that far.

"I did do it! I did it by myself!" he said in excited disbelief. Sonny gave him a high five.

"I knew you could do it!" Sonny said. Michael never rode his bike with training wheels again. And although he fell from time to time, he wasn't afraid anymore.

It wasn't long before the twins were tearing up blacktop and speeding down the parking lot of the complex in which they lived. They rode down the sidewalks in between the apartments, flying around like a couple of bats out of hell. They were the coolest five-year-old's in the complex and the envy of all the toddlers in the neighborhood. They blasted past the sandbox and jungle gym where their playmates were still playing. They learned to be more careful with their toys and were especially cautious with their new bicycles. They didn't want the three-legged kid, or any of his cohorts, to get ahold of them. They had found too many of their broken toys in the desert, and they wouldn't let the new bicycles suffer the same fate as that of Barbie.

The twins found freedom granted to them by their new bikes, and although they only had permission to ride around the complex, it wasn't long before they were cruising the block.

They pushed the boundaries of their freedom more and more every day. Their riding earned them a newfound respect from the neighborhood kids. They could go places and do things that the other kids could not. And when they got their bikes, it gave them automatic membership into a sort of unspoken club. The kids with bikes, as opposed to the kids without. Soon Michael, Michelle, and their little bike gang were hitting the trails in the empty desert lots. They found their way into the nearby shopping center and through the parking lots. They cruised along the back side of Lucky's and Pic and Save, splashing the gutters with their tires, and feeling the wind blow through their hair. They felt free. Cruising around on a bike is one of the most invigorating experiences a child can have. It was all so new to them.

It didn't take Mikey long to find himself cruising the isles if the Lucky's and the Pic and Save. The inside of the grocery store was a cool escape from the desert heat. As he walked by the candy bins, he casually grabbed a handful of chocolate-covered caramel goobers, while looking over his

shoulder to make sure no one was watching him. He would grab

a few chocolate turtles, or he might have grabbed some malt

balls, but never the trail mix. These bins were always full to the

brim and everything was sold by the pound. No one ever seemed

to be watching these bins. They were low to the ground, and

seemed an easy target for a free snack, and a quick sugar buzz. It

seemed so simple. He felt invincible. Although he knew it was

stealing and it was wrong, he didn't care, and it didn't stop him.

When he got away with it the first few times, he thought that he

couldn't get caught. Although he didn't realize it, he was five

years old and flying under the radar of suspecting eyes.

Soon little Mike set his eyes on a new set of Hot Wheels,

Lucky the green Care Bear, and some Star Wars action figures.

Return of the Jedi had just come out, and little Mike was

mesmerized. It would take some time before he learned the ways

of the force, and a little while longer before he learned that

nothing in life comes free. Mikey grabbed toys, the stuffed

animals, and whatever else he could get his sticky little fingers

on. He grabbed his loot, stuffed it down his Oshkosh overalls,

and ran out to meet up with his partner in crime. He handed off the goods to Michelle, and she would run around the corner and dump it in the bushes that landscaped the shopping center. They seemed to have a perfect system. When he'd collected enough booty, they'd retrieve the treasure from the bushes, and on their way, they would go. Most people think that the sweet innocent face of a child couldn't possibly hide the mind of a master criminal, but Mikey was clever and diabolical.

One afternoon, hungry from his and Michelle's bike adventures, Mikey decided it was time for a little snack. He scoped out the isles of the grocery store and spotted some delicious-looking Chips Ahoy. *Cookies! He thought as his mouth watered* He grabbed a pack, stuffed them in his pants, and made his way toward the front door. The store manager noticed a strange bulge sticking out of the overalls of the young boy. He moved in on the perpetrator, sneaking up behind him. With a sudden shock to his nervous system, Mikey felt someone grab him by the back of his overalls. He turned to see a long-sleeved shirt and a black tie.

"What do you think you're doing, little guy?" a loud voice boomed down at him. The man in the black tie grabbed the package and escorted the boy out of the store. "Don't you ever come back in here! Next time I'll find your mother and tell her what a little thief you are!"

Me a thief! What will my mother think? he thought with embarrassment, not too sure what a thief was exactly. He imagined the kind of spanking he would receive if she were ever to find out. His shame didn't last too long, and it wasn't long before he was cruising the isles again. He knew the manager would be looking for him at Lucky's and decided to turn his attention to the Pic and Save.

He walked in and found some yummy-looking candy bars, and it still being hot outside, decided to sit down and enjoy himself. There in the middle of the isle he peeled back the wrapper of his candy bar and cracked open a juice box. The Pic and Save was managed by a bunch of old gray-haired women. *This is where I should have been all along!* he thought. He was enjoying his chewy chocolate bar when he felt a sudden tug on

his ear. A blinding white heat took hold of him. He felt himself being dragged up the candy isle by his ear. He looked up to find one of the gray-hairs looking down at him, her gray fuzzy eyebrows frowning at him from above her horned-rimmed glasses. He sat in the manager's office as the older lady called the police. He was sitting there crying, knowing he had done wrong, and that he was busted. "Yes, this is Gladys calling from the Pic N Save on Charleston and Decatur. I hate to bother you again, but I caught another little thief in my store again. Yes, I know there's not much you can do, but maybe you can teach the little brat a lesson. Nothing but trash living in the apartments around these parts I tell you. Well I would appreciate it." She said. "Okay thank you officer."

When the police officer arrived, he knew he was in real trouble. His cry turned into a wail and the tears began to flow. "Am I going to jail?" he asked.

"You just might be son?" The policeman said. The officer escorted him back to the apartment complex where he lived. As they got closer to the apartment, Mikey tried to make a

run for it, but the officer was too fast for the five-year-old. He scooped up the little boy and squeezed him sideways onto his hip. The thought of a whipping scared him more than the idea of going to jail. Mikey kicked and squirmed, but the officer was just too strong. His mother opened the door, and he knew he was in for it. He knew he had a spanking coming. She didn't even wait for the officer to leave. His ass stung as his mother swatted him. She thanked the officer and dragged the little boy to his bedroom, where she continued to swat him. After she left, he pulled down his drawers. On his hind end were two little round red marks on two little round butt cheeks.

"Ouch!" he said with his eyes full of tears. He rubbed the heat from off his backside. That was the last time he would steal anything for a very long time. He spent the next few days grounded to his room, but when Jacky and Pete had left for work faith would let him out to watch afternoon cartoons.

Michelle sat eating her breakfast. She looked over to that her bike wasn't sitting next to her brother's. She realized she had

accidently left her bike out in front of the apartment the night before. She jumped out of her chair, worried something had happened to it. When she went out her fears were confirmed. The tassels had been ripped off the handle bars of her bike. Finally, she had had enough. Michelle knew it was the work of the three-legged kid, and she was going to take him down.

Michelle and Mikey talked about it all day. They talked about how they were going to get back at him. They sat in Mikey's room devising their plan. With some crayons and a crumpled-up piece of paper, they drew out the plan. They knew Faith and their mom were going shopping the following morning, and that Pete would probably be asleep like he always was during the day. It would be the perfect time to slip away. They talked of which ways to go and planned the perfect route. It was time to take the three legged-kid and his gang of tyrants down.

Jacky came down the hall after cleaning the dishes and watching her favorite nighttime soaps. It was one of those moments when she was able to get the night off. She passed Mikey's room and could hear them giggling and whispering.

What are those two doing now? she wondered. She stood behind the door with a grin on her face. She loved those two children. They always kept her on her toes. She never knew what they would be getting into from one moment to the next. She walked a little past the door just a short distance and raised her voice. "You two better get into to bed. It's getting late!"

"Okay, Mommy!" they said in sync.

They awoke to the smell of Jacky cooking breakfast in the kitchen, their tummies grumbling as they rubbed their eyes. They stumbled into the dining room, taking their seats at the table. They watched and waited as Jacky prepared their plates.

"Mmmmm. I love pancakes, I am soooo hungry!" Michael said with exaggeration.

"You're always hungry!" his mother said with a laugh. Mikey wasn't a picky eater. He loved food and he loved to eat. Anything Jacky put in front of him he ate without a fuss. Michelle on the other hand was an extremely picky. She had explicit orders for her mom on how to prepare her food. She asked specifically that the syrup be served on the side so that

nothing got soggy. She wanted her bacon and eggs on another plate so that it wouldn't get mixed up with her pancakes. And she liked her milk in her own designated cup.

Michelle wanted to save a few of her pancakes just in case they got hungry on their adventure. She was a little sleepy but managed to think up a plan on how to smuggle the pancakes out so as not to get caught. Their mother told them she had eyes in the back of her head, and Michael and Michelle thought for the longest time that she did in fact have eyes in the back of her head. Jacky went into the master bedroom to get ready for the shopping day she had planned with Faith. Michelle found it the perfect time to smuggle her flapjacks out of the dining room. She ran into Michael's bedroom and hid the pancakes under his pillow. She made a mad dash back to the table, her little heart pounding out of control. She sat down and winked at Michael. After they finished their meal, they got dressed and ready to go out.

"We're going out to play, Mommy," Michelle said.

"Okay, just don't be wandering off too far. If you ride your bikes, you are only to ride them around the apartment complex. And I want you two to stay away from that shopping center, Michael. Do you understand me?" she yelled from the master bedroom.

"Yes Mom!" He said as the guilt from his shoplifting returned to him.

"Sonny I want you to go out front and keep an eye on your brother and sister!"

"Okay Mom!" He said with an automated response. Sat in his bedroom with his headphones on and really wasn't paying attention to what she said. He got up and closed the bedroom door.

Michelle watched from the sandbox as Jacky and Faith pulled out of the driveway and made their way down the street.

"The coast is clear!" Michelle said, signaling to Michael. Michael ran into the apartment and rummaged through his closet, searching for the bag he and Michelle had packed the night before. The backpack had a few G.I. Joes and a Barbie

inside, and a beat-up baton sticking up out of the top. All the necessities needed for their plan. He slipped his hand beneath the pillow, reaching for the snack Michelle had planted there. Michelle was impatiently waiting by the front door.

"Come on let's go before Pete hears us!" she said in a quiet whisper.

They quietly shut the door behind them. Both trembled from the excitement and partly out of fear of waking up Pete. They jumped on their bikes and started pedaling as fast as their little legs would allow. They followed the route they had planned the night before, talking and laughing as they rounded the corner, and made their way toward the three-legged boy's house. It was hot and sunny out that day, another hot day in the endless heat of a Las Vegas summer. They felt so free and grown up on their new wheels. Down the familiar streets they rode. They came to a neighborhood park and decided to stop. It was a perfect place for a break. They pulled their bikes up to the water fountain and gulped down as much water as they could. Michelle and Michael sat on the park bench talking of their plot

of revenge against the neighborhood bullies. Michael reached to the ground and started picking up little rocks to use as ammo. He filled the front pocket of the backpack with as many rocks as would fit.

"We might need these for later!" he said, looking at his sister.

"Good idea!" she said as she started to fill her pockets with stones. They jumped back on their bikes and were once again on their way. It seemed they had been pedaling forever when in the distance they could see the bullies playing in the front yard. Michelle started pedaling faster as she neared the boys. She jumped off her bike as Michael following closely behind. With her fists clenched and her knees weak, she walked up to the bullies.

"Did you pull the tassels off my bike?" she yelled.

"No! And what if I did? What are you going to do about it?" the three-legged kid said. He saw her knee was trembling. "What? Are you scared? You going to pee your pants?" he said, taunting her. The other boys started laughing. "Pee-pee pants!

Cry baby!" he teased. This did not sit well with Michael and his face turned a shade of red.

He started yelling back at the boys, calling them every cuss word he knew. One of the little thugs suddenly pushed Michael to the ground, scraping his knee on the black asphalt. Michelle's anger rose as she reached inside her pockets. Grabbing for the rocks, she began chucking the rocks at the bullies with all her strength. The projectiles flew through the air as the altercation quickly escalated and turned into an all-out rock fight. Michael got up from the street and punched the older kid square in his nose.

An older kid stumbled a few steps back, then landed on his ass. His eyes welled up with tears. Michelle couldn't believe that Michael had just punched him. A sister of one of the boys came up behind her and pushed Michelle to the ground. Scrambling to her feet, she grabbed the backpack and started swinging. She hit the other girl until she ran off back toward the house. She then went after the boys. She swung the backpack as though her life depended on it. She wailed on the boys as the

contents of the bag came flying out. The three-legged boy and his cohorts began to return fire, throwing rocks from their front yard. The twins got on their bikes and tried to ride out of there as quickly as possible. Michelle stopped pedaling, got off her bike, and quickly picked up a few rocks for cover.

"Go!" she yelled to Michael. She threw her small fistful of rocks, hopped on her bike, and began pedaling again. She tried to catch up to Mikey as stones rained down on her. She looked behind her, trying to keep an eye on the kids that were chasing after them. The bullies began to slow down as they ran out of steam. Michelle pedaled hard and fast as she made her getaway. She could see Michael in front of her pedaling for his life. He turned down the next street and stared into the early morning sun.

Michelle heard the loud screeching of tires and breaks. She rounded the corner and she saw Michael crashing up against the windshield of an oncoming car. His body flew like a shadow high into the air. The little blue bike became nothing more than twisted metal crushed underneath the front tires of the car. She

couldn't believe what she was seeing as the breath was knocked

out of her. Michael's body landed on the ground with a thump.

His body lay in the street, twisted and mangled. Michelle

jumped off her bike and ran to her brother's side. She felt

helpless as she looked at his lifeless and unmoving body. Blood

was coming out of his ears, eyes, nose, and mouth. She began to

try and untwist his body. His leg was twisted and wrapped

around behind his neck. As she tried to untwist his limbs to pull

him back to shape, his body began shaking and convulsing with

a rigorous force. She placed her hands upon his stomach and

tried to put the weight of her body upon him to stop him from

shaking. She moved without thought and ran on instinct.

She looked up to the sky, crying out in agony. "Please,

help me! Please don't let him die!" she cried. She began to try to

pick up the lifeless body of brother. She didn't know how she

was going to get home. She didn't know how she was going to

explain this to her mother. She continued trying to pick him up.

She was crying and confused. She felt helpless and didn't know

what to do. The lady in the car got out for a moment. She saw

the little boy on the ground, bleeding and broken. She looked the little girl in the eyes. She got back into her car, and she sat there for a moment. Then she put the car in reverse, backed up, and took off down the street. Michelle sat there alone in the street holding her brother. She yelled and screamed for help. She looked down the street, wondering where everyone was. She wondered why no one was coming to help her. She kept pleading to the sky looking for help for what seemed like an eternity. Her mind was reeling. From the corner of her eye, she saw a very tall man running toward her. He carried a blanket with him. He saw Michelle trying to carry Michael's body down the road. He took the boy's body from her and laid Michael back down on the asphalt, wrapping him in a blanket of blue and green. He rested Michael's head on his lap. Michelle began crying.

"Please don't let him die!" she said repeatedly. The man gently reached out to the little girl.

"Don't worry, Michelle, he's going to be all right!" he told her. His presence calmed her. She looked at him in awe. She

did not remember telling this tall stranger her name. He told her that Michael's body would began to shake again, and before he could finish his sentence Michael's body began to convulse violently. The stranger placed his hands-on Michael as Michelle had done earlier, and Michael's body again lay there motionless and lifeless.

From a distance she could hear sirens and she knew that help was on the way. The police and ambulance began lifesaving procedures right there in the middle of the street. They soon had Michael on a gurney. They lifted his body into the ambulance, trying to resuscitate him. They closed the doors of the ambulance and sped off down the road. It all happened so quickly. A whirlwind of disaster had taken over them and turned a beautiful day into a nightmare. A police officer put Michelle into a police cruiser. She looked out the back window of the police car, looking for the man that had helped her, but he was nowhere to be seen. She sat back down with nervous anxiety, wondering how she was going to explain all of this to her mother. She didn't know how she going to explain that her

brother was dead. She didn't even know where they had taken her brother. She had up until now no concept of death, but instinctively she already knew what it was.

Chapter 7 Shadows in the Night

Twins are different than other children. They seem to have their own language, sharing an inner circle of private understanding. Michael and Michelle may have been young, but their perception had always been beyond their years. They were adventurous and smart. They always worked as a team, and between the two of them there wasn't much they couldn't do or get into for that matter. Michelle was always the instigator and Michael was always her willing coconspirator. They were always very protective of each other. They'd fought and argued about everything from the time they first learned to talk, but at the end of the day they were all each other had. They were best friends, and no one knew them better than they knew each other.

The family was spending day and night at the hospital. It was a scene like that of a funeral. Biggs, his brother David, and

his parents were there, as well as Jacky's father and her sister. Maybe they indeed were waiting for a funeral. The doctors had operated on Michael, trying to salvage his damaged body. They had revived him seven times before he became stable enough for life support equipment. After many hours the doctor finally emerged from the operating. Jacky rushed to the doctor to find out what was happening. A fear gripped her. The doctor looked somber and she prepared for the worst. "Jacky I'm doctor Anderson."

"How's my son? Is he going to be alright?" She asked as her hands trembled. Biggs put his arm around her to try and comfort her, but he had fear in his heart also. It was the first time he had comforted her in a long time.

"We were able to stabilize Michael. He is now in a state of coma. He suffered major cranial fractures as well as fractures to his pelvis. It is likely that he has suffered brain damage, but to what extent it is too early to tell." He explained. "We won't know the extent of his injuries until he wakes from his coma.

And the chances that he will be able to walk again are extremely small."

"I'm not going to have a vegetable for a son!" she screamed at the doctors. "You better do whatever it takes to make sure he's all right!" she threatened.

"He is young and his ability to heal are far greater than if this would have happened to him at an older age. At this point, only time will tell how much damage has been done and how fully he will be able to heal from his injuries." Doctor Anderson told her. "I wish I had more to tell you at this point, but he is resting, and it is unlikely he feels any pain from his injuries." She collapsed into Pete's arms and sobbed. They looked on her with helplessness, knowing that there was only so much they could do for the boy. And knowing that only time could tell how or if he would recover from his injuries. Biggs looked at Jacky in the arms of this strange man holding her and he wished he was the one comforting her. He knew he should be the one holding her, but he knew they were far from beyond that. He knew their

relationship was too far gone and that he would never be that man in her life.

Michael was eventually placed into intensive care. He was still in his coma, but his vital signs were stable. He was asleep in another world. A world free from pain and suffering. He was surrounded by white light and the sound of a soothing humming. He was floating, suspended from his broken body, and enveloped in the healing light. His family was allowed to see him but only for short intervals of time. As Michelle entered the room, she saw a little person lying on the hospital bed, but she could not recognize this person as her brother. His head was swollen to the size of a watermelon and his face was black and blue all over. It looked as if the slightest touch to his skin would cause him to bleed. There were tubes running in and out all over his body. Michelle could hear the hissing and pumping of the respiratory machines, and the beeping of the heart monitors. She became dizzy and fainted to the floor at seeing the shape her brother was in. They took her out of the room as she started crying uncontrollably, which in turn caused Jacky to start crying.

Jacky and Biggs were spending a lot of time down at the hospital waiting for Michael to awaken from his coma. He had been unconscious for two weeks now, but to Jacky and Biggs it was an eternity. Sonny, Faith, and Michelle were left to the care of Pete. When he wasn't working, he was sleeping, and when he wasn't sleeping, he was drinking. Sonny and Faith were going to school, which left Michelle with a lot of time alone. She was only allowed to see Michael sporadically, and only for a few short moments. It was the first time that they had been apart since they were born, and she wished that he would just wake up. The days dragged on into weeks. The household was filled with an eerie air of dread, and there was a sense of depression hanging over every one's state of mind. After a while Michael was released from intensive care and placed into a regular room. It had been three weeks before he started to respond and awaken from his coma. The room he was in was very dark with the shades pulled tight. He had opened his eyes, his throat raw from the tubes going down his throat. He cried and pulled at the tubes, yanking them out of his throat and out of his arms. The doctors

tried to explain to him that he needed those tubes to keep him alive, that he needed to stop pulling them out. Even though he understood their words, he didn't understand what they were saying. He just wanted the tubes out. The slight light entering the room would pass through his eyes, piercing his brain like an electric knife. He would cry and wail, but nothing seemed to stop the pain. His body ached all over and would throb him back to sleep. Sleep was the only place he seemed to be safe from the pain that his body was in. In his sleep he would find a place of white light. He could hear soft voices humming lullabies to him and the light of that other world would cradle him as he slept. It was warm and soft inside his sleep. He hated to be taken away from there.

It was late, and everyone was at the hospital, leaving Michelle alone at the apartment with Pete. She sat in front of the television set. Every so often she would glance over her shoulder as she could feel his eyes upon her. He crushed down one can of Budweiser after another. She did not like him. There was just

something about him that bothered her. The way that he leered at her made her skin crawl. His overgrown and untrimmed beard seemed to hide some dark secret locked up behind his deep-set black eyes. It was not long before she became weary and tired of her stepfather's invasive stares.

She made her way to Michael's bedroom and fell asleep in the bottom bunk. She felt closer to him when she slept in his bed. She missed him terribly and cried herself to sleep. She still had nightmares of the car accident. She could still see the image of his body flying through the air. She could still see his broken body lying, bleeding in the street, and all this made it hard for her to sleep. She awoke to the sensation of another presence in the room. A shadow stood in the doorway, looking over her as she tried to sleep. She raised her head and the shadow would move past the doorway. She put her head back on the pillow and fell back asleep.

Late into the night, she awoke to the presence of a man on top of her. The weight of his body was suffocating. She was frozen in fear, not understanding what was happening to her. Her

heart was pounding out of control and all she could feel was pain and terror. She could smell the stench of alcohol coming from his breath as he fondled her under her nightgown and kissed her on her neck. He touched her chest like she had the breasts of a woman, even though she had none. She was scared, not realizing what he was trying to do to her. Michelle just lay there, squeezing her eyes shut as hard as she could, wondering what was going on, and wishing he would leave. Her body was stiff and resistant to him.

He finally left the room, she could hear him open the refrigerator and crack open another can of beer. She lay in bed frozen and unable to sleep. She stayed awake as the light of the early dawn arose, and only felt a little relief when she heard Pete stumble down the hallway and close his bedroom door.

Michael slowly recovered from his injuries. The swelling in his head receded, though he still slept most of the time. He was unable to walk, and he was not able to move his right arm or leg. His right hand was locked tightly into a closed fist. They finally released him from the hospital after a few months and

into his mother's care. He stayed in the living room of the apartment on a bed provided for him by the hospital. Day in and day out, Michelle slept next to him on the couch. His blackened eyes saddened her, and she longed for the day when he would be able to get up and go outside to play with her. When he did happen to awaken he would cry out in pain. He drank a constant stream of Gatorade, orange juice, and liquified food.

Everything had a bland and unappetizing taste to Michael's tongue. Jacky would awaken him, trying to get him to stand and walk. His equilibrium was out of whack, and as he stood his head would start spinning until he felt like he would fall over. Jacky pushed him until he was able to steady himself upon his child-size walker. His right leg dragged, and his right hand curled into his chest.

He had partial paralysis of his right side, but with constant work, the physical therapist said that he might gain some of the muscle control that he had lost. It was an endless array of doctor appointment after doctor appointment. The physical therapist would stand by him as he walked his way

across the flat narrow ramp, holding on to the parallel bars. The doctor gave him discarded blood pressure pumps, having him squeeze them over and over, trying to rebuild the muscles in his right hand. He would cry at the pain of having to work his leg and arm. They felt dead to him and all he wanted to do was go back to sleep.

"If you ever want to walk and play like a normal boy again, you got to keep going. Now just a few more times! Come on! Do it for Mommy," Jacky said, trying to encourage him. Michael felt like he was being punished but didn't know why. He felt tired all the time and didn't understand the purpose of his constant exercises. Although it hurt Jacky to see her child in pain, she knew it was the only way that he was ever going to recover. They gave him a box of blood pressure pumps, Silly Putty, and tension toys to play with at home. He loved the Silly Putty and the squishy toys but hated the blood pressure pumps and wanted nothing to do with him. Jacky had to constantly remind him to play with the pumps; otherwise he wouldn't touch them. Jacky encouraged him to work with them, as she knew

that he needed to work with them the most. She would have to sit there with him as he squeezed and squeezed on those pumps, because if she didn't he would put them down and pick up the Silly Putty. Michael had to relearn everything. He had to relearn how to speak, walk, eat, and write. He had to relearn everything he had learned in the short span of his life prior to the accident. The doctors told him that it was better for this injury to have happened when he was so little, because he could recover more quickly and with less permanent damage than if he were an adult. Michelle waited, for what seemed in the mind of a child to stretch on forever, for him to get better.

Finally, after months of recuperation Michael was well enough, and stable enough, to walk on his own. He still had a concussion on his forehead from the impact with the windshield of the car that struck him. It had left a large knot on his head, a permanent reminder he would carry for the rest of his life. Sitting on the front porch of the apartment were the little blue bikes. Michelle's was still in perfect condition, while Michael's was a twisted wreck of metal. There were chips and cracks in the

paint where the frame of the bike had been bent, exposing the metal underneath. Michelle kicked the bikes.

"Those damn bikes!" she said, as Michael giggled at her.

"Yeah, them damn bikes!" he repeated. He wanted to kick the bikes as Michelle had done, but he was afraid he would lose his balance. He still dragged his right leg as he walked, and even though he had regained some muscle control in his right hand, it still curled into his chest unless he consciously chose to keep it from doing so. They played like normal children, even though Michael was slower than the rest of the kids. His dragging leg and curled hand did not go unnoticed by the other kids in the apartment complex. When Michelle saw children staring at Michael, she was quick to correct them. They knew she meant business, and so tried not to stare too long at Michael as he struggled to keep up with them. The doctors knew that Michelle would be key in helping Michael recover from his injuries. Without her constant encouragement, Michael wouldn't have healed as quickly as he did.

Jacky had begun to realize that Las Vegas was fast becoming a place she no longer wanted to raise her children in. The city was growing too fast with development. It attracted elements that she didn't want to bring her children up around. The accident had put fear into her, and she wanted to find a place that had wide-open places for her children to play in. She longed to get out of the apartment complex and into a real home. A home that she could call her own.

She was going through the Sunday paper one morning and she came across an employment advertisement for the California Department of Corrections (CDC). The prison system was building up fast and was hiring in droves. So much so that they even had advertised in nearby states such as Nevada and Arizona. She thought that it would be a great career for her new husband, and that it would provide them a stable income. She dialed the phone number in the ad and pretended that she was the one interested in the position of correctional officer.

She found out that they were doing testing near her father's home outside of Los Angeles within the next month. It

didn't take much persuasion on her part to convince Pete to go through the testing process, and soon he was off to train at the academy in Northern California. She asked her father if she and the kids could stay with him for a while, until Pete had finished his training.

While Pete was in Northern California, she moved the family out of Las Vegas and back to California, where she'd been raised. Biggs wasn't too happy about this, but he felt that there was nothing he could do. He didn't want to see his kids move so far from him. It was a four-hour drive from Las Vegas to where Jacky was heading. He tried to convince Jacky not to make the move, but she had already made up her mind. And when he became angry with her she quickly reminded him of the past, and he knew he was not in a position to win that fight. She reminded him that his life style was not conducive to raising children and she reminded him that it wouldn't take much for a judge to agree with her. All he could do was sit there and watch her leave, taking his children away with her. One weekend a month, she loaded up the kids in their Dodge truck and they

would go up to see Pete during his training. He told her that the nearest prison that was hiring down south was the CCI prison in Tehachapi and that it was probably where he was going to be assigned. It was a town she had driven through many times on her drives to see Pete in Sacramento.

On her way home, she decided to stop by this tiny town and see where she might make her new home. She came up the steep grade of US Route 58, heading east out of Bakersfield. She saw scantily clad pine-covered mountains. Alongside the highway ran railroad tracks that looped in and out of tunnels bored into the mountain sides. When it reached the mountains' summit, the road descended into the Tehachapi Valley. It was cool and breezy at its four-thousand-foot elevation. The mountaintops were green, and it seemed as if there was a peace that blew through the summit pass.

She decided she would stop and have a picnic there, not telling the kids that this could be their new home. She went into a local grocery store to buy some lunch meat, bread, soda, and chips for a picnic. The woman at the checkout counter greeted

her with a friendly smile and hello, which almost shocked Jacky. Jacky had grown too accustomed to the closed-off, defensive people of Las Vegas. The warm welcome of the clerk pleasantly surprised her. They sat in the cool breeze under the big trees of the city park, and it was then she knew that she had found what she was looking for. She knew that this would be a good place to raise the kids. Pete soon finished his training, and as suspected, got his assignment to CCI. It wasn't long after that they were packing up the Dodge and heading back up those mountains and toward their new home.

Chapter 8 On Someday Ranch

Tehachapi is a place of beauty, and a place of contrasting landscapes. To the east is the shoreline of the Mojave Desert, and to the west lies the gateway to the great central valley. It is a high-altitude oasis of oak- and pine-covered mountaintops. It was a place that had changed little over the years, and only in recent decades had it began to see much development. Change is not something that had been welcomed there, and that is the way the locals wanted to keep it. It was an alcove off the side of the highway that most travelers passed by without taking much note of. To most people it was just a rest stop and nothing more.

After the Southern Pacific came through and built the rail track, it marked this tiny spot on the map. Chinese laborers blasted their way through the hillsides with dynamite and muscle. With shovels and picks, they linked a trade route

between San Francisco and Los Angeles. The Southern Pacific built water towers along the way for the original steam engines to pipe their way up the mountains. Soon coal power engines took their place, and the old water towers fell into disrepair, most of them eventually dismantled.

The soil in Tehachapi is fertile, and the cooler temperatures in the winter make it an ideal place to grow apples and other produce. Co-op produce farms sprang up all over the valley, and trading depots were built along the train tracks to ship produce and products in and out of the valley. During harvest the produce was loaded onto trains destined for the larger markets of San Francisco and Los Angeles. The grasses in the valley grow tall in the spring rains. Ranchers moved out west from the South and Midwest, buying the land up on the cheap. The tall, rain-fed grass made for a reliable source of food for cattle. Large cattle ranches prospered. Keene Ranch and Fort Tejon, among others, were sealed into the history of California. A hundred and fifty years later, you can still find the descendants of the original settlers living in the area. With the

settlers came their cultures and their religions. With them they brought their ways of living and the ways of their beliefs. Churches sprang up all over the valley. Places of worship and denominations were many in this small town. The people showed up in promise of work and the hope of a small plot of land that they could call their own. The churches came in hopes of taming the Wild West with morality and virtue.

The house the family bought sat on the south side of the valley in the foothills of the double mountains. Atop this peak was Mountain State Park, an oasis of thickly covered pine mountaintops. Running down the mountains, and through the canyons were creeks fed from the winter melt-off of snow. For three hundred and sixty degrees, the view of the Tehachapi valley from Water Canyon is awesome. Jacky and Pete built corals and fenced in pins on the weekends. They took the kids on trips to live animal auctions where they bought up chickens, ducks, and a few geese. They eventually even bought a horse and pony. Life seemed to be coming together for them on their little ranch. The inmates at the prison where Pete worked made

crafts and goods in exchange for the guards putting money on the books for them. It was part of the state's rehabilitation program. The inmates would learn new trades and skills, making products in exchange for money to buy cigarettes and goods while incarcerated.

Pete had a wooden sign made out at the prison. "The Someday Ranch," it read in bold lettering burned into the surface of the wooden plank. At the bottom of the two-acre parcel, where the driveway came off the dirt road, Pete drove a post into the hard ground. Upon the top of the post he fixed the large wooden sign, christening the plot of land.

It was late April when they moved up to Tehachapi, and there were only a few weeks of the school year left. Jacky didn't see the point of making the kids finish the school year and decided just to enroll them in September for the following school year. Michael was still recovering from his accident and still walked with a limp in his right leg. The twins watched every day, staring out the window, as the kids walked down the hill toward the bus stop. They watched as the kids waited for the

yellow bus to cruise over the hill and come to a stop. With a plume of black smoke, it would take off, heading toward the next bus stop. Michael and Michelle wanted so much to join the kids down at the bus stop, to ride the big yellow machine, and to mix and mingle with all the other kids. It wasn't so much a desire to learn, but a desire to be among kids their own age. The weeks passed quickly, though, and soon summer set in with bright sunlight and warm breezes. The creek ran at full capacity and an endless amount of play time was ahead of them.

Sonny was pushing sixteen and didn't much care for the small-town life. He felt out of place there, and he felt he didn't belong. He missed his friends in Las Vegas and he missed the streets of Las Vegas. Pete tried to exert his own paternal control over Sonny, but Sonny wasn't having any of it. They fought and bickered over everything from chores to homework. Sonny, after living under the tight grip and control of Biggs, was no longer willing to be controlled by yet another stepfather. He longed for the bright lights of Las Vegas. It was all he had known, and every friend he had in the world still lived there. The kids in

Tehachapi had not yet caught on to the new wave and punk fashion that swept the country. It being a rural mountain community, they had not been exposed to cable television. The style and fashion of the cities had not yet hit main street America. They were unaware of MTV, and in their world, there was no HBO. The only television available in Tehachapi were a few local stations airing out of Bakersfield. And that was if the weather was clear and if you happened to have an antenna tall enough to catch the signals.

The kids in town eyeballed Sonny with strange stares. To them he was a freak come busting into their town. The kids in this town new nothing of the Sex Pistols, the Ramones, the Clash, or the Cure. Sonny stuck out like a sore thumb, and it was something he became dreadfully aware of. He had never been one to care for school. Due to his hyperactivity and learning disabilities, it was always a struggle for him. His teachers didn't know how to handle or react to him. He was often passed from one class to another, eventually ending up in classes designated for children with learning and behavioral disabilities.

The state runs educational institutions the way they run mental facilities. The normal kids are grouped together with children of their likeness, while kids that don't fit the norm are packed up like a can of mixed nuts. They try to keep the insanity of the few from contagiously infecting the many. Band-Aids are placed on their bleeding wounds with inadequate medications and treatment. It was not long before the new town, the overbearing stepfather, and the lack of friends drove Sonny to run away. He left like a hobo, hitching a ride on the back of an eastbound train. He packed some clothes, a toothbrush, a comb, some food, and some cash he took from Jacky's purse. He decided to go back to Las Vegas. To go back to what was familiar to him, and to where he felt accepted by his peers.

When he got back to Vegas, he hopped around from one friend's sofa to another. He hopped around until he wore out his welcome, and soon he found himself trying to survive on the streets. He did odd jobs and lived with odd people. He survived with the undesirables and soon became one of the undesirables. He got caught up and fell in between the cracks like so many

kids do. At first it seemed to Sonny that he'd found the nonstop party that he left behind, fast times of getting drunk and getting high. Jacky had tracked him down and tried to convince him to come home, but he was a free man and wanted nothing of Tehachapi. She was distraught over his running away, but it wasn't the first time he'd pulled this stunt. She figured that when he got cold or hungry he would find his way home. For now, Sonny was riding high and living low. He didn't mind the streets, and in Vegas quick money was easy to come by. He panned his way through one meal and one eight ball after another, begging from tourists coming to and from the casinos. It would be quite some time before the reality of his decisions would catch up with him. Jacky tried to hold onto him. She tried to do for him what she thought was best, but the more she tried to keep him in place the more he fell out of line. Every time she tracked him down and brought him back, she would turn her back, and he was gone again.

Jacky was a simple woman with simple pleasures. Her smarts were gained not so much out of books and texts, but out

of survival and life experiences. She had left high school before she could graduate, which was common for women of her generation. She married young with high hopes of producing a family and becoming a mother. The part of mother was easy to come by, but maintaining a family, and keeping it intact, proved to be a different feat altogether. Men of her generation were caught up in the great social changes that took place in the sixties and seventies. They often fell short of their vows and were swept up in the motions of the time. They become rolling stones, and many times these men rolled back when there was nothing to come home to. She'd always felt inadequate about never finishing her education. She felt hindered by the fact that she did not go back and finish what she had started. This became the model and mode of her life. She was always waiting for something to happen to her, instead of making something happen for herself. She wanted every man to be like her father, but what she didn't realize was that her father was a rare diamond.

She embraced the country lifestyle and filled the property with farm animals. She decorated her home with duck-printed wallpaper, and little salt and pepper shakers in the shape of cows. She had glasses with faded yellow sunflowers painted on their sides. She would reuse margarine and empty lunch meat containers, because to her Tupperware was an unnecessary waste of money. In the end, she just wanted a family. She just wanted to be a mother. She just wanted a simple life. And she wanted a home to raise her kids in a place to call her own. She thought she had finally found these things in Pete. After all the disappointing men, and disappointing relationships, she believed that this is what she'd finally found.

An Indian summer was in full bloom. It was late July and moving into August. The twins were spending all hours of the day at the creek. Mikey was getting stronger every day, and soon it became barely noticeable that he had ever gotten hit by that car. They built little damns and moved heavy rocks into the stream, restricting the flow of water to create large pools they could swim in. They tied ropes around the high branches of the

oak trees that sat on the banks of the creek. They ran and grabbed the rope and swung into the pools of water they had created. They hollowed out the insides of the larger oak brush, creating forts where they could see out in all directions, but not be seen by people looking in. Grabbing old blankets and sheets, they spread them out on the floor like carpet and created cool and shady places to hang out in the summer heat. They pretended to play house or college roommates living together.

They acted so grown up in their imaginary worlds. It didn't take long before Michael and Michelle grew accustomed to the country living. They spent most of the summer barefoot, romping and stomping through the creek bed. They splashed around in the creek, letting the cool water rush over their small bodies. There was a sweet smell of sage to the creek. There was a magic to that place. They found millipedes and centipedes down there. They would dry off on the large slabs granite rock, as blue-bellied lizards and horned toads scurried past their feet. It was said that if you stared at a horned toad too long, it would squirt a stream of blood in your eye, and you would go blind.

How true this tale was, only a child could guess, but like most children, the twins believed most whatever people told them. They dug in the black silted mud of the creeks, and if it were an extraordinary day, they might come across the sacred salamander. They found purple-tailed skinks. There were gophers, California king snakes, and of course California rattlesnakes. They didn't run across too many rattlesnakes, and they were lucky that they hardly ever did. The creek became their home and their refuge. They would stay in it until dusk had deeply set and they would see the headlights of Jacky's car going up the driveway.

It was Sunday and Jacky had gone to Lancaster to find work and add some extra income for the family. Michelle had spent the night before at Kimmy's house. Kimmy's family attended the Baptist church regularly and invited Michelle to join them. Raul and Frankie had gone to Sunday mass at the Catholic church with their family; this left Michael with nowhere to go, and no one to play with.

"Hey, you want to go to the store with me and take a drive?" Pete asked him. He sat on the floor of his bedroom playing with his toys by himself. Not much else was going on, and with no playmates in sight, he didn't hesitate.

"Okay." He said. He was anxious and wanting to get out of the house. It was Pete's day off, and he was itching to start drinking. They got in the truck and headed to Wild Rose, a local gas station. They went inside, and Pete let him pick out any candy he wanted. He searched the isles until he picked out some foil-wrapped chocolates, Lemonheads, and a box of Cherry Clans. They were ten cents apiece, and what he picked out amounted to less than a dollar. At the checkout Pete heaved a twelve-pack of beer onto the counter, and Michael unloaded his handful of candy in front of the cashier.

"That's a lot of candy for one boy." The clerk behind the counter said.

"The sour candy is for my sister. I don't like sour candy. I mean I'll eat it, but I don't like it." He explained.

"And, where is she?" The clerk asked.

"She's at church." He said.

"Well that's a good place to be." She said.

"Uh huh." The clerk rang up the beer and the candy. She put the candy in a small paper bag and handed it to Mikey. He grabbed the paper bag at of her hand quickly.

"What do you say Michael?" Pete asked.

"Oh, thank you." He said quickly as he ran outside and to the truck. They drove back up Water Canyon and passed the turn off for the house.

"Would you like to take a drive up the mountains before going home?" Pete asked him as he sipped on a cold can of beer.

"Okay." Mikey shrugged too busy with his bag of candy. It wasn't too often that Pete was in a pleasant mood. He normally didn't pay much attention to Michael, and if he did it was normally with irritation and anger. It was a nice change to feel affection. Most of the time Mikey felt like a nuisance to Pete. They drove up Water Canyon as the road twisted and turned through the crevasses of the mountains. The higher they climbed in altitude, the denser the trees became. Soon the road

was covered in shade as sunbeams broke through thin areas in the foliage overhead. The large black oaks soon became intermixed with the high-altitude pines as they came to the entrance of Mountain Park.

They drove up one steep hill after another until they came near the top of the park. A gray tree squirrel ran along the side of the road in front of the Dodge, its bushy tail shaking rapidly behind as it scurried up a tree. Michael thought how pretty the tree squirrels were compared to the brown dusty-looking ground squirrels found closer to the house.

They came to a rest at the top, and Pete pulled into an empty campsite. It was heavily shaded and out of sight of the nearby campers. Pete turned the engine off as Michael sat there eating his chocolate and sucking down a root beer that Pete had bought for him. Pete put his arm around Michael and started rubbing his shoulder. He periodically took sips of the beer sitting in his lap. It felt good to feel his affection. He was rarely nice to Mikey. They sat there drinking their beverages, and it gave Mikey a sense of belonging. It gave him a sense fatherly love he

had been missing since he had last saw his father. It was a side of Pete he had rarely saw.

"Would you like to try some of my beer?" he asked. Mikey was shocked that he would even offer. He had always been scornfully warned against drinking alcohol. "It's okay! Try some." He assured the boy. He took the cold can which was wet from dew. The cold bitter beer shocked his mouth. He choked down the bitter, sudsy beer and instantly felt the alcohol send a buzz to his brain.

"It's good, huh?" Pete said to him.

"Uh huh!" He said lying. He didn't like the bitter taste. It was too strong for the palate of his young taste buds. Mikey passed the beer back to him and Pete insisted that he have more. Mikey took another drink and the beer again burned his tender throat. He didn't like the taste of it, but he didn't say anything in fear of disappointing his stepfather. Pete then told Michael to put his candy on the dashboard as he continued to massage the young boy's shoulders.

Pete put his hand onto Mikey's lap and started to rub his groin. Michael became nervous and scared. He felt a stimulation rise in his pants. Being six years old, he didn't know what to think of it.

"Have you ever had anyone suck your wiener before?" Pete asked him. Michael shook his head from side to side. Pete leaned over and pulled down the elastic waist of Mikey's brightly colored shorts. He put the young boy's little penis in his mouth and started to suck on it. His little organ started to become erect. Pete started to massage his little testicles. Michael's penis quickly jerked up.

"Stop. I think I am going to pee," he said

"It's okay, go ahead," he said, breathing beer into Mikey's face.

"Just relax," Pete said as he continued sucking on the little boy's penis. A sudden shock of exhilaration and nausea swept over Michael as he peed into Pete's mouth. Pete drank the kid's urine. The boy's body trembled both from overstimulation and anxiety. Pete leaned back into the driver's seat and washed

Michael to choke and cough. He thought he was going to throw up.

"I can't do it," Michael said. "I don't know how to do it right." Pete became frustrated and, spitting into his hand, finished off the job he had tried to get the little boy to do. He grabbed a towel from under the truck seat and ejaculated off into it.

"You let me do it to you, but you won't do it to me!" Pete snapped at him in frustration. Michael felt confused and guilty. He felt as if he had done something wrong. He felt guilty for not doing what his stepfather had wanted of him.

On the ride back down the mountain, Michael's mind was reeling in confusion. He wasn't sure what had just taken place, and it was too much for his young mind to take in. He felt feelings of pleasure, of guilt, and of shame. He felt for the first time in a long time the affection of a father figure, but it was wrapped and twisted into this feeling of guilt, shame, and a pleasure he had never experienced before. Pete looked at him and rubbed the top of his head.

"Whatever you do, you can never tell your mom about this. You can't say a word. Otherwise your mommy will go to jail, and you will go to a foster home," Pete told him. "It will be our little secret. Okay?"

Michael just looked at him and nodded his head in compliance.

"Do you want your mommy to go to jail and get in trouble?" Pete asked him. Michael shook his head back and forth. They drove back down to the house. Mikey did as he was asked and didn't say a word to anyone, not even Michelle. The thought of his mother going to jail scared him. Pete locked himself in his room and drank himself to sleep. Mikey sat in his room playing alone and waiting for his sister to come home from church. He didn't know what to think of what had happened on that mountain. He had no way of processing it, but deep down he felt that there was something wrong. It was a perversion masquerading as the love of a father. It was a disgusting and unholy act in a place of beauty and spirit. A child's innocence and trust were lost there. Secrets and promise were made up on

that mountain that would remain there amongst the trees like

shadows. And the trees would remain silent witnesses, never

able to shed the secrets that they held.

Chapter 9 The Lion and the Lambs

In modern society people are so used to going to the grocery
store and picking up prepackaged, cellophane-wrapped meat.
They throw their goods onto the checkout counter as automatic
machines send them down a conveyer belt. With a buzz and
bleep, the products ring up through the scanners. In a flash, it
brings up the cost of the pre-weighed products. A bagging clerk
throws it into a brown paper bag and out the door people go. At
home, the cellophane wrapping is broken, the meat is thrown
into a skillet, and the meat is soon put onto a plate along with a
few side dishes. A thought is never given to the process it takes
to get the product from farm to plate. The blood that is spilled,
the gizzards that are gutted, and the skin and bone that have been
removed remain out of sight is remain out of mind.

Children watch Disney cartoons with talking animals, they're beds are filled with plush stuffed animals that they hold and caress at night. They do not hear the suffering of animals or smell the blood that is spilled to fill their empty stomachs at dinnertime. The prepackaged meat offers them no insight into the unavoidable truth that life feeds on life. It is a secret that is withheld from the children of a "civilized" world. Death and hunger are kept far away from their imaginations. Childhood soon ends when death and mortality enter the thought and dreams of a child. The moment a child realizes that they too will die one day is the beginning of the end of their childhood, and nightmares soon intermingle with their dreams.

Summer dwindled away, and early fall was on the horizon. It was still warm outside, but the evenings started to cool, and the mornings were crisp. The grasshoppers and crickets chirped away upon their violin legs, with smooth rapidity singing along throughout the day and night. The acorns had fallen from the oak trees, and the apples in the local orchards would soon become

fully ripened, picked, and shipped off to market. The memory of what Pete had done in the woods was still fresh in Michael's memory. Something deep inside told him that what Pete had done was wrong. With every bone in his body he knew it was wrong, but fear and manipulation kept him from speaking about it. On one hand, he enjoyed the attention that Pete had paid to him, but on the other hand he felt a lingering sense that something was wrong. Michael grew close with Frankie and Raul despite their differences in culture. Jacky had wanted him to stay away from their Mexican neighbors. She was old fashioned in her thinking and was unfamiliar with the culture of her neighbors. She saw the differences between her family and theirs, whereas Michael did not. There were not many boys for him to play with in the immediate neighborhood, and despite Jacky's initial objections, he started to play with them anyway. It started out as an occasional playtime in the afternoon, but before long he was spending morning, noon, and early evenings over at their house. Michelle and Kimmy started to become very close as well, spending the night over at each other's houses on the

weekends. Michelle starting to attend the Baptist church with Kimmy, her siblings, and her parents. These kids became their first true childhood friends.

Raul and Frankie's parents were the first generation out of Mexico. They had come to the United States in search of the promise land. They came in search of steady work, and they came in search of a better life. They had left old Mexico behind but brought with them the cultures and customs of their native country. They invited all their relatives, and the ranch and farmhands that they worked with over for a weekend barbecue. In fact, most anyone who had a friendly disposition was invited. They refused no one. There was always plenty of food to go around, and plenty of ice-cold beer and soda in the ice chests. They labored hard for the little scrap of the American dream that they were able to scrape together and celebrated their success's in their adopted country. The women were in the kitchen all morning getting all the fixings prepared for the feast. The salsa and the tortillas were always homemade and never store-bought. As was the tradition, the tortillas were always corn and never

flour. Fresh onions and cilantro were chopped and placed in bowls on the table. They had fresh grated *queso* from the *carnicería*, and there was a pot of frijoles boiling on the stove top. The men stood around the large barbecue pit dug deep into the ground, where wood was stacked up as the fire burned with an intense flame. They sat around listening to music, and traded jabs and jokes with one another.

Michael and Michelle woke in the morning to the crying of a goat. They peeked out the living room window to see a goat tied with rope to a tree just down property from Frank and Raul's house. Its cries echoed through the small neighborhood and grew louder by the hour.

"Time to eat. Breakfast is ready." Jacky said. They walked away from living room window and sat at the table.

"I think Raul and Frankie got a new pet goat." Mikey said.

"I know, poor thing's been crying all morning." Jacky said.

"It's cute mommy. It's pure white. Can we get a goat?" Michelle asked.

"Well, I don't know if that's a good idea." She said. "Goats can be a lot of trouble, besides we already have so many animals. We can barely afford to feed the animals we have now."

"Please mommy?" She asked. "I would love to have a little baby goat."

"Well I'll think about it, now eat your breakfast." She said with no intention of fulfilling Michelle wish. They ate their breakfast of fresh laid eggs from the chickens out back and store-bought bacon. They were relieved that Pete was at work. There was always a sense of tension in the house when he was home. They were always afraid of doing something to upset him. They felt they could be themselves when he wasn't home. They finished their breakfast, scraped their plates into the trash, and sat down to watch Saturday morning cartoons. The picture came in wavy and unclear. Mikey got up off the floor in front of the television and adjusted the rabbit ear antenna. He finally got it in

the right position and the picture cleared up. They sat there watching the cartoons with the cries of the goat and mariachi music playing in in the background.

The cries of the goat soon became screams. It was so loud that the twins could no longer ignore it. The screaming drowned out the sound coming from the television. With eavesdropping eyes, they peered out of the living room window. The goat was strung up from its hind legs, its cries growing louder as the blood rushed into its head. It swung back and forth with futility, trying to free itself from the grip of the rope. Frankie and Raul's father, Able, and another man walked toward the screaming goat with a bucket in hand. They placed the bucket on the ground, below the dangling goat. Able reached behind his back and removed a large blade from its sheathing. The other man held the goat steady, and with a quick movement, Able slid the blade across the animal's neck, slitting its throat. The blood from its veins first squirting, then running down the face of the goat, spilled into the bucket. It was still crying. As more blood fell and ran into the bucket, the cries of the animal

became quieter, and its jerking began to slow to an occasional twitch. Soon the nerves and the jerking ceased all together, but the blood continued to run. There were no more cries to come from the animal as it dangled lifeless from the tree.

Michael and Michelle watched in sheer shock. They ran to their mother crying.

"Mommy! Mommy!" They screamed as tears rolled down their cheeks. "They killed the goat! They killed the goat!"

"There's blood. It was bleeding!" Michelle tried to explain through tear-soaked eyes. An animal had been murdered, and with tearful eyes they cried out for justice. They wanted their mother to do something about this heinous crime. She sat them down, trying to explain this absolute truth to her crying children. Jacky knew they were going to eat that goat. She called her neighbors uncivilized, called them beaners, Mexicans. She told her children not to go over there to play with those kids any more. She told them that what the neighbors had done was barbaric, and that civilized people buy their meat in the grocery

store. She fed them the lie that Walt Disney had sold to the world.

For a few weeks this was enough to keep the twins away from the kids next door. But with boredom and a lack of playmates, they soon got over their fears, and it wasn't long before they were next door again. Michael and Michelle went down to the tree where the goat had been slain. For months afterward, the blood-splattered stain of where the goat had been slain remained. Michelle kicked dirt over the dry crusted blood, trying to cover the stain, but it remained there until the rains and snow of the winter had come. The smell of the slain animal remained for weeks. A smell only kept by flesh and blood. A smell that can be found near any slaughterhouse. It was nauseating to their young stomachs. Michael stayed over for dinner that evening. As he sat there eating the tacos that Rosa had prepared, he brought up the incident of the slain goat from a few weeks prior. It was then that Able informed him that that goat now sat folded in Mikey's corn tortillas. Mikey looked down at his food in shocked. He didn't know what to do. He felt

it would be rude to turn away the dinner that had been prepared.

He continued to chew his food, which tasted so good. He

shrugged his shoulders, continued eating, and put the thought of

the goat out of his mind.

School was gearing up to start as the summer was getting

ready to set and the fall would soon rise in its place. The kids

had met one of the neighborhood kids by the name of Doug. He

was a smart-ass kid who acted older then he really was. He was

a bit of a young punk and was always finding trouble to get into.

Doug lived on a dirt road on the opposite side of the creek. It

was a place the twins weren't familiar with and hadn't spent

much time. Doug came from a family of old world values. His

father was heavy-handed with Doug and his brother Jason. He

had a paddle hanging inside the pantry closet that he'd had made

out at the prison by the inmates. The paddle was large and

sanded smooth. Large holes were drilled in it so that as it flew

through the air, it was met with less resistance. There was only

one reason for his dad to have had this paddle made, and that

was for busting butts and spanking asses. Doug would get in

trouble often as it turned out, and his dad would yell at him to go

get the paddle. Anytime his dad said this, Doug knew an ass

beating was coming.

For a kid who got his ass spanked with a wooden paddle,

one would think he would be well behaved, but for some reason

he was always knee-deep in trouble. Maybe that's how he got

attention from his parents. His parents were always having

weekend parties and drinking in the evening when they got off

work. They both worked at the prison, which was a very

stressful job. It seemed his parents never paid much attention to

him unless he was causing trouble, and if a kid can't find

attention one way, he will find it another. All in all, they weren't

bad people, in fact they were very nice and well respected in the

neighborhood. But Dougie was a hell-raiser. It was this

dangerous side to Doug that not only intimidated Michael but

also enticed him. It brought out in him an attitude that Jacky did

not care for. What monkey see's, and monkey will do.

Kimmy had spent the night at the house with Michelle. It

was one of the few weekends left before they would have to

return to school. After breakfast Michael, Michelle, and Kimmy walked down to the creek. They played along the banks not wanting to get in the water, as it was still a little cold out. Doug came busting through the bushes. He sat down on a rock, teasing the kids, and even though they were all older than he was, he acted as if he knew it all, and treated them like they were just kids. "So, what are you guys doing today?" Doug asked

"We're playing in the creek. What does it look like?" Michelle said in a sarcastic tone. He stuck his tongue out at her and she replied by doing the same.

"So, have you guys ever been up to the top where the creek starts," he asked them.

They stood there all quiet, knowing full well that none of them had. They had all talked about it and wondered where the creek started but were always too scared to go far from the immediate area. What lay beyond was an intriguing taboo, but it was off-limits.

"Well, have you?" Doug asked again. Their silence gave away the fact that they hadn't. "Well, I stole a few of my mom's

wine coolers. You guys wanna go?" he asked in a manner that not only made them feel like small children, which they were, but also made them feel like chickens.

"Ooh, is that alcohol?" Michelle asked. "You're going to get in so much trouble!"

"Besides we are too young to drink alcohol!" Kimmy said, backing up her friend.

"Well, what about you, Mikey? You ever been to the top of the creek?" Doug asked.

"No!" he said with a scowl.

"What? Are you a scared? You little momma's boy!" Doug teased.

"I'm not a momma's boy!" Mikey said, defending his little masculinity.

"Well, you don't have to drink the wine cooler. I brought some water, too," Doug said, "So what do you say? You want to come? They sat there talking in a circle. Their parents weren't exactly keeping a close eye on them, and they knew they had time to kill.

"We'll go, but we need to stop and get some snacks for the road!" Michelle said. She was always the negotiator of the group. They all ran to the house and ransacked the pantry. They made a few peanut butter and jelly sandwiches, grabbed a few cookies and some chips. It was their first excursion into the woods, and they didn't want to leave home without a few provisions. Michelle grabbed her backpack and loaded it up with the food. Michael ran into the tool shed and found an old camping canteen. He rinsed it out and filled it with water. Soon they were out on the trail, or lack thereof.

"We should take a short cut over the hills. It'll save us some time," Doug suggested.

"I think we should stay along the creek, so we don't get lost," Michelle said.

Let's take a vote. Who wants to save some time and get to the top of the creek faster?" Doug said as he raised his hand. Mikey and Kimmy raised their hand. "Looks like you lost." Michelle reluctantly agreed, and they began walking up the steep hill. The grass along the hill was tall and dry. It came up above

their kneecaps, and the foxtail stickers began to burrow into their socks. It got to the point where it became too painful to walk. They had to constantly keep stopping to pick the stickers from their shoes and socks.

"Nice shortcut, Doug!" Michelle said sarcastically.

"Yeah, nice shortcut!" Michael and Kimmy said, agreeing with her.

"Well, it was a lot clearer in the spring!" he said in his own defense. "And the grass was a lot lower."

"Let's just follow the creek up. It will be a lot quicker!" Michelle said.

"Whatever!" Doug said. "You know you got a smart-ass mouth on you!" he said, irritated at losing his position as navigator. They tore off their socks and shoes, cooling their itching feet in the creek water. It felt refreshing on their skin. They sat there picking the golden stickers from their stockings. They walked for a few hours before deciding to take a break. Michelle broke out the PB&J's along with the cookies and

crackers. All four of them sat under the shade of a large ponderosa pine eating their food.

"Hey, you guys, want some strawberry soda?" Doug said. Soda sounded so refreshing at that moment. It began to become hot as the cool morning air started to burn off. Doug got out some plastic cups and poured each one of them some of the fizzy drink. Everyone drank theirs with a gulp and held their cup out for more. Doug cracked open another bottle and poured the others another drink. They finished up their food, and as the stood up they started to feel light-headed from the drink. They giggled as they stumbled around to gather up their belongings. They marched their way up the creek singing campfire songs. Mikey stumbled across the surface of some slippery, algae covered rocks. He lost his balance falling hard on his butt. The other kids looked at him in shock. He sat there for a few moments, expecting his backside to hurt. When the pain refused to come, he looked around to see the other kids staring at him. When they realized he was okay, they all started laughing

hysterically, himself included. He got up, rubbed his butt, and they continued.

As soon as their buzz would start to wear off was about the time they would start to get thirsty again. Doug didn't hesitate to crack open another one of his magical sodas and start pouring. They walked until the oaks gave way to the pines. The cover overhead began to get thicker as the mountains surrounding the crevasse of the creek began to get steeper. The farther up the mountain went they went, the stronger the flow of the creek became. They suddenly heard a rustling in the bushes coming down the ravine. They all stopped. The rustling got louder, and it was coming closer and closer to them. Their initial thought was that it was a boulder getting ready to come crashing down on them. They could hear the breaking of branches, the snapping of twigs, and the rustle of leaves. As the noise drew nearer to them, they realized that whatever it was, was coming right in their direction. They sat there frozen not sure what direction to turn in.

Suddenly, a deer fawn broke from the low-lying oak brush above them. It jumped the ravine and ran along the upper embankment of the creek near where they stood, then took off down the creek side like a bolt of lightning. It had light spots on its side like Bambi. Off in the distance, there came more noise. The snapping of twigs and branches along with the rustling of leaves came again. Out of the foliage closer to the creek bed, a mountain lion broke free of the oak brush. They felt they were suddenly caught in some trial of life. It rushed toward Michael as he stood frozen, dead in his tracks. He was standing on a large rock as the mountain lion came pummeling toward him. He closed his eyes just waiting for the beast to attack. He thought he was done for. It pounced near his footing as it bounced off the rock he was standing on. It made its way in the direction the little deer had disappeared, and it, too, disappeared into the bushes. As it left their sight, they could hear it snarling and growling. Its body moved almost quicker than their eyes could follow. Its body looked as if it were made of pure muscle. They could hear the snapping of branches and the rustling of the oak

brush as the mountain lion raced down the ravine. The squealing of the young fawn and the snarling growls of the mountain lion soon followed as it caught up with its prey. It sobered up their buzz damn quick. Michael stood there in a cold white panic.

"Oh my god, we could have been food!" Doug said.

"Holy shit! Holy shit!" Michelle said. "What was that?"

"That was a mountain lion!" Doug said.

"Are you all right, Mikey?" Michelle asked.

"I...I think so!" he said as he patted himself down in disbelief. They stood there in stunned silence before Kimmy turned and whispered something into Michelle's ear.

"Oh no! Not my Kulaks," Michelle said as Kimmy grabbed her arm, pleading with her to be quiet. She looked like she had seen a ghost. She dragged Michelle into the scrub brush as Michael and Doug could hear them whispering. Michelle had gotten a new pair of Kulak shorts at the begging of the summer. She had allowed Kimmy to wear them so long as Kimmy didn't allow anything to happen to them. The two young girls soon emerged from the bushes, and everything seemed normal except

for the fact that the Kulaks that Kimmy was wearing were now entirely wet.

"What happened to you? Did you piss your pants?" Doug asked her.

"No!" Kimmy said sharply. "I just fell into the water!" she said quickly. "Right, Michelle?"

"Yeah, she just fell in the creek," Michelle said quickly. Michael and Doug never thought anything of it, but Michelle later told Michael in private that the mountain lion had literally scared the shit out of Kimmy, and that she had dropped a load in Michelle's Kulaks.

They continued their hiking trip until they came upon a large pool of water. It had been carved out of the ravine by the creek. They swam and played in the creek until late in the afternoon and polished off the wine coolers Doug had stolen from his mother. On their way back home, they instead decided to take the paved road, instead of foraging back along the creek bed. The story of the mountain lion and the fawn was something they decided to keep to themselves and not tell their parents.

That and the story of the shit-stained Kulaks. The twins walked home after the small group of kids broke up and headed in their own directions. They had escaped the clutches of one predator and were walking into the waiting arms of another.

Chapter 10 Thanksgiving

It had stayed warm throughout the summer and into the early

fall. The warmth would not give way to the cooler northern

winds. There were mornings where the temperature had dropped

down enough to start turning the mountaintops shades of orange

and red, but the tree leaves still clung to their branches. The frost

of autumn had not set in, and the days seemed as bright and

warm as if it were August. Late November came as families

across the country prepared for the arrival of their extended

families for the Thanksgiving holiday. Turkeys and hams poured

into grocery stores by the thousands. People were traveling all

over the country in anticipation of feasts and family gatherings.

Jacky purchased Sonny a bus ticket from Las Vegas to

Bakersfield. He had not been back to Tehachapi since he had run

away. He called from time to time to ask for some money, but

other than that he'd remained a stranger. She had felt a sense of failure when it came to Sonny, she felt she was at a loss with him, but she hoped that maybe she could convince him to stay. She thought that maybe the harshness of being out on his own might be enough to persuade him to come home. She was excited to have her whole family together again. She drove down to Bakersfield and picked him up from the Greyhound station for the big holiday. She planned for everyone to stay at the house during the holiday and wouldn't accept anybody staying in a hotel. Next to Christmas, Thanksgiving was her favorite holiday. They didn't have much room, but it was enough for everyone to have a place to sleep. Jacky's sister Barb and her boyfriend came up from the coast, as did Barbs grown daughters and their boyfriends. Jacky and Barb stayed up long in the night before the big day, preparing the food. She made pies, the stuffing, deviled eggs, and all the preparations for Thanksgiving dinner. She made pecan, pumpkin, coconut cream, and chocolate cream pies. She made all the crust from scratch as she'd been taught by her grandmother. She was a true master in the kitchen, and

everyone was delighted that she once again would be entertaining. Everyone arrived for the holiday as promised. The house was brimming with as many aromas from the food as there were people who had come to enjoy it.

In the morning there were so many people sleeping throughout the house that Michael and Michelle had to tiptoe around to avoid stepping on people. Jacky's father, Curly, drove up early on Thanksgiving Day with his girlfriend Mary. He had given marriage a few tries after the death of Jacky's mother, but it never panned out. As much as he tried he could never get over the death of his first wife, the love of his life. Curly and Mary were making plans to buy up rental properties and to build a shopping center in the Antelope Valley. Both Curly and Mary was a successful business owner, and she was a person who loved her vodka as much as she loved her money. Sometimes it was hard to tell which she loved more. Curly had a fondness for the bottle as well and loved to drink Jim Beam straight on the rocks. This was a drinking family by and large. Everything from beer and vodka to bourbon and champagne was either in the

refrigerator or in ice chests on the floor. Cousins, aunts, uncles, and grandparents played card games while the turkey was roasting in the oven.

In the Sanchez house next door, it was a similarly festive story. A house full of out-of-town relatives and an oven stuffed with a turkey. There was mariachi music playing full bore, and the Mexican family's relatives and guests danced on the front lawn. They had their ice chest full of beer as well, and inside the kitchen there was little room for the kids running around. All the adults were busy entertaining their relatives and preparing their holiday feasts. There were so many kids running around both households that the adults couldn't look after them all. They were all busy catching up with one another and sharing stories of what had happened since they all had gotten together last. This gave the children free rein to do pretty much whatever they wanted.

Michael had been back and forth between his house and the Sanchez home. The countertops were filled with food in preparation. Half-drunk cocktails, soda, and beer cans littered

the countertops and coffee tables. Mary was a heavy smoker. She loved her Marlboro Lights 100s, and her vodka tonics to go with them. She had this dazzling yellow cigarette lighter that kept catching Michael's eye. He walked by the counter looking at the yellow lighter. It was just sitting unattended, waiting for him to snatch it up. He circled the lighter like a shark circling its prey in the water. He was waiting for the perfect moment of inattention. He knew the adults were too busy to keep a close eye on him. The alcohol running through their systems and the festivities had made them inattentive. When everyone had a blind eye to him, he quickly grabbed the yellow Bic and shoved it into his pocket. He bolted out the door and made his way back toward the Sanchez house. He caught up with Raul and Frankie, who were playing down by the chicken coop with a few of their cousins.

"Hey guys, what you doing?" Michael asked with a sly grin upon his face.

"Nothing, just hanging out, waiting for the turkey to get done," Raul replied.

"Yeah. So, you want to go make smoke signals?" Michael said mischievously.

"Smoke signals? What's that?" Raul asked, with confusion.

"You know smoke signals, like the Indians make," he replied. "See the mountains over there?"

"Yeah!" Raul said.

"There's Indians in those mountains, and we can send them smoke signals, and they will send us smoke signals back," he explained.

"Yeah, that sounds cool," Frankie said. They walked to the far end of the Sanchez property and ducked down behind a large sage bush.

"Go gather some twigs and grass," Michael told them. Raul and Frankie went around and gathered as much debris as their small hands could carry. The summer had been long and dry, and that had left plenty of dry brush and grass on the ground. Michael crouched down and made a small pile with the debris that the other boys had gathered. Raul and Frankie stood

over him as he sparked up the pile of twigs and grass. The small pile of twigs and grass burned quickly. They had not cleared all the grass around the pile, and it wasn't long before it started to catch fire as well. The three boys stood back and looked on with amazement.

Soon the fire spread from the grasses and leapt into the sage bush. The sage bush blew up like a roman candle. With wide eyes they looked at each other as the fire soon grew out of control as it hopped from the one bush to the other nearby bushes.

"Run!" Mikey screamed. Raul, Frankie, and their cousins ran toward their house, and Mikey ran toward his. He ran inside and sat in his bedroom as the fire burned on without supervision. Meanwhile Raul and Frankie ran up to their father. He was sitting out on the front lawn drinking beer with his relatives and friends, listening to music and waiting for the thanksgiving dinner.

"Mikey started a fire, Mikey started a fire!" they squealed.

"What?" he shouted at them.

"Mikey started a fire! Come look!" The boys dragged him by the hand around the house. He looked down the hill to see the end of his property ablaze.

"Chinga tu madre?" he shouted. All the adults ran toward the fire with buckets and water hoses in hand. Michael peered out his bedroom window trying to remain inconspicuous. He saw all the adults running from his neighbor's house. Soon everyone poured out from his house, running down the driveway with water hoses and buckets of their own. Mary, the smoker with the shiny yellow lighter, ran as fast as she could to the flames. But the hose she was pulling stopped short, halfway down the driveway, and yanked her to the ground. Everyone was down at the end of the property line where the fire burned. With a quick response, they were able to knock down the flames. The fire had been doused but not before taking out a fence post and leaving a large burned circle in the dry brush.

Michael quickly ran into the kitchen and replaced the yellow Bic he had taken from on top of the Marlboro cigarette

pack. He was nervous and shaking. He was afraid that when the adults returned Jacky would give him a spanking that he would never forget. When they came back, he could hear them all talking and wondering how the fire had started. Nobody ever seemed to have noticed the missing lighter, and the spanking that he was so afraid of never came. He slowly emerged from behind his bedroom door, and after the trepidation wore off, he gained enough nerve to go into the kitchen.

Everyone had finished their holiday meal. The turkey had been picked apart like a carcass thrown to the vultures. Aunt Barb, Jacky, Michelle, and Faith were in the kitchen putting the leftover food into old butter containers for refrigeration. The holiday had reached peak intoxication, and the turkey and stuffing couldn't absorb the alcohol fast enough. Grandpa Curly's turkey dinner had set in along with his Jim Beam, and he had retired to the couch and coasted off to sleep with a snore. He dreamed of the pies and desserts that awaited his stomach to settle.

Pete was in his usual state of intoxication and contamination. Going to the ice chest, he realized that they had already plowed through two cases of beer. He asked Barb's daughter Brandy if she would like to drive down to the gas station so that he could get some more.

They drove to Wild Rose, which was the only place open on the holiday. After purchasing the beer, they headed back up towards Water Canyon. Pete decided to take a shortcut up a deep rutted dirt road that cut across a field, instead of going around on the paved roads. He parked underneath the shade of a large oak tree that sat in the middle of a field and shut the engine off. He handed Brandy a beer from one of the newly purchased cases and cracked one open for himself. She lit up a cigarette, and even though she was legally an adult, she felt even more grown up sitting there drinking a beer with her uncle Pete. He sipped a few drinks from his brew and slowly put his arm around her.

"I can't believe how much you have grown up; you really have developed into a full-grown woman!" he said to her as he stared at her breasts.

"Uh…yeah, I guess I have," she said uncomfortably. He started to rub her shoulders and neck. "How's that beer?" he asked her.

"Um…It's cold. Pretty good, I guess," she responded. She began to feel uncomfortable. She thought about her aunt Jacky. He slowly moved his hand down her arm and over to her left breast as he massaged it. She looked at him, afraid to make a move. He bent forward and kissed her as he forced his beer-stained tongue into her mouth. She pushed him back away from her.

"I think we should be heading back. I-I don't think you should be doing this," she stammered. "I want to head back now!" she said demandingly.

"I'm sorry. I shouldn't have pushed myself on you. I…I…I'm just a little drunk," he said in defense of himself. "Please don't say anything to your aunt Jacky, or your mom. This…this won't happen again."

"Let's just go!" she insisted again. He started up the truck and pulled out from the cover of the oak tree. The truck moved as it rattled up the dirt road and toward the house.

Back at the house, everyone was in high holiday spirits as they became more intoxicated. Sonny had snuck Curly's bottle of Jim Beam and had started getting a pretty good buzz on. He walked out onto the front porch and lit a cigarette. After a few moments Mary joined him. She had not seen him in a few years. Their conversation soon moved on towards religion and politics, two conversations that should never be discussed under the influence of alcohol. Their simple conversation began to develop into an argument. Neither one of them even knew what had set the other off. With the flames of their tempers fueled by alcohol, their voices became louder and louder. Jackie stood in the kitchen cleaning up the holiday meal when should heard Sonny yelling. "Fuck you! You don't know what the fuck you're talking about old lady!"

Jacky walked outside and grabbed Sonny by the back of the arm. She pulled him around to the side of the house.

207

Michelle stared out the window and watched the heated exchange escalate between them.

"What the fuck is wrong with you? Why would you talk like that to your grandfather's girlfriend?"

"She's a fucking bitch, Mom!" he said belligerently.

"You are totally disrespecting your grandfather, and you're embarrassing me!" she said. "Are you drunk? You seem drunk? Have you been drinking?" Even though she was short in stature, she was tall with anger. She could strike the fear of God into her children. Soon Sonny's belligerence had got the best of him and he turned his anger onto Jacky.

"She's a bitch, Mom, and I don't fucking trust her," he said. "She basically called me a loser and a drug addict."

"I don't care if you trust her and I don't care what she called you! She's your grandfather's girlfriend. You're really starting to embarrass me." She told him.

"Why are you taking her side? Why can't you be on my side for once?" He said to her as his words stumbled off his tongue. She stood there and looked on him with disappointment.

"You've never been on my side. You've always chosen yourself over me, me always chosen your husbands over me, you've always chosen everyone over me!"

"You know what, I was so happy for you to be here with us, to be part of a family, and this is what happens. She's right. You are a drug addict and you are a loser. You need to clean your shit up. Grow the fuck up!" she screamed at him.

"Fuck this! I don't have to put up with this shit," Sonny said to his mother. "You fucking bitch!" She stopped for a moment and stared at him dead in his eyes.

"I'm a fucking bitch, huh? I'm a fucking bitch?" she said as she slapped him in the face. "You've embarrassed me. You've become nothing but an embarrassment." She continued to slap him repeatedly as he backed up against the house.

"Get off me, you fucking bitch!" he yelled. Michelle stared in wide-eyed wonder at what was taking place outside the front window. She could hear Sonny's head thump up against the wall. It rattled the window in front her and their argument could be heard throughout the house.

"I'm sending you back to Las Vegas right now! I want you to go in and pack up your shit. You'll be leaving on the first bus back," Jacky said. "You want to live on the streets and be a fucking drug addict, see if I fucking care! I will never fucking help you again!"

She went inside and grabbed her purse and car keys. Sonny stumbled in and grabbed up his dirty backpack and dirty blankets. As he passed Mary sitting in the den with her vodka tonic, she smiled at him, raised her glass, and blew a plume of smoke in his direction. He flipped her off and slammed the front door on his way out.

Michelle ran to the front window of the house and watched as Jacky peeled off down the driveway. The tires of the car sent gravel flying up against the house. It would be a long time before Michael and Michelle would see their older brother again, and even longer still before he came back around the house for any of the holidays. The kids sat there eating their slices of pie. Grandpa Curly and Mary left soon after. The rest of the adults continued to drink and play card games. They

pretended not to notice what had taken place. They did not talk about it, and instead continued as if it had not occurred.

Chapter 11 A Holly Jolly Christmas

There had been a few storms that came in and dusted the mountain pass with frost, but it was not enough to call it snow. The snow usually started in December, but the valley wouldn't normally see the heavier loads until January or February. In years gone by it seemed that the annual snow season lasted for months, burying the valley in its frozen grip. It was measured in feet, where now it is measured in inches. When the snow did fall it covered the high desert with illusions of a winter wonderland. People that grew up there recognize the difference in the winters over the years. They always noted the difference in snowfall. The old-timers talked in the coffee shops about how it didn't snow up there like it used to, just as they talked about how the summers weren't as cool as they used to be. The change in the weather cycles was evident.

As winter finally made its arrival, the air was cold and clean. The wind blew across the valley of the summit pass dropping the temperate drastically from the tepid autumn. Michael and Michelle were anticipating the arrival of Christmas, the arrival of Santa Claus in his load-bearing red sleigh, and the beginning of the long-awaited winter break. They were lucky in that Santa seemed to always stop by their house as he flew over the valley. He never seemed to miss them, whether they were good or not. Sometimes they wondered how on earth they had made it onto the nice list. Maybe their good deeds had somehow outweighed the bad? All week long the only thing the children at school could talk about was Christmas this and Santa that. The school teachers had the children making ornaments of papier-mâché, sprinkled with glitter of red and green. The sort of Christmas ornaments only a mother could love. It was a festive time of year, and the children in class easily caught the Christmas spirit.

That last week before winter break seemed to last forever, but finally the last bell rang and the school went into

recess. The twins spent a lot of their time over at the Sanchez house. Michael played with the boys next door all the time, and when Kimmy wasn't home, Michelle would be the tomboy and play next door with Mikey. Today again the twins were talking about Christmas and Santa Claus, and about reindeer, presents, and toys.

"I can't wait for Santa to come. I hope he brings us lots of toys! I asked him for a Rainbow Brite doll!" Michelle said joyfully.

"Yeah and I asked for a Nintendo and some Star Wars toys," Michael said. "I want Super Mario Brothers, and a light saber like Luke Skywalker."

"My dad says Santa's not real," Raul said in defiance. The talk of Christmas made him uncomfortable. "He said that we probably aren't going to get any presents this year." He was older than Frankie and thought the idea of Santa Clause was a bust. Santa didn't stop by the Sanchez home the previous year, and from the sound of it, wouldn't be stopping by this year either.

"He is, too, real!" Michael said in heated defense. "He comes to our house every year. We even leave cookies and milk out for him, and when we wake up in the morning they're all eaten up!"

"Yeah, so if there's no Santa, then who eats all the cookies," Michelle said in support of her brother, and in support of her present-bearing saint.

"Well, if my dad says he's not real, then he's not real. My dad wouldn't lie," Raul said. Frankie looked caught in the middle of this heated debate, his eyes darting from one talking mouth to the other.

"Tomorrow, after I wake up, I'll bring my toys over and show you that Santa's real," Michael said. "If you guys are good, Santa will bring you toys, too."

"Well I think it's bullshit!" Raul said emulating the language he often heard from the adults around him.

"Well you'll see." Michelle said. "We have to go make cookies for Santa. Come on Mikey let's go." They left the Sanchez home with seeds of doubt planted in their minds.

Michael and Michelle stayed up, with Jacky and Faith baking up all sort of cookies. Jacky made sugar cookies, chocolate chip cookies, and pecan sandies. She made gingerbread and large flats of fudge. She set out her silver holiday tray on the coffee table filled full of cookies and fudge. Next to the cookie tray she filled candy jars with candy canes and an assortment of hard candies. Michelle wrote the note for Santa explaining to him that the cookies and the glass of eggnog were for him, and the carrots were for his reindeer, the extra-large carrot being for Rudolph, who was their favorite.

Jacky gave each one of them two cookies of their choosing. Michael always chose the chocolate chip cookies. While Michelle chose one sugar cookie and one chocolate chip. The twins sat in the den looking at the sparkling Christmas tree. They sat in front of the wood-burning stove as it blazed behind them and warmed their backs. Michelle looked over the stove with its narrow smokestack.

"Mom, how's Santa going to get into our house if we don't have a real fireplace? How is Santa going to fit through that? He's too fat!" she asked with the curiosity of a child.

"Well, he's magic. He can fit through anything," Jacky said.

"Well, what if you don't have a fireplace or a wood-burning stove, how is Santa going to get in? Kimmy doesn't have a fireplace. How does he get in her house?"

"Well, Santa's got a magic key. When someone doesn't have a fireplace, he can use his magic key, and open their front door," Jacky said.

"Frankie and Raul's dad said that Santa's not real!" Mikey said. "And some of the kids at school say he's not real, too!"

"Well, don't believe those kids!" Jacky told him, trying to keep the myth and the legend alive for at least a few more years. After their cookies they waited by the window, hoping to catch a glimpse of the reindeer-driven sleigh as it glided through the air. Next door Frankie and Raul looked out into the sky,

wondering whether Santa was real. They wondered whether they had been good enough throughout the year for him to stop by. They wondered whether they would wake up to a tree full of presents like the kids they saw on television.

"If you two don't go to bed soon, Santa's going to know you're not sleeping, and he is going to go right past our house!" Jacky told the twins. "Then you will have to wait until next Christmas to get your toys." That was all it took, and they were off to bed in a heartbeat. They kept trying to fall asleep, but the more they tried the harder it was to keep their eyes closed. The idea of what might be lying under the Christmas tree when they awoke in the morning was too much for their imaginations to wrestle with. Michael couldn't help wondering why Frankie and Raul's dad told them Santa wasn't real. He wondered how Santa could have missed their house last year. They seemed like pretty good kids. They never did anything too bad, nothing worse than anything Michael had ever done. He thought to himself that maybe there wasn't any Santa. Maybe his mom had made it all up. But why would everyone lie about it? His mom, his teachers

at school, all the movies and TV shows, could they all be lying? He tried to push this thought out of his head, hoping that Santa couldn't hear his thoughts. He fell asleep uncomfortably, wondering what the truth might be.

Jacky stood in the kitchen, still cleaning up the dishes from the long day of baking. She looked out the kitchen window, wondering where Sonny was. A large cold front was coming in, and she worried that he was out there somewhere caught in the cold. After doing the dishes, she and Faith went to the closet where she had hidden all the presents. They brought them down and one by one, placing them under the tree. They stayed up late doing some final wrapping before turning in for the night.

In the morning Michelle woke up first. She stumbled into the living room to see the Christmas tree stocked full of presents. She looked out the living room window and was blinded by white light that flooded into her early morning pupils. When her eyes adjusted she saw that Christmas had delivered a fresh blanket of snow across the valley. She ran into Michael's room.

"Wake up, Mikey, wake up. Santa came last night, and he brought the snow!" she squealed with excitement. "Wake up!" she said as she shook him. Michael's eyes shot open like a gun blast had torn through his dreams. "Look out the window, Mikey, look." He got up and looked out his bedroom windows. The ground was covered in snow. The white glistening light reflecting off the snow hurt his eyes. He blinked as he tried to focus his vision on the white-covered hills and mountaintops. He suddenly felt himself being dragged out of the bedroom and into the den where the Christmas tree was. Under the lights, the ornaments, and all the tinsel, lay the gifts that Jacky and Faith had stayed up late wrapping. Boxes covered with ornate wrapping paper and topped off with beautiful bows were stacked one on top of another all the way around the tree.

Jacky and Pete were soon woken up by the rustle of noise coming from den, and they knew the twins were awake. Jacky wrapped herself in her bathrobe and started to brew some coffee to get the sleep out of her eyes. Faith woke up and started helping Jacky go through and hand off presents to their rightful

owner. Faith was the kind of girl that slowly unwrapped each present, making sure not to tear the wrapping. She then would fold it up neatly, after the present was open, and place the wrapping back in the box along with the gift. One by one she would slowly do this with each present. She was always the last one to unwrap all her presents. Michael would tear through his presents. If the present was socks, underwear, or clothing, he would give some quick thanks and toss it aside until he came to a toy. He opened his Star Wars toys and played with them as the rest of his presents sat unopened. He picked up his plastic light saber and pretended he was Obi-Wan Kenobi or Luke Skywalker, fighting off the Galactic empire. Meanwhile Michelle would tear ass through her presents one after the next, stripping off the paper and tossing it aside. When she ran out of gifts, she looked around at everyone else still unwrapping their presents. This always made her feel shortchanged, as if she'd gotten fewer presents than everyone else. Her eyes filled with tears and she put her head into her arm and started to cry.

"What's wrong? Why are you crying?" Jacky asked.

"Everyone got more presents than I did," she answered with a sob.

"No, they didn't. Everyone got the same. You got the same number of gifts as Mikey and the same as Faith," Jacky said, trying to cheer her up. "You just opened your presents a lot faster than everyone else." Her speedy unwrapping habits led to many disappointing Christmases, but no one seemed able to explain this to her. There was one last present sitting under the Christmas tree. It was stuffed way in the back and out of sight. "To all the kids, Love Santa," the label claimed. All three kids got a hand in on unwrapping this present. They tore open the paper wrapping, and as soon as the printing on the box could be read, they realized they had gotten their Nintendo. The twins squealed in excitement as they ran around the den, unable to control themselves. After the wrapping had been thrown out, and the boxes put away, Jacky brought out unwrapped presents and placed them under the tree.

"Who are those for?" Mikey asked.

"Those are for your brother Sonny!" she said.

"Where is Sonny?" Mikey asked

"He's in Vegas, somewhere I think," she said with uncertainty. She started breakfast while Pete hooked up the video game to the living room television. The twins sat there in wonder and amazement as the cartoon characters came to life on their television screen. The little characters jumped and ran back and forth across the screen, all in glorious 8-bit graphics. Up until then, it was something they had only seen in arcades. They all sat there in the living room and ate their breakfast. Pete and Faith sat there and played it for a few hours, not letting the twins have a turn. It was not until after they got bored with it that they finally let them play. After an hour of playing the games, Pete decided that he didn't want them playing it all day.

"All right turn it off. I don't want you to rot your brains out. You two can play it again later in the evening," he said. They looked at the television screen, then at the gaming console, and wondered how it could possibly rot out their brains. They looked at their stepfather and felt they were being bamboozled.

"But you and faith got to play it longer!" Michelle said.

"And if you two want to play it again later I want you to turn it off and go out and play for a while."

"But…," Mikey said.

"No buts. Get up, get dressed, and go outside." Pete said. Feeling cheated and disappointed, they decided to go off to their friend's house and show off their Christmas presents. Michelle walked down the road to Kimmy's to see what she had gotten. She took some of her new clothes, her plastic jewelry, and a few toys to compare with. Meanwhile Michael gathered up his new toys to show off to Frankie and Raul. He carried his blaster strapped to his hip, and the light Saber he carried in his hand. He put on his snow boots and trudged through the snow toward the Sanchez house. He left his new clothes behind. "See what Santa brought for me! This is my blaster," he boasted. As he pulled the trigger, the little black plastic gun lit up and made strange noises. Frankie was enthralled and in awe of the plastic gun. "But see this! This is my light saber, it is the true weapon of a Jedi master!" he said, reiterating the words straight out of the movie. He pulled it from the little plastic belt around his waist and

swung it around like he was wielding a sword. The cone-shaped pieces of plastic extended out to full length and lit up, the saber making buzzing noises as he swung it around.

"Wow!" Frankie said. "Can I try it?"

"Sure!" Mikey said as he handed him the plastic sword.

"Santa didn't bring that for you. Your mom bought that!" Raul said in jealousy.

"Uh, Santa brought it for me. My mom didn't buy it," he said in defense.

"Santa's not real. My dad told me not to believe in that stuff," Raul said back with anger as he stormed off.

"Why's your brother such a jerk all the time?" Mikey asked.

"He's mad because Santa didn't come last night," Frankie said.

"Santa didn't come to your house last night?" he asked in shock.

"No, maybe because we didn't get a tree and decorate our house like your mom," Frankie said. Michael looked around

the living room and didn't see a tree; he saw no decorations or presents. There were no lights in the windows, no garland, and no tinsel. He suddenly felt bad inside about bragging about the things he had gotten. He thought for sure Santa would have come and dropped off some toys for them. He didn't realize how short on money their parents were. How they were just barely making ends meet with bills and putting food on the table. To them there were more important things to spend money on. Making ends meet was their priority.

"Where are you going?" Frankie asked as Michael bolted toward the front door.

"I'll be right back," he said. He ran back to the house and into his bedroom. He grabbed some of his older toys from his toy chest and ran back to Frankie's house. *I guess Santa isn't real*, he thought. He ran back over to the Sanchez house with his hands full of toys.

"You can have some of my toys," he said. That was the first time that Michael realized that Santa wasn't real, and that

his mother was the one behind all the Christmas presents. The rumors on the playground had been true.

The Christmas snow had melted a few days after, but winter soon came on with an obscuring vengeance. The late-season snowfall more than made up for its tardiness. The thick clouds rolled in and blotted out the sun with their gray heavy masses. The clouds were so heavily laden that they moved across the sky like a ship against an iceberg. The lights from the little town below faded in and out of vision as the passing clouds waxed and waned. The snowflakes fell first as little specks. The snow drifted across the roads and blew easily in the wind. As the air became thick and cold, the small balls of ice started to stick upon the stalks of the foxtail grasses. It fell between the cracks and crevasses of the gravel on the dirt roads. The flakes became bigger, and soon they fell like white stars from the sky. They stuck to each other like cotton balls, and the small piles soon grew into drifts. The patches of snow, like that of a quilt, became sewn together into a large blanket of white. The old contours of

the landscape became obscured as the white snow distorted the land into a smooth puffy blanket. At night the clouds lay low and blocked out all light from the stars above.

When winter is at its height, at its coldest density, the days become gray and the evening becomes pitch-black. The lights from town and of nearby houses fades out and a sense of isolation falls in. Sometimes it can be a comforting isolation and sometimes it can be an isolation set with depression. The coldness can awaken your senses and make you feel alive, just as it can dampen your spirits and make you feel alone. When the coldness of winter sets in, you instinctively take stock of what you have, and what you are lacking. On an instinctual level, you start to add more food to the pantry. The heavier quilts and comforters come down from the closets and replace the lighter blankets that covered the beds during the spring and summer. If your home is heated with a fireplace or wood-burning stove, you stock up on cords of wood. You must be careful that the wood is not too green, so that it will burn through and not die out early in the night. If you have horses or cows, you make sure to buy

enough bales of hay to see the livestock through the lean times of a long winter.

Pete began spending a lot of time at the bar at night and away from the family. He was drinking the family into poverty, and when he did spend a night at the house, he was usually sleeping off a hangover. Jacky would have to drive to town from time to time and peel him off a bar stool, and often she would have to peel him off another woman. During the winter construction would slow down, and with that so did the extra money Jacky brought in. They were living paycheck to paycheck, and hand to mouth. The money that Pete made out at the prison was a decent income, but it wasn't enough to quench his thirst, pay the bills, and feed the family. Jacky grew bitter over his relentless drinking and spending. Things could have been better, more affordable, had Pete learned to live within certain limits. But limits and boundaries were not within his thinking. Jacky was buying a quarter of a cord of wood at a time, because she couldn't afford to buy a whole cord. When you live in a rural community, and far enough outside of town, you heat

your water and cook your food with propane. And to offset the costs of propane, you heat your home with wood. This propane is trucked up the mountainside in large tanks. They go from one rural home to another, filling up the residential propane tanks, and replenishing the needs of those families for a short time.

The Sanchez family seemed to always be well prepared for the wintertime. Able would go out in the late summer and cut all the wood his family needed for the season. He replenished the wood supply early enough to give the wood plenty of time to dry and cure for the burning. He and the boys piled up the wood along the fence line that separated the families' two joining property lines. One cord of wood after another stretched up and down the fence.

As winter dragged on, the small amounts of wood Jacky bought were never enough and dwindled to nothing very quickly. When there was no more, she would send Michael over to ask if they could have a few logs to get them through the night, and Able and Rosa never hesitated to offer them help whenever it was asked of them. Whether it was wood, a cup of

sugar, even some labor of help that was asked of them, the Sanchez family never hesitated or refused. They were true friends and neighbors. It seems that the only difference between the haves and the have-nots, is not necessarily what you have, but what you do with what you've got.

The Nintendo that was bought at Christmastime was soon commandeered by Pete. After a few days, Pete started to complain about the cords lying around. and the games being out of their boxes. Mario Brothers, Ninja Gaiden, and Duck Hunt started to become restrictively controlled. It wasn't long before Pete moved the video game system into the master bedroom, hooking it up to his television. At first, he was working on Saturdays and Sundays, and that gave Michael and Michelle enough time to play games and clean up afterward. They would sit in the master bedroom at the foot of the bed and lay the many different video games. They hated being in that room. They hated the smell of the place where Pete rested his head. But to get to the games they had to play them in his room. Their weekends consisted of a few hours of cartoons after breakfast,

then a few hours of video games, finished off by a few hours of outside play time with Kimmy, Frankie, Raul, and occasionally Doug. Pete came home after work, and if anything was out of place, he would spout off like a teapot. He would often look for any reason to start complaining. Just as soon as he walked through the door, his eyes would scan the house, looking for anything to get upset over. He ranted and raved throughout the house. No one was immune from his objections. An unsettling unhappiness resided with in him and he always looked for a reason to project that unhappiness onto everyone in the house.

"Those kids have been in my room again!" he yelled to Jacky from the master bedroom. She rolled her eyes and walked into the backroom to see what he was upset about. "I told them that if they were going to use my things, they need to pick up after themselves, and put things back the way they found them!"

"It looks like they did a pretty good job cleaning up after themselves to me," she said in their defense. "I don't see what you're talking about?"

"Look all this stuff is out of order." he said. She looked around wondering what he was talking about. All the games were put away, the controllers were rolled up and placed next to the console. Everything looked neat and orderly. She couldn't see what he was seeing.

"I still don't understand why you had to move that thing into our bedroom! I hear that damn thing in my sleep." She said. "Besides, didn't we buy it for them. I mean it is a children's toy, isn't it?"

"Well, they don't know how to take care of things. That video game was expensive. If they appreciated things, and took better care of things, then we wouldn't have to be going through this. I don't want them in my room unless I am there to watch over them," he demanded.

Jacky rolled her eyes as she walked down the walked down the hallway to finish getting dinner ready. The video games had started off as fun. A tool of entertainment geared toward amusing children. Michael and Michelle loved playing them. It was like controlling the main character of a storybook.

Each different game was an electronic adventure, a journey to an imaginary world. From saving princesses to ninja assassins, the world of fantasy had finally become available at the touch of a button. But Pete found a way to drain the fun out of things for the kids the way he always did. He turned an instrument of entertainment into a tool of manipulation and control.

Pete soon switched his days off to Saturday and Sunday, leaving him more time to be around the kids. Jacky spent most of her time down in Lancaster cleaning houses, while Faith spent a lot of time after school with cheerleading practice, volleyball, or whatever extracurricular activity she was doing at the time. Jacky worked as often as she could, trying to bring in extra money.

It was a cold Saturday morning. Too cold to be outside in. The twins sat in front of the television on the floor at the foot of the bed. As they played the games, Pete sat on the bed behind them and drank beer. They took turns handing off the controllers between themselves and Pete. He became unusually friendly with them. He uncharacteristically joked around with them.

Depending on which twin's turn it was, he played with their hair or flicked them in the ears, trying to distract the m while they played their games. Soon he started to rub their shoulders.

After a little while, he became aroused, and his erection became apparent as it protruded out from the crotch of the sweats he wore. He had Mikey pause the game and told the kids to get onto the bed, which they reluctantly did. He started to kiss them and fondle them. Michelle got scared as her head started to swim with anxiety. She started to pout and cry a little.

"No, no, no, don't cry! It's okay!" he said in a quiet and calm voice. "This is what big people do. This is love," he said to her. She looked at him unsure of what to do. He kissed her as he forced his tongue into her mouth. The beer and the cigarettes on his breath stank and filled her mouth with a bitter taste. His tongue was large and rough. It felt awkward and intrusive.

"You want a sip of my beer?" he said, hoping the alcohol would calm her. She reluctantly took a sip. The bitter foam filled her mouth and caught in her throat. She swallowed it down and after a moment felt a buzz in her head. He made them both drink

until he knew they were feeling a buzz. After he knew they were intoxicated, he led the kids into performing oral sex on him. The video game music played in the background. The characters of the game were paused and frozen in action. Michael and Michelle felt trapped and wished they had gone outside to play instead of being stuck inside with Pete. Pete soon got up and went into the master bathroom. He came back with a jar of Vaseline that he threw onto the bed. He went to the closet and retrieved a videocassette. He turned off the video game and popped the tape into the VCR. Soon screaming orgasms filled the air. A woman appeared on the television screen. She moaned as her body writhed and turned. Her large breasts were moving up and down, as a large penis penetrated her vagina. Michael and Michelle didn't fully understand what was happening. They just wished they could leave.

Their stepfather was always harsh toward them, and at first his unusual affection felt good to them. At first it felt good to have his attention, but soon his affection changed, and they didn't enjoy doing the things he was having them do. They were

young, and their minds could not comprehend what their bodies were being subjected to. It always started off with the video games, or a movie, and somehow it always ended up in Pete's bed. It was him performing oral sex on them, or them performing oral sex on him. Sometimes he'd turn it into a game. He would use whipped cream or candy when the kids complained about the foul odor of his genitalia. He would force oral sex upon the children for a few hours, often ejaculating onto a towel while having the two small kids jerk him off.

Afterward he'd sit the kids down and tell them not to say anything to their mom. He told them that if they did, he would go to jail and that she would be very mad at them. Sometimes he would say that their mom would go to jail, and that they would end up in an orphanage or a foster home. He tried to convince them that what he did was normal, and he would tell them how much he loved them. He normally fell asleep after cleaning up his mess and covering up his tracks. He then sent the twins out to play for the rest of the afternoon, whether it was extremely cold or in the middle of the hot summer. But they didn't mind;

they were just glad to be away from him, and not doing the things he had made them do. As much as he tried convincing them that what he was doing was okay, they hated having to do it, and they knew it didn't feel right.

He'd wake up just in time for Jacky to come home and put on dinner. He was a real smooth liar and a master manipulator. This would be the start of a vast web of lies he would begin to spin. Maybe it had all always been a lie? The twins' mother hadn't really known this man very long before she married him and moved in with him. She really had no idea who he was.

It could happen any ordinary afternoon, and it soon turned into a weekly event. Every chance that Pete got time alone with the kids, he molested them. He took advantage of the trust Jacky had for him, and the trust the children had for him. He had an opportunity to be a real father figure to this family, and he turned into something dark and twisted. He set the course for what would become a very dark future.

The easy days of childhood were over. What should have been the innocent days of their youth became a dreadful terror of sexual enslavement, wrapped around a Hershey kiss. There was the much-needed affection of a father figure, disguised in a perverse and destructive sexual being. In one moment they would feel loved, and the next moment they would feel used and disfigured. Fear soon locked them in place. Pete meticulously carved his puppets, and one by one, each was strung. Fear blanketed their world like a black fog. Their small, only recently discovered voices were stolen and silenced. And they felt they could not move. The brightness of life became blotted out as they were faced with situations that were far beyond their ability to understand. They began to feel different than other children. They knew that what was going on in their home didn't happen in every home. They knew that Kimmy's and Frankie and Raul's daddies didn't do those kinds of things to them. The underlying feeling that something was very wrong permeated their lives. A life filled with perversions and manipulations began sowing the seeds of a horrific storm.

Chapter 12 Family Ties

Michael Biggs hailed from a family with deep roots in southern
Mississippi. They were cotton farmers of Scotch Irish decent.
Life on the farms of the old South was tough, and not for the
faint of heart. One had to have sheer determination to carve out
an existence as a farmer in the hot and humid South. Michael
Biggs's father, Benjamin, was raised by the iron hand. There
was no room for questioning, not from a woman, and not from a
child. Any sign of falling out of line was met head-on with a belt
or fist. One did as they were told and raised not even a single
sigh of resistance.

Benjamin Biggs was as hard as the Depression era from
which he came. He was a farm boy hardened by the plot of land
that his family tilled. The family awoke early in the morning to
feed the stock, and to start on a long day under the humid sun of

the South. They plowed the land, they tilled the land, they worked the land, and reaped the rewards of her bounty. In the end they made a meager living on the crops their lands yielded, and when the season was over they prepared to do it all over again. It would be long after sunset before they would wash up for dinner. When dinner was through, it was off to bed, and another early sunrise would soon be on its way. Every breath, thought, and action was for the survival and progress of the entire family.

Ben knew that life on the farm was not what he intended for himself, and he knew at a young age that his father would be the last in a long line of cotton farmers. When he was seventeen, he'd enlisted in the navy, and was sent off to World War II. It would be through his service that he would meet Ellen, a pretty woman a few years his elder. She was of French descent from Portland, Maine, and the prettiest Yankee Ben had ever laid eyes upon. She was one of those women who are rarely spoken of who enlisted in the services during the war. She would go on to marry Ben and produce two boys, Michael and David. After his

tour with the navy ended, he went on to enlist in the air force, where he was to be stationed at Nellis Air Force Base near Las Vegas. When his service obligations were met, he worked for the military out at the Nevada test site. There he worked on top-secret projects developing the high-altitude spy planes for the US government. Las Vegas was little more than a windswept desert valley at the time.

The winter snow melted away and signs of spring were coming to the Tehachapi pass. Plants broke free from the dead husks of the last season, casting off their skins of the past to bloom in the sun for another season. The yellow stalks of foxtail were soon swallowed by the green grass that sprang from their dead roots, and the hills were turned to emerald once again. All the trees in the orchard were blooming as the cold air was warmed by the southern winds.

Michael and Michelle were waiting impatiently. Their grandma Ellen and grandpa Ben had phoned and said they would like to stop and visit the kids on their way to Pismo beach. They owned an RV and traveled frequently to escape the desert sun.

There was an RV park on the outskirts of town that sat among the old apple orchards, and at the base of the mountains. When they came through Tehachapi, on their way to the coast, they often stopped by for a few days to see the twins. The twins were their only grandchildren. Michelle grabbed a pink Strawberry Shortcake backpack from the closet she shared with her sister. She packed some underwear, a couple pairs of socks, some shorts, a dress, a couple of shirts, her sandals, and some sneakers. By the time she was done, the little backpack was filled to the brim. She heaved it onto her back and waddled into the kitchen.

"Where are you going?" Jacky asked.

"Grammy's coming! I going to see Grammy!" she said with enthusiasm.

"Well, you're only going to be gone until tomorrow evening. What do you need all that stuff for?" Jacky asked her.

"Well, you never know," the girl answered in complete seriousness. She was half-hoping her grandparents would kidnap her and take her back to Las Vegas with them.

"Come on, let's put some of this stuff away. You are only going to need a few things," Jacky said. She walked into the girls' room and helped her repack her backpack. When she came back into the living room Michael was sitting on the couch with his backpack on.

"Okay, mister, and what did you pack?" she took his backpack and looked inside. She found a pair of socks, some flip-flops, and a few toys inside. "You're not going to get far with this," she told him. She heard a car pull up the gravel drive way toward the house and knew her former in laws were there. "Shit!" she said as her heart skipped a beat. It still made her nervous whenever they came to visit. They stilled blamed Jacky for leaving their son and taking the kids away from them. She had never felt comfortable around them. They had a way of making her feel as if she didn't belong. As if she was never good enough to be with their son. They had for many years turned a blind eye to the problems that plagued their son. And they'd turned a blind eye to the bruises he left on Jacky when they were together.

She ran quickly into Mikey's bedroom and quickly repacked his bag. The gravel popped and ground into the dirt as the car pulled in front of the house and was placed in park. Jacky rushed to the door as the doorbell rang. She greeted her former future in-laws with a nervous smile.

"Hello!" Ben greeted her with a deep southern drawl. Michael always got amused at how much his grandpa sounded like Foghorn Leghorn. The kids were given hugs and kisses and were showered in attention by their grandmother. The grandfather wasn't the most affectionate man, but he had his own way of showing the kids how much he cared for them. Pete hid in the bedroom while the formalities were being made in the living room. Jacky excused him as getting ready for work, which he was not. She showed them around the house, and then around the property.

"So, you are heading to Pismo for the week? That sounds pleasant," Jacky said, trying to make conversation. "I haven't been there in years!"

"Yeah, we are heading down there for another season. We wanted to get out of Vegas before that wretched fireball heat came," Ben said.

"Yeah, well I am glad it stays pretty cool here during the summer. It hardly ever gets above ninety," Jacky said as if to show yet another good reason for having left Vegas.

"Jacky, we were thinking that if it were all right, we would like to take the kids for a week to Pismo with us over the summer," Ellen said, trying to open the topic of custody and visitations.

"Well, we will have to see. Pete and I have a busy summer planned this year," she responded abruptly. There was a superficiality to their pleasantries. Underneath the facade of pretense, they really didn't like each other. "So, you will have them back tomorrow evening?" she said as if to change the subject.

"Yeah, we have got to pull out of here around five thirty or so in order to get a head start on the road. We're getting older now, and I don't much like driving at night anymore," Ben said.

"It would only be for a week. Even if it were for just a few days, I am sure you could fit it in somewhere!" Ellen said, bringing up the visitation topic again.

"We'll see how it goes," said Jacky. "Like I said, we have a lot planned. We're thinking of heading east to visit some family. Well, you kids have a good night and I will see you tomorrow." Jacky bent forward and kissed the kids as they loaded up into the car. They backed up and pulled out of the driveway. The twins got up and looked out the rear window and saw Jacky standing in the drive as they left. They both waved and blew kisses to their mom. Jacky had failed to mention that while registering the kids for school she'd registered the kids under Pete's last name. She had pretty much changed their names by all accounts except through the courts. This was a fact that would not have sat well with Ben.

"So, you kids excited about summer? I know your birthday is around the corner as well," their grandmother asked.

"Yeah, we're real excited," Michelle said.

"Yeah! No more school!" Michael shouted.

"Well, your grandfather and I were talking, and we were thinking that maybe you kids could come and stay with us out in Pismo for a week over the summer. What do you think about that?"

"That would be cool," Michelle said.

"Yeah that would be awesome!" Mikey added.

"We are going to go back to the RV and put your things away, then we are going to the poppy fields outside of Lancaster," Ben said as he looked into the rearview mirror. "All the hills turn orange this time of year!"

"Yeah!" the kids said synonymously. They pulled up to the RV and parked with the motor running. Ellen hurried as she put the kids' things away.

"Grammy, I have to pee," Michael said as he stood before her squirming.

"Okay," she said. "But you got to hurry. Your grandfather can be a little impatient." Michael finished his business and they were on their way. They took the back road out of Tehachapi. They passed tall windmills as they climbed the

mountain pass before dropping back down into the antelope valley. As the road curved in and out of the mountains, they saw patches of pinks, purple, oranges, and yellows along the hillsides. The hills were brushed in pastels that reaffirmed the spring season in brilliant color.

They dropped down into the Antelope Valley and drove along the desert road. The antelope of the valley's name sake had long ago been driven into extinction. Little yellow flowers clung to the edges of the black asphalt. The tall lanky Joshua trees stuck out of the desert brush like scarecrows in a cornfield. They drove for a while, and soon the road flattened out along the desert floor. They found a turn out on the side of the road and got out of the little car. They found themselves in a sea of orange. Across from where they parked was a dirt road that cut right down the center of the desert foothills. On both sides of the dirt road the foothills were covered in bright blazing orange. The California poppies were in full bloom, and the abundance of rain in early spring had made them that much more beautiful and abundant. There were cars parked on both sides of the paved

road where they had parked. People were walking up and down the dirt road in the foothills, taking pictures of the poppy fields. The road was worn with deep ruts from the heavy rains. The side of the road was lined with tall purple lupine stalks. As they walked Ellen struck up a conversation with Michelle.

"So how is school going?" she asked.

"It's fun. I like Mrs. Powell my teacher, and I like a lot of the kids in my class. Except Jamie, he picks his boogers and eats them. I saw him do it," Michelle told her.

"That's gross." Ellen said laughing.

"Yeah, that's gross." Michelle giggled.

"And your mom? How is she? Do you like your new stepdad?" she asked.

"I hate him, Grammy. I miss my daddy?"

"Oh well, your daddy misses you, too, sweetheart. And you shouldn't say you hate anybody. It isn't very polite."

"Well, I do hate him; he's mean to us," Michelle said.

"Well, your mom has chosen to be with him. But you can still visit us in Las Vegas in the summertime, and we want you to come with us to Pismo."

"Pismo! That sounds like fun! We've never been there before!" Michelle said in excitement.

They finally got to the top of the hill and stood overlooking the valley. There was orange for as far as they could see. "Would you look at that view!" Ben said. "Okay kids, go over there and stand next to your grandmother so we can get some pictures." He said somewhat impatiently. Their grandmother stood behind them as they stared blindly into the sun. Mikey squinted out of one eye and tried to smile. "Alright that should just about do it." Ben said. "Now let's get the hell out of here!" They began the trek down the rutted hillside. Ben and Ellen walked with caution, trying to avoid the deep ruts in the road. Michael skipped down the road. He jumped over ruts, darting back and forth like he was playing hopscotch. He had healed well from his car accident. It was barely noticeable that he had been so mangled at one time. He had gotten halfway

down the road when the sound of a barking dog and people yelling caught up with him. He stopped and turned around, looking back up the rutted road he had just run down. He saw Michelle, his grandparents, a couple, and their dog standing over the rut he had just jumped over. He ran up to the small crowd as the dog continued barking wildly at the deep rut in the road.

"Look! It's a rattlesnake!" Ben said to Michael. Sitting in the rut was a coiled viper. Its head was tucked into its body, its tail raised. It shook its rattle in an eerie rhythm, a warning for those nearby to keep their distance. "Boy, you sure are lucky your ass didn't get bit jumping over that snake like that," his grandfather said. "You must have someone looking out for you." Michael just stared at the snake in wide eyed-silence. He couldn't believe he had come so close to getting bit.

They left the poppy fields and grabbed some lunch before heading back up to the mountain. The Joshua trees gave way to the oaks and the scruffy brush gave way to green grass. The windmills cast tall shadows on the desert mountains in the

afternoon light. When they pulled up to the RV, there was a red pickup truck parked beside it.

"We have a surprise for you kids waiting inside," their grandmother said excitedly.

"What is it?" Michelle asked.

"Well, it wouldn't be a surprise if I told you, now would it?" Grammy said. They got out of the car and made their way into the RV, and when they flipped on the light Michael and Michelle saw that their dad was sitting on the sofa.

"Daddy!" they both screamed in excitement. They rushed upon him and were showered in hugs and kisses.

"Awe! I missed you kids," their father told them.

"We missed you, too, Daddy. We missed you so much!" they said.

"But, hey, listen to me…Are you listening?" he said, trying to get their attention. The both nodded their heads simultaneously. "Whatever you do, you can't tell your mother I came up here. We haven't exactly worked things out yet. Okay?" he said somewhat sternly.

"Okay, Daddy," they said. "We won't tell." He scooped them up and hugged them again. Since Jacky and Mike had separated, the couple had barely spoken on the phone, and when they did it usually ended up in bitter arguments. Mike knew that he had made some terrible choices in life and Jacky would make certain that he would never be able to live it down. Everything from the drugs and alcohol to the abuse would forever cloud his life. Anytime he even brought up custody or visitation rights, she would bring up his abusive behavior and his drug and alcohol addiction. It was a catch-22. For Mike there was no way out. It was a losing situation, no matter how he might approach it.

Grammy cleared the small table and brought out board games for the kids to play. They played Monopoly, Life, and some UNO until dinner was ready. Fried chicken, mac and cheese, and some frozen peas and carrots is what Grammy prepared. She served everything up on paper plates. When it came to staying in the RV, paper plates were invaluable. Not only did they cut down on water use, but they saved on time as

well. When they were finished eating, the kids helped clear the table.

"You kids want to take a walk through the orchard after we're done?" their father asked as he dried the dishes with a hand towel.

"Okay," Michael said.

"That's a good Idea. I'd like to walk some of this meal off," Ben said.

"Yeah, I need to walk some of this off, too," Michelle said in response.

"Walk some of what off?" Grammy butted in. "You walk anymore off, you might disappear, little girl." She laughed.

After they were finished cleaning up dinner, they all put on their shoes and light windbreakers. The sun had started to settle into twilight by the time they got going. It was slightly breezy, and the evening air had cooled to a chill. They made their way up a dirt road that led out of the backside of the RV park and into the large apple orchards. Acre after acre of orchards sprawled out in front of them. Every section of ground

was tilled and sectioned off in perfectly neat rows. Line after line of apple trees ran parallel to one another, and in the distance, it appeared the rows ran together. They walked between the trees as the tightness of their bellies loosened. The blossoms from the trees were beginning to fall away, and now were replaced with little nuggets of fruit. The fruit was still not ripe and was bitter to eat. It clung to the trees in little clusters. Tiny bits of foil were tied up in the trees, and an air gun would pop off every few minutes to scare the birds away. The air gun had the same noisy ferocity of a shotgun blast. Every time it went off, Mikey jumped a little, and a flock of birds would shoot up out of the orchard, only to find refuge on a nearby telephone line.

After passing a few rows of trees, they came to a section where the apples looked a little bigger. Some had even begun to get spots of blushing red. Michelle ran over to the tree.

"Look, these apples look ready!" she said with excitement. She picked one and ran up to Grandpa Ben and

handed him the apple. He took it from her and rolled it over in his palm.

"Hmm…doesn't look ripe to me," he said. He pulled out a pocket knife and cut into the fruit. "See? It is still green inside." He held it out to her to show her the inside. She grabbed the apple from his hand and took a bite. Her mouth puckered, and her eyes winced. It wasn't the sweet taste of apple she was expecting.

"Sour, huh?" Grandpa said. "I told you they weren't ready yet."

"It's not sour," she said as she swallowed and took another bite. It wasn't sweet, but she could handle the bitterness.

"Can I try some?" Michael asked. She handed him the apple and he took a bite. They both ran back toward the tree and grabbed as many apples as they could fit in the pockets of their jackets. Out of the corner of his eyes Mikey saw something drop out of the tree. He looked down on the ground and saw the most perfectly red apple lying in the dirt.

That one's going to be a sweet one, he thought as he reached down and picked it up. He held it up to eye level in between his thumb and forefinger. Its redness was beautiful. He rolled it around and exposed a soft bruise on the other side with a hole at its center. *Damn worms,* he thought. He was getting ready to toss it back on the ground when a yellow face with black eyes suddenly popped its head from the hole. He threw it to the ground as wasps came forth from the rotted fruit. Before he could run, he suddenly felt a painful sting come from just under his arm. It was a blinding white-hot sting of unexpected pain.

"Ahhhhhhh!" he screamed with the highest of pitches his little throat could muster. His father and grandfather looked up, startled by the young boy's scream as he came running toward them with tears in his eyes.

"What happened?" Mike said in a slight panic. The boy tried to explain to him what had happened in between gasps of breath.

"He picked up an apple from the ground and it had wasps in it," Michelle explained. "He must have got stung."

Michael's dad lifted his jacket and shirt, exposing the soft tender flesh that covered his rib cage. The skin was red and swollen. There was a red knot the size of a marble just below his arm pit. The pain burned red-hot and bright as the sun.

"My god, you scream like a little girl!" Grandpa Ben said as he rubbed the rattling from his eardrums. "You would have thought somebody died." He chuckled as he bent down to look at the boy's side. Ben walked over to a spigot and turned on the water, making a small pool of mud. He grabbed a handful of mud and started applying it to Mikey's sting.

"What are you doing?" Mikey asked him afraid of the touch to his wound.

"I'm making a mud pack for your sting. It'll take the burn out," Ben told him.

Mikey thought the mud pack idea was a little weird, but the cold mud press felt good against the hot sting, and the pain seemed to recede a bit. He felt ashamed he had screamed so

loud, but that wasp had stung him hard. He thought his grandpa would be a little more sensitive to his wound, and he certainly didn't like his primal scream being compared to that of a little girl. *Not even a bumblebee bites that hard, for crap's sake!* he thought. After a few moments the chaos of the wasp-filled apple would be over, but the sting would last long into the next day.

After the tears had dried up, and the echo of little Mike's screams had stopped reverberating throughout the valley, they moved on down the row of trees. The twins walked down the road with their elders as they gobbled up one sour apple after another. They made their way beyond the boundaries of the orchards and into the open foothills of the mountains. Lonely oaks sparsely populated the grassy fields. The road made its way past the foothills and carved its path like a scar up the mountains in the distance. Ben looked down at Michelle whose cheeks were still full of sour apples.

"You know you're gonna get the trots if you keep eating those green apples!" he warned her.

"What's the trots, Grandpa?" she asked, looking at him in bewilderment.

"You know. The skidders, the…uh…Hershey squirts," he said as he still saw the puzzled look in her eyes. "Diarrhea," he said finally.

"Oh! Diarrhea!" she said. "I know a song about diarrhea," she informed him. "Like to hear it."

"Okay. I guess so," he said with a chuckle.

"When you're sliding into first and you feel a juicy burst, diarrhea, diarrhea. When you're sliding into third and you feel a juicy turd, diarrhea, diarrhea. When you're sliding into home and your pants are full of foam, diarrhea, diarrhea," she sang.

"That's disgusting," Grammy told her with a chuckle. "Who taught you that song?"

"We heard it at school," she said.

"That's awful, the things you kids come up with these days!" her grandmother said.

The road came to a bend, and around the curve it opened to a large gravel pit filled with machinery. Everything from

tractors to gravel belts and skip loaders sat in the large open pit. The kids hopped up on the idle machines and played. They pretended they were driving the tractors, loading and unloading dirt.

"Beep, beep, beep," Mikey chirped as he pretended to be backing up in the skip loader. Their father pulled out a 35mm camera.

"Hey, kids, get down from there and let's take some pictures," their father said. They got down and posed for a few shots. It was getting late and the sun was far below sunset. The wind whipped up a bit as they made their way back down the road. The tiny lights of the town below started to twinkle. Michelle and Michael walked as their stomachs started to churn. There was uneasiness in their bowels, a churning and an irksomeness.

"Grandpa, I think I got go to the bathroom," Mikey told him.

"A number one or a number two?" Ben asked.

"A number two," he said as he squirmed.

"Okay, well, then go, but there's nothing to wipe with out here. Are you sure you can't wait?" he asked. Mikey shook his head no, and quickly bolted off behind a sage bush. Ben turned to find Michelle, but she was nowhere to be found.

"Not you, too!" he said. "I told you two to stay away from them apples," he shouted over the bushes at them. "I guess you know what the trots are now!" All the adults laughed as the kids kept peeking from around the bushes.

They walked back to the RV park as the kids raced off to hit the shower. They got dressed in their pajamas and watched a little television before falling asleep, one in each of their father's arms.

In the morning they dressed and ate breakfast. They drove to a nearby field full of poppies and took some more pictures before their father had to drive back to Las Vegas.

"I love you two kids very much. I want you to know that. I want you to come and stay with me. If not this summer, maybe next. I'll have to talk to your mother about it first, but there

aren't any reason you kids shouldn't be more a part of my life!"
he told them as he held them close to him.

"Remember not to tell your mom you saw me!" he said.

"We won't!" they both said.

"And remember that no matter what happens I will
always love you!" he told them.

"We love you, too, Daddy," they said. He hugged them
once more before getting into his red truck and driving back to
Vegas. Their grandparents dropped them off at home and headed
west toward the ocean. Although it was hard for them not to slip
up to Jacky that they had spent time with their dad, they were
able to keep the secret and she never found out.

Chapter 13 A Birthday Wish

It was the middle of spring, and the fever of life was in full

bloom. And with another spring came another birthday for the

twins. They were coming out of the early stage of youth. Their

legs and arms had started to grow longer. They were not

teenagers yet, but they were no longer little kids, either. Because

their birthday fell toward the end of spring, for gifts their mother

would always buy new summer clothes for them to wear.

Fluorescent clothing was flying off the racks. Fluorescent

sunglasses, T-shirts, and shorts were the new fad. Parachute

pants of supremely bright pink, yellow, and electric blue were

the craze of the day. And it seemed that everyone was sporting a

fanny pack. It was the end of spring, and almost the end of

another school year. The long hours of daylight had arrived, and

this meant the twins were able to play outside until late into the

dusk. The creek down below reached its crest. The bullfrogs were in full chorus, and the crickets were backing them up on strings. Every night was like a natural symphony of sound.

The twins waited impatiently at school all day long until the final bell rang, and then they were out. Thoughts of birthday cake and presents danced around in their heads. They had tried to locate their mother's secret hiding place but were unsuccessful. Michelle was normally pretty good at sniffing out presents, but this year she'd had no luck. Many were the Christmases and birthdays celebrated early in their mother's closet, where the presents had always been hidden. Jacky had never really been very good at hiding things, but she was getting better at it every year. She had been preparing for the kids to get home all afternoon. She and Faith had hung streamers and balloons all over the house. There was a banner hanging over the china hutch mirror screaming, "Happy Birthday!" The house was filled with the smell of cake baking in the oven and dinner simultaneously cooking on the stove.

The kids got off the bus, heaved their heavy backpacks over their shoulders, and started trudging up the hill toward the house. They hated that long walk up Water Canyon Road.

"So, are you gonna come to my house for my birthday party?" Mikey asked Frankie and Raul. "We are going to have a piñata!"

"We have to ask our dad. What time does it start?" Raul asked.

"I don't know. Just come over when you're done with your homework," Mikey said.

"Okay," Frankie said, butting in.

"What about you, Doug? You want to come?" he asked.

"Um, yeah. I guess I could come," Doug said impartially. "I mean, I really don't have much else to do."

"Cool!" Mikey said.

"I hope my mom buys me some new Kulaks. I sure do miss my old ones," Michelle said with a sly grin. Kimmy's eyes bolted from the road as she stared at Michelle.

"You promised not to talk about that!" Kimmy implored her.

"Okay, okay!" Michelle giggled. "I promise!" The boys looked at them, wondering what they were talking about.

The walk up the hill was hot and windless. The anticipation made the house seem that much farther away from the bus stop. Kimmy and Michelle walked some paces ahead of the boys as they talked about the birthday party. They didn't want to be seen walking with the boys. They were too mature for that. They turned off the dirt road that led to the driveway as the kids went separate ways. When the twins entered the front door, Jacky and Faith ran in from the kitchen. "Happy birthday to you, happy birthday to you, happy birthday, Mikey and Michelle, happy birthday to you!" they sang. When they were finished, they ran toward the twins and gave them a big hug.

Michelle and Michael finished up their homework as quickly as they could. They couldn't wait to get the party started of which they were the guests of honor. It was not long afterward that the doorbell started to ring, and the neighborhood

kids started showing up. They all gathered on the front lawn under the oak tree. Faith strung up the donkey piñata and gave Michael and Michelle the first whack at it. She spun Michelle around blindfolded. "One, two, three!" She counted as she spun her little sister around. The girl swung the stick at the piñata she could not see. Dizzily she walked in circles, swinging, then missing. The donkey piñata came down and struck her on the shoulder. She backed up, took a whack at it, and knocked its head clean off. A few pieces of candy spewed from its broken neck. As the candy fell to the ground the kids dove upon it like a pack of wolves onto fallen prey. After five swings her turn was over.

Then it was Michael's turn. "One, two, three!" Faith counted again. He ambled around blindly as the piñata came down and bopped him upside the head. He turned and swung at the air but struck nothing. Five strikes later he was out, with the donkey still left largely intact. Every kid went up and struck out until it was Michelle's turn again. Again, Faith blindfolded her eyes, spun her around, and set her off. Two whacks into it, she

tore into the donkey's side, busting it completely open. The large cache of candy rained down onto the grass. All the kids ran around and gathered up as much candy as they could. They packed their mouths full, chewing on big wads of colored sugar. After the piñata, the kids gathered in the den and played board games until dinner was ready. They were all hopped up on a sugar buzz. The dogs were barking and chasing around the kids through the house.

Jacky had cleaned the house before all the guests had arrived. She was thorough and had even cleaned the back-sliding glass door to a spotless shine. Frankie, with his sugar buzz, was antagonizing the dogs as he ran through the house. He came around the corner and into the dining room where the large glass door was. The dogs were gaining on him. He looked in front of himself and charged full steam ahead as the dogs were nipping at his heels. He hit the glass with such a force that it vibrated with a hum and rattled in its tracks. Straight backward he fell and hit the floor in a daze. Jacky heard the commotion and ran into the dining room.

"Oh my god! Are you okay?" she asked him. He got up, nodded his head, and proceeded on undaunted. Jacky walked back into the kitchen. She stared at the clock. It was almost four and Pete was still not home. He got off at two, so he should have already been home by then. *If he's at the fucking bar again I swear to God!* She said to herself. Dinner was ready, and she couldn't wait for him much longer. She didn't want to serve cold food to the kids. She had Faith set the table for dinner and she called the kids in to eat. The kids sat down as they filled their plates with mac and cheese, corn, and barbecued chicken. They had worked up such an appetite in their frenzy that they devoured their meals like wild animals. She made a plate for Pete and stuck it in the microwave.

The kids ate quickly, and soon Jacky and Faith were clearing the table. They brought out the presents, which had been locked in the shed out back, and put them out on the table with the cake. "Happy birthday, Michelle and Michael," it said in yellow cake frosting, written in their mother's handwriting.

They called the kids, who were outside playing, into the dining room one more time. It was now five thirty and still no Pete.

The kids walked into the dining room to a table filled high with presents and a birthday cake blazing with candles. The candles were spilling their wax upon the white and yellow frosting in little colorful streams. Jacky and Faith started the chorus. "Happy birthday to you, happy birthday to you." The kids followed in sync. "Happy birthday Michelle and Michael, happy birthday to you!" they sang. The twins crept in close to each other. They were both wishing in their minds that Pete would somehow go away. That he would just disappear from their lives. They blew out the candles, the flame turned to smoke, and the smell of wax filled the air.

Jacky and Faith handed the presents to the twins, starting with the smaller ones first. It was mainly new shirts and shorts for summer, which of course blazed brighter than the candles on the birthday cake. Some summer dresses for Michelle, and a new pair of Kulaks, which Michelle proudly waved in the air. They got two new Super Soakers, which had just come onto the

market, and a new Slip 'N Slide for the front lawn. Faith threw away all the wrapping paper and organized the presents. Jacky grabbed some paper plates, plastic forks, and a knife from the kitchen. She went back into the dining room as she heard the keys jingling in the door.

Pete flung the door open as he sauntered in. Jacky gave him a raised eyebrow as he stumbled around carrying a case of beer. He walked into the kitchen, trying not to make eye contact with Jacky.

"Here, why don't you cut up the cake?" she told Faith, handing her the knife and following right behind Pete into the kitchen. He bent over and loaded his beer into the fridge. He got up and turned to come face-to-face with Jacky.

"So where have you been?" she asked him.

"I, uh, stopped for a drink at the bar after work, and then I came home," he answered her.

"That's what I thought. Did you forget it was the kids' birthday?" she said starting to grill him.

No, I didn't forget about the kids' birthday! What? I can't stop and have a few drinks with my friends after work? Am I not free to do that?" he said with sarcasm.

"It's five thirty Pete! Having one or two beers is one thing, but to be coming home wasted on your kids' birthday is another!" she snapped at him. "And what? You couldn't not drink for just one day?"

"*My* kids, huh?" he said.

"I'm sorry. My kids, I don't want you coming home to *my* kids' birthday party drunk!" she said as she started to raise her voice. "You know what? Why don't you just go into your room and drink yourself to sleep another night? We really don't want you around anyhow! You're embarrassing!"

"You know I really don't need to hear this shit from you!" he said. "I put up with enough shit at work. I shouldn't have to come home and listen to this kind of shit when I get off." He grabbed a few beers, headed into the master bedroom, and slammed the door shut.

"Yeah, go ahead. Do what you always do!" she yelled at him. "Drink yourself into a stupor!" She walked back into the dining room, and when she entered all eyes were on her. She cleaned up the table once more, removing paper plates and cups half-filled with juice. She sent Faith out with the kids to go play on the lawn. As soon as all the kids were outside, Jacky stormed into the back bedroom. The kids could hear the arguing out on the lawn. Faith sent all the neighbor kids home. She, Michael, and Michelle stayed on the lawn while Pete and Jacky had it out.

It was well into twilight when things quieted down and Jacky came outside. When they went back into the house, the door to the master bedroom was closed and a television on low volume hummed in the background. This was a constant in this household. Pete really knew how to make people feel special. For some reason Mikey and Michelle's birthday would always end in arguments, bitterness, and tears. It was as if Pete couldn't stand to see any of them happy. It was as if he would try to find some way to ruin it. Mikey and Michelle's wish had not come true. Many moments of would-be celebration were almost

always spoiled by the presence of their stepfather. The misery and self-loathing he felt inside he projected onto everyone around him. If he felt like shit, he was sure to make everyone else around him feel like shit.

Chapter 14 The Green Van

It was late summer, and all the wild grass from spring had turned from a beautiful emerald green to a straw yellow. Michelle called Kimmy on the telephone and told her to meet her and Michael down at the old green van that sat next to the barn on Kimmy's parents' property. The broken machine had sat there for many years and made a perfect place to play and pretend. The kids kept this place top secret. They had rules and a secret knock for the door to be opened. They wanted no one to know of their newfound hiding spot. They'd found some old rolled up carpet and horse blankets in the barn. They'd laid the carpet down on the floorboards of the gutted van and placed the blankets over the busted-out windows. Its tires were flat and rotted. The tall yellow grass grew up and around the marooned vehicle. The engine and its cover had long ago been removed,

and dry grass was now growing on the inside of the van where the engine used to sit.

They quietly packed snacks and sodas into their backpacks, thinking their stepfather was in his room napping. They were just getting ready to jet out the door when they heard his door open.

"Where do you two think you are going?" Pete asked, surprising them.

"Um, we're going over to Kimmy's to play. Mom said we could before she left this morning," Michelle said quickly

"Good idea. You two can stay outside and play!" he told them. In disbelief they opened the sliding glass door and took off like bats out of hell. They had thought for sure he was going to want them to play video games with him. They heard Pete lock the sliding glass door behind them, and they felt they were in the clear. Pete stood in the glass doorway and watched as they ran toward the old green van. They ran as fast as they could, before he had a chance to change his mind. Their freedom seemed to come at a price and always with strings attached.

Down the hill the green van rested in the shade of the oak tree next to the old red barn. The twins tapped on the door with the secret code and Kimmy flung the doors open. They liked to play house in the van. Michael and Kimmy would pretend to be married, and Kimmy and Michelle would pretend to be sisters-in-law. Michelle sat in the driver's seat, pretending she was driving them all to Hollywood, that they were escaping from Pete. She so wished she and Kimmy could really be sisters. Kimmy was the closest thing Michelle felt to having a sister. Faith never spent much time with her little sister. She was always busy with cheerleading, high school, and boys. There was too large of an age gap between them, and Faith wasn't interested in doing the things little girls did anymore.

"God, what took you guys so long!" Kimmy complained.

"My stepdad woke up! I didn't think he was going to let us come!" Michelle explained. "We brought snacks and some sodas," she said as she opened the backpack. Michael and Michelle knew exactly why he wanted to be alone in the house. He wanted to drink and watch his porn. It normally came on as

soon as Jacky left. They were just relieved he didn't keep them locked up in the house. This was the way life was for the twins. If they told him they didn't feel like playing video games or watching movies with him, he would get angry and normally wouldn't let them out to play. They didn't care if they had to stay out all day, as long as they were out of the grips of the slithering snake. They could care less where they were, as long as they were together, and as long as they were safe. Kimmy did not like the twins' stepfather, and only tolerated him because he was an authority figure. He was scary and always made her feel awkward. He would stare at her with his black beady eyes and big bushy black eyebrows. She loved the twins but hated going to their house. She knew that Mikey and Michelle hated Pete, but she didn't know why.

They had a picnic on the old wooden dock down by the creek, not far from the van. They waded in a small pool of water keeping cool from the sting of the sun. The sun was burning down on them like ants under a magnifying glass, and the creek was a sure way for them to beat the heat. They laughed and

played for a few hours and after a while made their way back to the little green van. They had just closed the doors when there was a sudden tap at the door. In their bewilderment they all looked at one another.

"Who's that be?" Kimmy said in a whisper. Nobody but the three of them knew of this place. At least that's what they thought.

"Maybe it's Frankie and Raul!" Mikey said. Michelle's heart began pounding in her ears, for she knew who it was.

"Who is it?" Kimmy asked, thinking her mom or dad had returned from church early.

"It's Pete! Open up!" he said as if they were in trouble. They looked at one another as he pounded on the door again.

"He must have been watching us!" Michelle said. Kimmy slowly opened the doors to the old van. He stood with a beer in one hand and a plastic bag in the other. Michelle suddenly felt sick to her stomach. She knew what he was doing there. She knew exactly what he wanted. Michael was thinking of a way to run and hide, only there was nowhere to run and

there was nowhere to hide. Pete had them trapped. He climbed into the van as the kids sat there not able to do anything. Their hiding place was exposed. Kimmy wondered why Pete wanted to play with them. Her dad never came down to the green van to play with her.

Pete was clearly drunk. The stench of yeast from the beer he was drinking came off his breath and began to fill the van. He sat down with them and asked Kimmy if she wanted some of his beer. She looked at him apprehensively

"My mom and dad say I can't drink until I'm an adult," she said.

"It's okay. I'm an adult and I say you can have some. Just don't tell your parents. She took the beer can and began sipping it. She sat there proudly with her beer, feeling all grown up and slightly buzzed. She started giggling. Pete leaned over her and asked, "What's so funny?"

"I just feel funny!" she said, still giggling. She looked down and saw the plastic bag sitting next to him. "What's in there?" she asked him.

"Oh, just something you probably won't like. It's for grown-ups," Pete told her, trying to manipulate the girl into looking at the contents of the bag.

"I wanna see. I'm a grown-up," Kimmy stated proudly as she kept sipping on the cold beer.

"Okay, are you sure?" Pete asked her.

"Yes," she said as she rolled her eyes at him. She reached for the bag, pulling out its contents. Her eyes widened and then squeezed shut. "Ew, what are they doing?" she said as she opened the magazine to take another look. "My boobs are never going to get that big, are they?" she asked.

"I don't know. Let me see and I'll tell you!" Pete said in a playful manner. The twins just sat there in silence as Kimmy lifted her shirt to expose the little tiny bumps she had for breasts.

"Can I touch them?" Pete asked. His hands shook as he reached out to touch the little girl's underdeveloped chest. He touched them softly, trying not to scare her. Suddenly Kimmy flipped her shirt down and started to giggle again.

"Now you show yours, Michelle," Pete told her.

"No, I don't want to," she said, trying to get out of it.

"Oh, come on. Kimmy did it! Now let's see yours," he said. Michelle reluctantly lifted her shirt as Pete sat there fondling and cupping her bare flat chest. He started rubbing his penis through his jeans. "Now, Kimmy, you kiss Michael on the lips."

"Oh no. I don't want to kiss her!" he said in protest.

"Michael, kiss Kimmy on the lips. You will like it!" Pete told him. Michael puckered up and quickly gave Kimmy a kiss on the mouth. Pete grabbed Michael's hand and placed it on his erection.

"Just touch it and rub it like I taught you, Michael." He unzipped his pants and pulled down his jeans and underwear.

"Now, Michelle, you suck on it!" She felt sick to her stomach but did what she was told.

"Pull down your shorts and panties!" he told Kimmy. She reluctantly lowered her pants, as asked. Pete fondled her between her legs.

"Is it all right if I kiss you down there?" he asked. She was shaking slightly from fear and because she felt sensations she had never felt before. Pete put his face between her legs.

"It's okay. Just relax!" She lay there with her eyes closed, not knowing what to expect. Her body tingled, and waves of feeling flowed through her

He pulled his head up from between Kimmy's parted legs and motioned for Michael to come sit next to him. He told Michael to continue licking the little girl's vagina as he took his stepdaughter and began to pull off her shorts. He parted her legs and did the same thing to her.

After a few moments of this, Pete had Michael climb on top of Kimmy.

"Try to put your penis inside of her. It feels good." Pete reached out, and with his hand he tried to assist Michael in pushing his small organ inside the girl. Michelle lay there on the bottom of the rusted floor of the van wishing she was somewhere else, anywhere else. She now wished she had never met Kimmy. She wished that Kimmy had never had to do this

stuff. Her mind raced with thoughts, and guilt began setting in. *If only I never would have made friends with her*, she thought.

Suddenly she was snapped back to reality when Pete grabbed for her ankles and began to pull her closer to him. He climbed on top of the small girl and whispered to her, "Don't worry. I am not going to really put it in. I am just going to rub it up against you and pretend." Michelle lay there stiff as a board, her heart pounding as her stepfather moved up and down on flesh that belonged to her. A couple of times he tried to stick the tip of it inside her. She cried and winced in pain. He stopped before ejaculating and got off her.

"Have you ever sucked on a pee pee before?" he said to Kimmy. She looked at him with uncertainty in her eyes. She placed her mouth around the man's large organ as instructed and closed her eyes tightly. She stopped only to gag between breaths.

"Now, you kids lay next to each other!" he said as he built upon his fantasies. He knelt in front of them masturbating as the kids looked on at him in bewilderment. He looked possessed and overcome by his own sexual deviance. He started

moaning and then ejaculated. He looked like some kind of arcane beast. His body shook in complete compulsive desire. After he was finished, he looked at all three kids.

"Don't ever tell anyone what happened here! This is our little secret! Okay? You don't want your parents to go to prison, do you? Because I am a cop and I can put them all in jail," he told Kimmy. She shook her head from side to side. Unsure of what had just happened, she swore she would never tell. "Now go down to the creek and wash yourselves off!"

The kids silently walked back down to the creek and began to wash their small bodies clean. Michelle wished the creek would also wash away their memories of what happened that day. Everything felt different and looked different for Kimmy after that day. Pete had stolen the innocence of another child. He took from Kimmy her innocence, making her aware of things her mind was not yet ready to handle. In a single moment, and in a single act, all the purity of her childhood was gone forever. Things that were to be experienced on her own, moments that were to be cherished and sacred, were demeaned

and distorted into moments of perversion and disillusion. Forever sex for these children would be clouded by the events that were occurring to them now. They would never be allowed to lie down freely next to another without thinking of the things that were being perpetrated upon them by this man.

The kids slowly walked back toward the van. Pete was gone. He'd gone back home to wash off the sins he had just committed. They walked in complete silence, occasionally looking up from their feet and glancing at one another with an uncertainty in their eyes. They were all so lost, so confused and scared. They stood by the van, but it didn't feel like the same place anymore. The feeling of security and refuge it had once provided was gone. They said their good-byes and made a pact never to tell a word. They would never go back to play in the old green van again.

Michelle and Michael walked home as fear welled up deep within their souls. The only security they had upon entering their house was that their mother would soon be home. They walked inside hoping that Pete would be asleep. His bedroom

door was closed, and they knew he was probably sleeping. The twins walked into Mikey's bedroom and waited for hours until their mother's headlights to come creeping up the driveway. Michael reached out for Michelle's hand and squeezed it as tears welled up in her eyes. He whispered to her that everything was going to be okay. They knew the things their stepfather was doing were not right and were not okay. Even though they had no control over what Pete was doing, it would be a burden for them to carry for the rest of their lives. Pete was a cancer or disease, and now he was beginning to corrupt and infect people around them. Michelle hated him for this. She squeezed her eyes shut and silently began to pray. "God, please help us!"

Chapter 15 Portals and Corridors

Michael fell into a deep sleep. Light danced inside his mind. The light formed pictures and moments that existed beyond the confines of the physical realm and beyond the confines of time. He began dreaming. Inside his dreams he found himself holding hands with Michelle and Faith. Both girls were wearing dresses, and he wore a little suit with a bow tie. They were walking next to Jacky and Pete, who were to their left. They were all dressed very formally. They came to a large gray building with a stone facade and long narrow stained-glass windows. There were large stone steps leading up to two extremely tall solid oak doors. Pete grabbed the long handle of the door and pulled it open. He held it open for the family as they moved into the building. Before them lay a long corridor with narrow stained-glass windows to the right, and more corridors leading off to the left. They passed

two of the corridors before making a left turn down the third. They walked a short distance down the hallway and came to an open room. Centered in this room was a large silver casket. The lid to the upper half of the casket was open, as the lower half was closed. Flowers were lining both ends of the coffin. A ribbon streamed across a floral reef. "Rest in peace" was the promise it made to everyone at the wake. Michael approached the casket with caution. He saw a woman with gray hair lying in the coffin. He looked at her face. It was as if one moment he recognized the woman and the next he could not. There was an inscription on the inside of the open casket that Michelle began to read aloud. Jacky started sobbing uncontrollably.

Michael suddenly felt a pulling sensation. The room with the casket broke apart as he was torn from his dream and thrust back into the waking world. He opened his eyes to find himself back in his bed. The coffin and the large gray stone building were nowhere to be found. He walked into the living room as the dream quickly faded away into his subconscious mind. His mother sat talking on the telephone in the dining room.

"Mom!" he said, trying to get her attention. "Mom!" he said a little louder. Jacky waved her hand at him to go away. He walked into the kitchen and poured himself some cereal. The dream was slipping out of his mind the more awake he became, but it left a lingering feeling in his heart. He poured some cereal and milk into a bowl and sat at the dining room table next to his mother. Jacky was visibly upset. He tried to listen to his mother's conversation in between the chomps of cereal he was eating. He was not sure what was going on, but he could tell that something bad had happened. He soon heard Jacky hang up the phone. She was crying, but she tried to find a little composure.

"Mikey," she said to him.

"Yeah?" he said.

"Your grandma Bessie died early this morning," she tried to explain to him. Bessie was Jacky's grandmother. Her father, Curly's, mother. She was a solid southern woman. She had raised Curly and his two sisters by herself after her husband had run out on her. She had been in and out of the hospital over the last few months with plagues of pneumonia. She had lived to the

ripe old age of ninety-eight, a feat very few people accomplish. She saw everything from the invention of the automobile to the landing on the moon. She came from a time when horse-drawn carts were the normal means of transportation. She saw two world wars, Vietnam, Korea, and the first Gulf War. Her father had served in the Civil War fighting with Confederate forces trying to secede from the Union. Her time on earth was an epoch of unfathomable change.

"Her wake is in a few days and her funeral will be held the day after that," Jacky mumbled, not really paying attention if he was listening or not. She spoke the words as if she were speaking to herself. Michael remembered the grass-covered knoll in front of Bessie's senior community. He and Michelle had spent hours rolling down the grassy hill that sat right out front of her little apartment. Their heads would be dizzy and spinning when they got up and their backs would itch all over.

"I guess you kids will have to take the week off from school," Jacky muttered to him as she walked out of the dining room.

Jacky's sister Barb drove up from the coast, where she lived. The two sisters and Faith began packing up the little apartment Bessie had lived in. Curly, and his last living sibling, Bernice, made all the final arraignments for Bessie's funeral and for the settling of her estate. There was an assortment of handmade dolls, some as old as sixty years. There were baby girls and baby boys, some in bonnets and some in overalls. All their clothing was hand knitted. There were crocheted doilies and handmade rugs littering her little apartment. Bessie had spent hours knitting, crocheting, and sewing, necessary talents she'd picked up in a time when new clothing was a luxury.

Jacky started to pack up Bessie's dolls and put them into boxes. She grabbed Michelle's favorite dolls and began to pack them. They were twin dolls, one boy and one girl, just like Michelle and Michael. Bessie had made them while Jacky was pregnant. She had always promised Michelle that the twin dolls would be given to her if anything were ever to happen to her.

"Do you have to pack up those ones, too?" Michelle asked her mother. Jacky looked at the dolls, then looked at her daughter.

"Okay. I guess you can have them, but you better take care of them!" she told Michelle as she handed them over. Michelle grabbed up both of them and gave them a hug. She ran into the living room and onto the sofa, where she pretended to change their diapers.

Michael was watching television. He was bored and getting antsy. Jacky had made him sit down in the living room and ordered him to stop getting into things.

"I want you to sit here, watch television, and stay out of stuff," she'd demanded. He was always into something, and it usually didn't take him very long before he began snooping into boxes and cabinets. He flipped through station after station on the old turn-dial television, but he didn't find anything that interested him.

"You want to play house or have a tea party?" Michelle asked him.

"No, I don't want to play stupid teatime, or stupid house!" he said out of aggravation and boredom. He got up and started fooling with the figurines on the end table next to Bessie's knitting chair. He found an old cylinder-shaped tin about the size of a cork. He remembered Bessie on many occasion pulling off the lid and sticking her finger into. She would pull out a fine brown powder upon her fingernail and sniff it off her fingertip. She always told him it was Grandma's cocoa, that it was for grown-ups, and that he couldn't have any. He pulled, and he tugged but couldn't get the lid off. He turned the lid, then pulled, and it finally gave. The brown musty powder spilled all over his arms and onto the floor. He could smell a sweetness to the dust. He raised the can to his nose and took a deep breath through his nostrils. His nose started to tingle, and he began to sneeze as his eyes filled with tears. When the sneezing sensation subsided, he took his pinky finger and drove it into the sweet brown powder. He raised his powder-laden finger to his nose and deeply inhaled the powder into his nostrils. The powder struck the wall of his nasal cavity and the

back of his throat with a burning punch. He sneezed, and he coughed. Then came the buzz, buzz, buzz, and the bump, bump, bump inside his head. His face felt warm and buzzed with electricity.

"You're stupid for getting into that stuff! You're going to get in trouble!" Michelle said to him in a scolding manner. She was older than Michael, and even though it was only by twenty minutes or so, she never let him forget it.

"No, I'm not," he told her. "You want to try it?" he asked as he held out the little tin. If trouble were to come, he didn't want to be the only one getting into it.

"No!" she said. "I'm not getting in trouble!"

"You chicken. Just try it once," he implored her, still holding out the tin. She looked at him with a wary eye as she stuck her finger into the tin.

"Now hold it up to your nose and breath in," he instructed her. She took a deep breath as the powder lifted off her finger and into her nose. She started sneezing and coughing as the snuff went into her nasal cavity. After the coughing and

sneezing came the whomp, whomp, whomp. It was as if helicopter blades were pulsating through her head. When the pulsing stopped, the electric buzzing around her head began. Her face felt hot and her cheeks turned red.

"What are you kids doing in there?" Jacky shouted to them from the bedroom.

"Nothing!" they said. Jacky knew immediately they were up to something.

"Will you go in there and check on them?" she asked Faith. Faith walked into the living room. Michael quickly turned to face her while simultaneously hiding the tin behind his back. Faith looked at the twins, noticing brown rings of snot crusted to their nostrils, and brown powder on their cheeks. *Well, they haven't been outside, so it can't be dirt*, she thought.

"What're you hiding back there?" she asked Michael.

"Nothing," he told her. Looking as innocent as he could through guilty eyes. She reached behind him and grabbed his hand. She unrolled his tightened fist to find the can of snuff hiding in his brown-stained hand.

"Mom, they got into Grandma's snuff!" Faith yelled from the living room.

"What?" Jacky said.

"The snuff. They got into Grandma's can of snuff!" she said again. Jacky walked in from the back bedroom.

"Are you kids trying to get sick? That stuff will make you sick!" she scolded them. She looked at their brown tobacco-stained faces and couldn't help laughing. "Well, I hope you two don't throw up! Why don't you go play out front? Go roll in the grass or something and try to stay out of the way! We've got a lot of work to do around here!"

She walked back into the bedroom and Faith cleaned their faces with a washrag. They blew their noses as brown snot stained the tissue. They went outside to play on the lawn as they were told to do. Jacky packed the little old woman's apartment up. The smell of her Grandmother still clung to the air. Her presence seemed to still linger there in the apartment. Her clothing was still hanging in the closet, as if she might come

back for a jacket or a sweater. A half-finished doily sat on her night stand waiting for her to come home and finish it up.

Jacky began to dismantle Bessie's bed. She needed more floor space as the boxes had begun to pile up in the bedroom. She pulled the hand-sewn quilt off the bed and folded it up along with the sheets.

"Will you grab the other end of this mattress and help me set the bed against the wall?" Jacky asked Barb. They grabbed the top mattress and pulled it up, exposing the thousands of dollars in money that had been hidden underneath it. Their eyes popped open as if they had just seen Bessie's ghost. None of them had ever seen so much cash at one time in their entire lives. To Faith's eyes it might as well have been a million dollars.

"Geez, Grandma was rich!" Faith said, her eyes popping out of her skull.

"Well, I don't know about rich, but she definitely wasn't hurting for money," Barb said.

"How much do you think is there, Mom?" Faith asked.

"I don't know; it looks like ten, maybe fifteen thousand," her mother said.

"Dollars?" Faith stammered.

"Dollars."

"Well, it looks like we should probably call Dad and let him know what we found," Barb said. Jacky walked into the living room and picked up the telephone. She called her father and told him what they had found. It seemed that the last time Bessie had ever trusted a bank was just before the Great Depression hit. She had scrimped and saved to make even small deposits. Just before the banks failed, she had saved up five thousand dollars, which in that time was a considerable amount of money. It had taken her many years of picking cotton and fruit in order to save up that money. She was planning on using it to move out west. She was heading to California, to the land of gold and sunshine. There were only a few thousand bushels of cotton and fruit in between her and the golden state.

Soon things went from bad to worse, she lost her jobs working on the farms, and there were rumors going around town

that the banks would be closing. She went down to close her account, but it was too late. The banks had already put up closed signs, trying to stop people from making runs on deposits. The banks disappeared from town along with her five thousand dollars, never to be heard from again.

Bessie had saved the money they found in her apartment while living off social security. She made ends meet by canning preserves, making quilts, and crocheting doilies. She would sell these items to some of the other elderly residents in her senior community. She saved a little bit here and a little bit there. In the end they found fourteen thousand dollars hidden under her bed, and another four thousand tucked away in a shoe box hidden in her closet. In her checking account they found two hundred, forty-two dollars, and thirty-one cents. She did not have a savings account.

They all headed to Lancaster, where the wake was being held. They pulled up to the funeral home, they got out of the car, and made their way up the sidewalk. They came to the steps leading up to the main entrance of the funeral parlor. The steps

were covered in gray slate stone slabs. Michael's head hung low, his eyes were affixed to the ground as they walked. They got to a short flight of stairs and he looked at the gray slab stones and something started to become very familiar. He raised his eyes from the ground and saw two large oak doors. Pete grabbed the long handle that hung from the oak doors and pulled the door open. The family entered the building, and something started to click in Michael's memory. They walked into the main corridor. To the right were narrow windows of stained glass. Sunlight came through the stained glass, casting slits of colored light onto the floor. To the left were corridors running off the main hallway. They passed two corridors and made a left turn. They walked into an open room. There was a silver casket centered on the back wall of the little room. The top half of the casket was open. Grandma Bessie was lying inside. Flowers were arranged at both ends of the casket.

Every moment and every detail seemed to be speaking to Michael. There was a disorienting familiarity to everything that was happening. They approached the casket to pay homage to

the woman who had forged an existence and a family out of next to nothing. Without her perseverance, they would not have existed. Without her determination, their lives would have been very different. Michael stood there experiencing this as if it were a memory. He remembered all of it as it all came back to him. The memory of his nearly forgotten dream came back to him. And he knew that he was now, somehow, living his dream. It was very confusing to him. It was the first time the kids had ever seen a dead person. To the young kids it seemed as if she were sleeping, and if they looked out of the corner of their eyes they could swear she was still breathing. She looked more alive in death than she had for the last few months of her life. A look of serenity was upon her face. Maybe the promise of rest and peace had been fulfilled. Michelle started to read the inscription on the inside of the casket. "Footsteps in the sand." she spoke. A flood of images passed behind Michael's eyes and a sense of déjà vu crept over him. He knew that he had in fact dreamed of this place before, and not only the place but of this very moment. He looked at the floral wreaths and the banner promising rest. He

looked at the silver casket and the gray-haired woman. Even though he had not been able to make out her face in the dream, he knew it was her. Why she came to him he did not know, and how he'd seen this before it happened, he did not understand.

The funeral was held the following day as tears of loss filled the eyes of the bereaved. Michelle and Michael did not know how to feel. They did not cry for her at the funeral. It was something that they felt guilty for. It wasn't until a few months after that, when they were watching an episode of *Punky Brewster* that the tears would start to fall. It was an episode in which Punky's best friend Cherry had lost her grandmother. It struck a chord with the twins as guilt filled their hearts and their tears came down like rain. They felt guilty for not crying over the loss of their grandmother. The funeral ended and soon after the tears dried up. They gathered at Curly's house for one last meal in remembrance of his mother.

On the following day, Jacky and Barb finished packing and loading Bessie's belongings into Curly's truck. Jacky made one final walk through the little apartment before going to the

manager's office to turn in Bessie's keys. The place was empty.

Nothing hung on the walls and the floors were barren. She

walked from the living room and into the back bedroom. It was

empty like the room before. She walked out of the bedroom, and

something in the bathroom caught her attention. She had packed

up the bathroom and cleaned it a few days earlier. When she was

finished, there was nothing in the bathroom but a roll of toilet

paper that hung from the side of the sink. She looked in the

empty bathroom and saw a piece of parchment on the

countertop. Jacky quickly flipped the light on. On the paper was

a note scrawled in Bessie's handwriting. "I just want everyone to

know how much I love you, and how much I will miss you all.

Love, Mama Bessie." Jacky's hand began to tremble. A shudder

of disbelief washed over her, and tears came to her eyes.

"Faith!" she screamed. "Faith!" she yelled again. Faith

ran into the bathroom, thinking something awful had just

happened.

"What, Momma, what's going on?" Faith asked in a

panic.

"Did you put this note in here?" Jacky asked almost yelling at her.

"What?" Faith asked.

"Did you put this note in here? Jacky asked again.

"No! Why? Who is it from?" Faith asked.

"It's from Grandma Bessie!" Jacky said.

"How did it get there?" Faith asked.

"I don't know. Are you sure you didn't put it in there?" Jacky asked again

"Yes, I'm sure, Mom. And it definitely wasn't there this morning when I used the bathroom!"

"It wasn't there when we locked up last night, either," Jacky said. "You don't think she…"

"What?" Faith asked.

"Oh, never mind. Just go wait for me in the car," Jacky told her. She held the note in her hand. She had a strange sense that she was not alone. It was the same feeling she'd had ever since she started to clean out Bessie's apartment. A feeling of another presence with her, that Bessie had been with them all

along. She had just been passing off the feelings she got in Bessie's apartment as jitters, thinking that she was just psyching herself out. She never figured out how the note got in the bathroom or when exactly Bessie had written it, but she knew that it wasn't there when she had arrived at the apartment that morning. She asked everyone, even the twins, if they knew anything about the note. No one had ever seen it before and no one knew how it got there. Bessie's passing was a milestone for the family. It marked the end of an extraordinary life and marked the memory of an extraordinary woman. Forever afterward, when things got rough for Jacky, she could still feel that presence lingering around, and she knew that she was with Bessie.

Chapter 16 The Boy Who Cried Wolf

The summer began fade slightly and signs of early autumn were starting to appear. The mornings were cooler as southerly winds started to give way to the strength of the north. The days were still warm but didn't burn with the intensity of midsummer. It was the weekend, and much to the reluctance of Jacky, she allowed him to stay at the house. The boys got up early that morning. They were planning another weekend hike into the mountains.

"Hey, I know this place where somebody started an old tree fort. I figure we'll take a rest there," Doug said as they packed their backpacks for the short-day trip.

"That sounds good," Mikey responded.

"It's a little rickety, but it seems safe," Doug said. The thought of a rickety old tree fort sounded intriguing to Mikey.

The idea of an old abandoned fort spurred his imagination. They packed Mikey's backpack with a canteen of water fresh from the tap, some chips and cookies, and a couple of sandwich bags full of dry cereal. They well water was always cool and sweet.

"We won't need much food, will we?" Mikey asked.

"Naw, we're not going to be gone that long. We'll just go for a few hours," Doug said.

"And where are you boys going?" Jacky asked as she walked into the kitchen.

"Ummm…we're going hiking," Mikey told her.

"That sounds like fun. It would do you good to get out of the house," she told them. She liked that they would be out of her hair for the day. Even though she wasn't fond of Doug and thought he was a troublemaker, she liked the fact that he got Mikey out of the house. Doug was always dragging him along on little hiking trips. It was good for him to be active and to work the muscles he'd injured in his accident. He still dragged his right leg when he was tired, but she noticed it less and less as he grew.

"Just stay out of trouble! Don't let your common sense get loose of you," she warned them with a raised brow.

"Yeah, yeah, we know!" Mikey said with a tone of sarcasm.

"Hey, don't get snotty. If you knew, then you wouldn't be getting into trouble, and I wouldn't have to say something!" she told him. He was getting older and was starting to push the boundaries of authority. He was testing adults to see what he could get away with, and what he could not. "Now get out here!" she told them. They grabbed up the pack and were soon knee-deep in foxtail. They hiked some ways up the creek bed, along the trails that had started to become very familiar to them.

"So where is this fort you've been talking about?" Mikey asked.

"It's up the trail up bit, kinda by Cappie and Steve's house," Doug said, an older retired couple the neighbor kids use to have bible study with. "It's on the property across the creek from their house." When the trail dropped down and crossed the

creek, Mikey and Doug almost immediately began taking off their shoes and socks, which were covered in foxtail stickers.

"My mom hates picking these fucking stickers out of my socks," Doug said.

"I know. My mom started making me do it. I hate these fucking stickers," Mikey said. "They really dig into the skin." Mikey liked the fact that Doug cussed so much. It made him feel free to cuss also. He liked the uninhibited, uncensored form of communication. It made him feel more grown up, more like an adult. He'd learned most of his cuss words from Doug, and what he didn't learn from Doug, he learned from his parents. He'd even started learning cuss words in Spanish from Frankie and Raul.

They walked through the creek, and up on the hilltop they could see Cappie and Steve's house. The couple allowed the neighborhood kids to sled on the steep terrain of their property in the winter. They would even bring out hot chocolate for the kids to drink. In the summer they used their van to take the kids to vacation Bible school, and they would let the

neighborhood kids swim in their pool. They were one of the few people in the neighborhood who owned a pool. They were truly Christians and showed by their actions what it meant to be a person of the faith. Doug knew they were close to the tree fort. He looked off to the opposite side of the creek, and soon saw the oak tree with the two-by-four steps nailed into the side of its trunk.

"There it is!" Doug said in excitement. They scrambled barefoot through the brush, their shoes tied together and hanging over their shoulders. They scurried up the homemade ladder into the old oak tree. The tree fort was nothing but a few two-by-fours nailed to the side of the tree and some plywood nailed in place in the center of the tree. Acorns had fallen from the canopy of the oak tree and were lying strewn about all over the plywood platform of the rickety treehouse. They sat on the creaky wood. Doug unscrewed the cap of the canteen and guzzled a swig of water. Afterward he let out a loud belch. He went to the corner and unzipped his shorts and started whizzing off the side of the platform.

"You taking a piss?" Mikey asked.

"Yeah, why? You want to hold it for me?" Doug said sarcastically.

"Hell no! I wouldn't touch your dick if you paid me," Mikey retorted.

"Well, I don't have any money anyhow, so I guess you're lucky." He laughed at his own smart-ass remark. Mikey felt obliged to man up and whiz off the side of the fort as well. As he was peeing, he noticed a single-wide trailer sitting near the top of the hill crest.

"Look. There's a trailer up there. Looks abandoned," Mikey said. Doug zipped up and turned around to see the trailer.

"Let's take a walk up there and check it out," Doug said. Suddenly Jacky's voice rang through Mikey's ears. *Don't be getting into any trouble.*

"Naw, let's just keep hiking," Mikey said.

"Come on, you pussy! We'll just check it out!" Doug taunted. "We won't get in any trouble." They walked up to the little trailer and peeked through the dusty windows. Boxes full of

314

odds and ends were stacked up against walls and in the little hallway of the single wide trailer. It looked like more of a storage shed than a place you would call home. They walked around the corner of the trailer. Doug tried turning the knob of the front door.

"What are you doing?" Mikey asked him.

"What? Just checking!" Doug said, trying to look innocent. Mikey didn't buy Doug's innocence. He had learned early on never to trust Doug. His mom was right. He was a smart-ass troublemaker, but in the same turn, he sure knew how to have an interesting time. He always kept Mikey on his feet.

Around the trailer they walked, peeking into the windows, half afraid somebody would be peeking back at them. They got to the back side and Doug turned the knob of the rear door.

"Click!" the knob turned, and Doug swung the door open in amazement.

"You think someone just left all this stuff in here!" Mikey asked.

"Sure fucking looks like it. Look at all the weeds in the driveway! No one has driven up that in a while," Doug said. He started to walk in.

"Wait!" Mikey said. "Don't go in there."

"What? You need to stop being such a puss all the time! I guess you can wait out here for me!" he said as he walked in. Mikey reluctantly walked in behind him.

The trailer was small and crammed full of stuff. In the boxes they found an assortment of knives of different shapes and sizes. There were a few sitting chairs and a couch covered in boxes. They were either half unpacked, or half packed up. There were a few decals hanging on the walls, along with strands of dust-covered webs. Doug walked into the back room. He stubbed his toe and looked down. He found a naked woman stretched over a motorcycle staring up at him from inside a box. He reached down into the box and picked up the magazine. Underneath the magazine he found another naked woman on another cycle. The box was full of them.

"We've got porn back here!" he yelled in excitement.

"What!" Mikey yelled from the living room.

"Porn. Boxes full of porn!" he repeated. Mikey ran into the back room to see a redheaded woman and her red furry bush staring back at him. She had large breasts and nipples that looked like large pieces of pepperoni. She had one leg stretched up over the seat of the silver motorcycle, with two fingers spreading her vaginal lips apart.

"Goddamn, that's disgusting! Still, I am getting a hard-on looking at this shit," Doug said.

"Find a better one," Mikey said. Doug pulled another magazine from the box.

"Yeah, that's better. Less lips and less ass!" Doug said, chuckling.

"My stepdad has a bunch of porn like this. Just without the motorcycles," Mikey said.

"I think everybody's dad has a stash of porn somewhere," Doug responded. It had never occurred to Mikey before, but Doug was probably right for the most part. They

spent all day in that trailer rummaging through someone else's personal property. Soon the twilight was upon them.

"I wonder why someone would leave all this stuff here?" Mikey said.

"I don't know, but it doesn't look like they're coming back for it anytime soon," Doug said. "We should take some of this back with us."

"Steal it?" Mikey said in shock.

"They left it here. It's not stealing if they left it," Doug reasoned.

"How are we going to explain where we got it all?" Mikey asked.

"We will hide it up in the fort and take it home a little bit at a time. They won't notice it then," Doug explained. It sounded like a good plan. They loaded up a few boxes full of knives, some porn, a few maps, and a bunch of trinkets and junk. They started hauling the boxes down to the fort. They were lifting them up into the tree when Mikey heard Jacky's voice echoing through the canyon.

"Michael, it's dinnertime!" she called.

"Shit. I have to go," Mikey said. He picked through his box of junk, carrying what he could fit in his pockets.

"Michael, dinnertime," Jacky's voice beckoned him again.

"I'll catch up with you at school," he told Doug. He cut his way back through the foxtails. He walked on the untrampled dry grass, leaving a new trail in his footsteps. When he got to the house, his dinner was waiting for him.

"It's about time. You look filthy. Why don't you wash up and change before you sit down to eat?" Jacky told him. He ran to his bedroom and unloaded his pockets. He hid his loot under his bed and went into the bathroom to wash up. He was hungry and chowed his food down in no time.

"Why don't you slow down, Michael. This isn't a feeding trough around here," Pete said in his usual controlling tone. "How many goddamn times do I got to tell you to mind your manners?" he said. Mikey finished his food, excused himself from the table, and went into his room to check out the

stuff he had taken from the trailer. He couldn't help thinking that Doug was going to take some of the stuff they had agreed to split up.

"I want you to get ready for bed. You got school tomorrow," Jacky told him. He jumped a little and turned around to see his mom standing in the door. "What? Did I scare you?" she asked him.

"Oh yeah, a little," he said with his eyes bugging out. "I'll get ready in a sec."

"Okay. I'll see you in the morning," she said as she walked away. He started thanking his lucky stars she hadn't notice the loot he'd pushed under the bed.

He awoke the next morning still nervous from the experience of the day before. He met Doug at school and they talked about the stuff they had found, and the things they had seen inside that trailer. After school Mikey and Michelle walked up from the bus stop. When they neared the house, they could see a cop car parked in the driveway.

"I wonder what's going on!" Michelle said. "Maybe it's about Pete? Maybe they are here to take him to jail?"

"I hope so!" Mikey said. "I hate that fucker!"

"When did you start cussing?" she asked him in shock.

"I've *been* cussing!" he stated proudly.

"You better hope Mom doesn't hear you talk like that! She'll wash your mouth out with dish soap!" Michelle said. The memory of liquid Dawn quickly came to his mind.

They walked slowly up the driveway. By the time they reached the house, they were convinced that the police were there for Pete. They entered the house and saw Jacky and the police officer seated at the dining room table.

"Michael, go and put your stuff in your bedroom and then come in here and have a seat!" Jacky told him. "Michelle, go into your room!" Michael did what his mother told him to do. He was nervous, and so was Michelle. He put his backpack away and seated himself at the table.

"Michael, I want you to meet Officer Johnson," Jacky said. The officer got up and firmly shook Michael's small hand.

"He is here because somebody broke into a trailer up the road. They stole a bunch of stuff, and trashed the place," Jacky said. Her words seemed to come out in slow motion as the blood rushed to his face. His heart plunged into the pit of his stomach. He suddenly felt short of breath. He felt shaky and nauseous.

"You don't know anything about that, do you?" she asked. Michael shook his head with a silently horrified no. "Are you sure?" she asked him again. Again, he shook his head with a silent no. "Have I ever told you the story about the boy who cried wolf?" she asked him.

"Yes," he said meekly.

"What?" Jacky asked him.

"Yes," he said a little bit louder.

"Well, let me tell it again so that you remember it a little more clearly. You see there was this boy. He was a special boy because he was in charge of looking after the villagers' sheep. And if he saw a wolf it was his job to blow the horn to alert the villagers that there was a wolf trying to eat the sheep," she began to reiterate the old tale.

"I know the story, Mom!" Michael interrupted.

"Well, you're going to sit there and listen to it again!" she continued. "Now this boy was up in the hills above the village one afternoon, and it was lonely and boring just watching the sheep. The boy sat there with his horn laying against a tree, and decides he is going to play a trick on the villagers and blows the horn. All the village men come running up the hills with pitchforks and torches, expecting to find the wolf. But when they get to the top of the hill, they find no wolf. The boy tells the men he was able to scare off the wolf and the wolf ran away. So, the villagers return to the village and praise him as a hero.

"Well, the next day the boy is up on the hill bored again, and again he decides to blow the horn. All the village men come running up the hill with the pitchforks and torches again, and again no wolf. Instead they find the boy rolling in the grass, laughing at all the sweaty little fat men running up the hill. Well, the villagers got mad, but they walked back to the village and continued about their day.

"On the next day, the boy found himself bored again. He was laying on the grass when he saw a wolf come out of the forest and nab one of the sheep. The boy blows the horn and blows the horn, but none of the villagers come. They think he is blowing the horn just to fool them again, so no one comes to help him. That night the boy never returned to the village. So, the next day the villagers go looking for the boy up in the hills, and all they find is pieces of his shirt. The wolf had eaten him," she said, concluding her story.

"And the moral of the story is, never tell a lie, or when the time comes to tell the truth, no one will believe you!" Michael said, cutting her short.

"That's right! So, is there anything you want to tell us?" Jacky asked him again.

"No," he said again.

"You know, I already talked to your friend Doug and he confessed to everything!" Officer Johnson said, finally speaking up. "In fact, he said it was all your idea!"

"What? He's the one who wanted to go up there! He's the one who opened the door! I mean the damn door wasn't even locked!" Michael blurted out, exposing his lies. Michael didn't even think that he had just seen Doug on the bus, and that it was entirely impossible for the officer to have talked to him. The officer had played him against his friend, and he fell for it hook, line, and sinker.

The cop left that day with his confession in hand. The owner of the trailer had bought the property as a weekend retreat. He was a big fella with a long beard who built custom bikes. When he found out that Doug and Mikey were so young, he had dropped all the charges. It took Mikey and Doug two weekends in a row of cleaning up their mess, and helping the man to clean up the property, before he called it even. They had gotten off easy, and Mikey never again broke into anyone's home. They had returned all the items they had taken. And every time they had to go back to that trailer to make good to the man they had stolen from, they carried with them a sense of shame. Luckily for them the man was a forgiving man.

Chapter 17 The Boy Who Cried in Vain

The autumn nights grew to a chill, but the days were still warm. The trees started to change their usual color. Another season was coming as surely as one was passing away. The twins began to be plagued with nightmares. In their sleep they dreamed of creatures swooping down upon them and stealing their breath. They gasped for air but found none. The incubi and the succubae were afoot, and with them they opened a doorway. The house creaked and moaned in the night with strange noises. There were ghosts walking in the hallway of the small house. Maybe it was the age of the land wearing through to the present, or maybe it was the negativity drawn in by Pete that brought these forces forth. In sleep there were dungeons, and Michael and Michelle were strapped to their beds. Something had stolen their breath. They tried and tried to scream, but nothing would come from

their chest. No voice would spring from their throats. And the succubae would swoop down upon them, sucking any breath they might have gathered from their lungs. The menacing black floating beings hovered in the corners and thrived in the darkness. They would awake panic stricken and gasping for air. It was as if they were held under water and then reemerge, swallowing up the air with gasps. The darkness seemed devoid of any light. Michelle slept next to a night light, but the darkness of her sleep seemed to absorb any illumination the little light could offer. There was a pull in the rafters of the house. A war was brewing. The light and the dark began to battle. The light of an idea of how they knew life could be, and the darkness of the life they were now living.

At school Michael started acting up. He and Doug bullied kids younger than them. In their minds they ruled the playground, although they still cowered to the bullies that were bigger than them. Mikey was drawn to the troublemakers, the kids that seemed to have emotional problems, the kids that had problems expressing themselves constructively. Michael had

anger and confusion in him. Sex had been forced upon them at a young age, and that had spread confusion in the twins' minds. They had no way of processing the things that they were exposed to. Their minds were not mature enough to fully understand what was happening to them. All they knew was that they felt different than the other kids. They felt apart from their peers. It was a sort of isolation and a feeling of being out of place.

Michelle was good at blending in with the popular kids in a way that Michael was not. She was able to funnel her emotions in a different way than he was. She was better at making friends than he was. She was good at building a believably solid outer facade, even though on the inside she felt broken. Although she hung out with the popular kids, and she blended well into their social circles, she could never shake the feeling that she didn't belong in Tehachapi. She dreamed of hitting it big and becoming famous even at a young age. She wanted to live in L.A. and become an actress. She dreamed of

328

taking her family away from Tehachapi and away from their stepfather.

School seemed to be a drag, and the two had a hard time focusing on schoolwork. They knew the work but never cared to complete their assignments on time. They didn't put any effort into their school work and would often get D's and F's. Jacky just put it off as laziness and a lack of trying. She never set the bar very high and would settle on them getting a C average. She was never the kind of parent that sat with them through their homework to guide them through it. But their minds were too occupied with what was happening at home. They focused on getting through it and dreamed of leaving the isolated mountain town. They had come from a bigger place, and they knew even at a young age that they had to return to the city if they were ever to make their dreams come true.

It was Friday after school and Michael wanted to go over to Frankie's house as soon as he dropped off his backpack. Pete was home drinking in his bedroom. The lights in the master bedroom were off and Mikey could see the glow of the cold blue

light of the television. *Mom must be cleaning in Lancaster,* Michael thought. He tiptoed into Michelle's room.

"Shush, be quiet," he said in a whisper as he pointed toward the master bedroom in the back of the house. Michelle nodded in acknowledgment. "We'll sneak out the back door," Mikey told her in a hush.

"Michael, Michelle? Is that you?" Pete's voice came from the master bedroom. They snuck quietly out the side door of the garage and ran over to Frankie and Raul's house as quickly as they could. They found the brothers swinging on a large rope that was hanging from the old oak tree in front of their house. The kids swung from the large oak tree into the early evening. As the summer began to wind down and autumn began to take hold, the sun had begun setting earlier and earlier. They missed the long days of summer as they knew the cold days of winter were approaching. The long summer days afforded them more time away from the house, a freedom the winter didn't offer.

Before they knew it, twilight was upon them and the bats came out to feed upon the flying insects. They soon got bored with the swing and became interested in the bats flying over their heads. They had a fear of the bats. They saw them as an embodiment of evil, a side effect of watching too many vampire movies. The long shadows of the western mountains at dusk fell upon the earth. The bats danced in and out of the glowing ember of the sun that was quickly sinking on the horizon. The rural houses had electric lanterns fixed to the sides of the garages; they were bright and stood out for miles. Flying insects and moths were drawn in by the light, and the bats would follow for an easy meal.

Frankie, Raul, Mikey, and Michelle stood in the twilight, throwing small rocks at the bats. The bats swooped in on the rocks, thinking they were insects. Their sonar hearing told them that there was a large object coming near them. Sometimes the bats got hit if they weren't quick enough to avoid the rocks, but it was rare for one to be killed with a rock. Their hearing was far too acute and precise. The orange ember fizzled out and the

oranges soon gave way to a red and purple sky. The kids knew the adults would be calling them in soon. The kids had lived next to one another for years now and had become well acquainted as long-term neighbors often do. They were all one another's best friends. Michael and Michelle would often spend the afternoon and evenings over at their house. Although the kids knew that their inherent cultures were different, they never allowed that to become a boundary between them. Michael grew so close to them that it was rare that he didn't spent the whole weekend at the Sanchez house.

"I think I got it!" Raul said. He suddenly bolted off.

"Where do you think he's going?" Michelle asked in a sarcastic tone.

"Who knows!" Frankie said with equal sarcasm.

"Ugh…Boys!" she mumbled, pretending to be annoyed, but happy to be hanging out with them. When he returned he had a Wrist-Rocket wrapped around his arm.

"Where'd you get that?" Mikey asked with enthusiasm.

"My dad bought it for me!" Raul replied, showing his gratitude.

"He bought it for us!" Frankie said, correcting his older brother.

"Well, I'm in charge of it," Raul said. "Besides we can take turns with it." He picked up a rock and loaded it into the leather pouch dangling from the rubber bands. He squeezed the pouch and pulled the bands past his elbow. He caught a bat in his sights and fired. The bat swooped for the rock, then suddenly made a hard turn as the rock shot past the flying mammal.

"Damn!" Raul said in frustration.

"Okay, my turn! Hand it over!" Frankie said with his palm open. Raul reluctantly gave up the slingshot. Frankie grabbed a small rock and loaded his ammo. He pulled the rubber bands back, aimed, and fired. The bat went in for the kill. It went to turn away, but it was too late. The rock hit it, and the bat fell into the darkness of the grass down the hill from them.

"I hit it," Frankie said. "I think I killed it."

"It just looked like you hit it," Raul said jealously.

"No, I think I hit it! I saw the rock hit it," Mikey said in Frankie's defense.

"Well, go down there and find it and then we will know," Raul said, trying to steal his little brother's thunder.

"I'm not going down there!" Mikey said, fearful of the little creature. "I don't want it sucking my blood!"

"Me, either!" said Michelle.

"We'll find it tomorrow, then you will see when there is more light out. I know I hit it," Frankie said again.

"Hey, do you think your dad will let me stay the night?" Mikey asked Frankie.

"You stay the night every weekend," Raul said. "Don't you ever want to go home?" he teased him.

"Go ask your dad if I can stay over?" Mikey asked Frankie again. Frankie ran off to the house. He soon returned.

"He doesn't care! As long as I don't get in the way of the TV," Frankie said. They soon heard Pete calling them in. The rule was for them to be in by dark, and it was late into the evening already.

"Guess it is time to go," Michelle said.

"I'm going to go ask Pete if I can stay the night," Mikey said. "Meet me by the fence in like twenty minutes!" he said to Frankie and Raul. He thought for sure that Pete was going to let him. He and Michelle walked toward the house.

"If you're staying at Frankie's house, then I am staying at Kimmy's," Michelle said. They both hated asking Pete for anything. It was like the world hinged upon his decisions. He never let anyone forget that he was the one in control. They walked into the house and closed the door. Light from the television in the master bedroom was pouring into the hallway, but the rest of the house was dark.

"You ask first, then I will ask," Michelle said.

"What? No, you ask first. I'm always the one who has to ask for everything!" Mikey said.

"But you wanted to spend the night at Frankie's house first!" she said.

"How about we ask together," Mike suggested.

"Okay, but if he wants us to play video games or watch movies with him, then we are out of here," she said. They walked toward the back bedroom. The television was on a low hum. The closer they got to the threshold of the bedroom, the sooner they realized that it wasn't a hum but the moaning of a woman that they could hear.

"Maybe we should just forget it!" Michelle said. She recognized that sound just as quickly as Michael did, and they both knew he was watching porn. They could almost feel the lust in the air. The humidity of breath clung to the walls and the stench of his sweat was dense and permeating. The animal had control of this man, and the beast inside would not soon let go.

"Let's just get it over with," Michael said. He softly knocked on the frame of the bedroom door, but they did not enter. They were afraid of what they knew was going on inside, and they were afraid that he would try to get them caught up in his dehumanizing behavior. He jumped at the sound of the knock and quickly pulled the comforter over his naked body.

"Is that you, kids?" he asked. He was caught off guard and his voice trembled at the sudden interruption. "What do you want?" he said.

"You called us in. We were wondering if I can spend the night at Frankie's house, and Shelle wants to stay the night at Kimmy's," Michael asked in a quiet voice.

"Why don't you kids stay in tonight? You want to play some video games or watch a movie?" he asked.

"No, we want to go play with our friends," Mikey said.

"No, you kids need to stay in," he said. "Besides your mother will be home soon."

"But she would let us if she were here," Michael implored him.

"Well, she isn't here, and I said no. So that's the end of it," he said. The kids walked away before Pete could say anything else and quickly went to the fence to meet Frankie and Raul.

"He said no!" Michael said in defeat.

"Why?" Raul said.

"I don't know. God, I hate that guy!" Michael said.

"Well, it's not like he's your real dad," Frankie said.

"I know. I shouldn't even have to listen to him. He's just a fucking jerk." The more he thought about it, the angrier he got. Thoughts swirled in his head and anger fueled his heart. The thought that he should tell his mom about all the stuff that Pete made them do spun through his mind. If she were here, they wouldn't be going through this, and she would surely let them stay the night with their friends. The thought of telling his mother kept swirling in his mind. And every time he ran the scenario in his head he would get nervous and his hands would start to sweat.

"I should tell my mom the shit he makes Michelle and me do when she's not around," he said.

"You should tell her. That guy's an asshole. I bet my dad could kick his ass!" Frankie said. Frankie did not know what Mikey was talking about, but he liked egging him on.

"Your dad would kick the shit out of him," Michael said.

"Yeah, he definitely would!" Michelle said. Headlights crawled up Water Canyon Road, and the car made a right onto the dirt road that led up to their house.

"My mom's home," Mikey said excitedly. "Thank God!" The headlights bounced along the surface of the dirt road.

"I'm going to do it!" he said. Suddenly he bolted off down the driveway to meet her before she reached the house. As the headlights came closer, nervous anxiety rattled his determination. Jacky pulled up next to him and rolled down her window. A cloud of dust that had been kicked up by the car came brushing passed him.

"Hi, Mom!" he said. His legs felt like jelly and the thought of telling her everything that had happened continued to nauseate him.

"Hey, honey. What's going on?" she said with a smile. She'd had a long day of cleaning homes and was tired.

"Dad won't let me stay the night at Frankie's!" he said.

"Well, I guess you have to stay here tonight," she said. "Besides it's only Friday night. You can stay over tomorrow night."

"Mom, I hate him!" he said.

"What? You shouldn't talk about your father that way," she told him.

"Stepfather!" he corrected her.

"Well, you shouldn't talk about him that way. And I thought you kids wanted to call him dad," she said. The old Buick she drove was humming and rattling in idle.

"You don't understand, Mom," Michael told her.

"What don't I understand? What are you talking about, Michael?" she asked him. He hesitated. "Michael I'm tired. I've been working all day and I still have to make dinner," she told him. He started to get real nervous. His stomach had butterflies flying around at Mach speed. He rubbed his sweaty palms together.

"He makes us do stuff when you're gone?" he told her. It suddenly just started coming out.

"Stuff like what?" she asked him. "Like chores and homework-type stuff."

"Like sex stuff, Mom," he told her. His voice broke under stress. He was shaking and scared of the floodgate he had just opened. He thought she wouldn't believe him. He thought that after breaking into the trailer that she would never believe him again. He felt like the little boy in the village who was left to be eaten by the wolves.

"Sex stuff! What are you talking about Michael?" she asked him, seemingly getting irritated. She couldn't believe what was coming out of his mouth. She didn't believe her own ears. A panic set in.

"I don't know. Sex stuff!" he repeated.

"You need to be more specific, Michael. Are you lying about this to go to Frankie's?" she asked him.

"No, Mom, I'm not lying! He makes me, and Michelle put his wiener in our mouths, and he makes us rub his wiener. He makes us watch sex movies. He…he tries to put his wiener in my butt," he said. Tears streaked down his face and cut clean

paths down his dust-covered cheeks. He wiped the tears off his face, creating a dirty smear. His words could not convey the severity of what was happening to them. His vocabulary could not paint the whole picture. But it was enough to send the message. Jacky sat there in stunned silence. She couldn't believe what she was hearing.

"Go to Frankie's house and play for a little while!" she told him.

"Can I stay the night at his house?" he asked.

"No!" she said as she stepped on the gas and hauled ass up the driveway. The back tires sent rocks, dirt, and debris flying behind the Buick. Small pebbles hit him in the shins with a stinging pain. He had started walking toward Frankie's house when he heard the screaming start. He knew that his parents were in an argument that he had caused. It was not long afterward that he was joined at Frankie's by Michelle.

"What's going on?" she asked.

"I told Mom about Pete!" Mikey said to her.

"You told her?" Michelle asked, completely stunned. "What did she say?"

"Nothing, really, but she seemed real pissed!" he said.

"Good. I hope she divorces him!" Michelle said excitedly.

"Me, too."

The yelling could be heard by all the nearby neighbors. It broke the quiet breeze that blew through the mountain pass. Faith came home from cheerleading practice. She sat outside with the kids not knowing what they were arguing about. She assumed that it was just another one of their arguments. She didn't want to hear all the screaming and yelling. Soon Raul and Frankie were called in for the night, and the three kids sat on the lawn for a few hours while the argument raged on inside the house. They could hear doors being slammed; they could hear the sound of breaking glass. The front door opened, and Pete stood there as he and Jacky exchanged verbal assaults. Pete opened the door to his truck slammed it shut and started the

engine. They watched as he peeled off down the driveway in his pickup.

"Looks like Pete's leaving," Faith said.

"Good! I hope he never comes back!" Michelle said. Faith looked at her little sister wondering where those thoughts would come from, where those emotions would come from.

Inside the house, Jacky picked up the phone and called her sister. She tried to speak to her sister, but the words kept catching in her throat. Her body was trembling. It seemed like everything she had worked so hard for, the family she had worked so hard for, was being pulled out from under her. It felt like her world was being torn apart from every direction.

"Jacky, is that you?" Barb asked. "You need to slow down and catch your breath, I am having a hard time understanding you."

Jacky sobbed into the receiver and was having a hard time catching her breath in between sobs.

"I…I…" She choked on her words as she tried to say that she thought Pete was molesting her kids.

"What?" Barb asked her to repeat. "I can't understand you."

Jacky started crying hysterically.

"Why don't you come down here and stay a few nights? It sounds like you need to get away for a few days," Barb suggested. She wasn't sure what was going on but knew it must be something serious. Jacky called Faith back into the house to help her get packed. She packed up clothes for herself, the twins, and for her mother as Jacky sat on the couch crying loudly. She was still crying as they drove down the road. Between the tears she didn't know how she was going to make it all the way to Barb's house.

It was almost a three-hour drive from Tehachapi to Santa Barbara, where Jacky's sister lived. Halfway to Santa Barbara Jacky was fading in and out of sleep. After ten hours of work, plus the few hours of arguing with Pete, the drive to the coast was too much for her tired body. Her head kept nodding down and her eyes would close. She suddenly swept her head back up and popped her eyes back open. She swerved suddenly as she

corrected herself back into her proper lane. She kept hitting the rumble strips carved into the pavement. But she kept driving, forcing herself to stay awake. She had stopped for coffee, but it wasn't enough to keep her up. The arguing and the crying had taken their toll. She had thirty minutes left of driving, and she knew she wouldn't be able to make it. She didn't want to pull the car over and sleep on the side of the road with the kids in the car.

"Faith, are you awake?" she asked.

"Yeah, Mom, I'm wide-awake! How 'bout you?" Faith said sarcastically.

"Do you think you can drive?" Jacky asked her.

"Me? By myself?" she asked in shock. "I've never driven on my own before. I don't even have my learners permit yet."

"Well, you won't be alone. I will be right next to you," Jacky said.

"But you'll be asleep!" Faith said.

"No, I won't be. I'll stay awake," Jacky said, trying to reassure her.

"Yeah right! You keep nodding off over there!" Faith said.

"If I fall asleep just wake me up." She said. Jacky pulled over and they switched seats. Faith slid into the driver's seat and nervously took over the wheel. She went down the highway, staying way below the speed limit. Jacky kept nodding in and out. Anytime Jacky's eyes closed, Faith would shake her and yell at her to stay awake.

They made it to Barb's house late into the night. They stayed in Santa Barbara for a few days. Jacky never once brought up the phone call she had made to Barb. She never mentioned why she was sobbing so hysterically on the phone and Barb never broached the subject. They sat and had coffee in the mornings. They went out to eat and hung out on the beaches in the afternoons, but still the subject did not come up. Barb could tell that Jacky was deeply troubled and had something weighing on her mind. She assumed it was about Pete, but she did not ask. She assumed that when Jacky was ready to talk about it she would open up.

After a few days, they returned to Tehachapi with Jacky never talking to Barb about what had happened. Pete mostly stayed away from the house, only coming there to change and shower. If he did stay at the house overnight, he slept on the couch. He got ready for work and started walking out the door. Michelle and Michael were sitting in the living room, watching television, and trying to ignore his presence. He opened the front door and then he stopped. He turned to Michael, still sitting on the floor.

"You know, I never made you do anything!" Pete said snidely. "I only did what you wanted me to do!" He stared at the kid coldly for a moment, then slammed the door and tore off down the driveway.

"Don't listen to him, Mikey. He's just an asshole!" Michelle whispered in his ear. She leaned over and hugged her brother. "Everything will be okay! One day we will leave this place. We'll move to L.A. and become famous. Then everyone can come and live with us in our mansion. And we'll be safe and happy. And Pete won't come around us anymore."

A few days later, Michael and Michelle were outside sitting on the lawn. It was late afternoon and Pete was due home. Like clockwork he turned down the dirt road and rolled up the driveway. He got out of the truck and slammed the door shut. He stopped and stared at them sitting on the lawn for a long cold moment. Then he turned heading into the house and slammed the front door. It was as if he wanted to send a clear message to them. To let them know he was the master of this house. He soon came out of the house and walked toward the them.

"Go in the house, Michelle!" he told her contemptuously.

"No. I think I'll stay out here in the sun," she said in disobedience.

"I said get your ass in the house. I want to talk to your brother," Pete told her again. She got up slowly, brushed the grass off herself, and slowly walked into the house. She turned every so often to make sure Pete didn't do anything stupid and to give him dirty looks as she walked away.

"Look, I just want to let you know, I didn't make you or your sister do anything. You wanted me to do those things to

you," he said, trying to convince Michael that he was innocent, trying to push the responsibility of his actions onto the two young kids. Michael sat there in silence, not knowing how to feel. On one hand he felt glad that he had stood up for himself, but on the other he somehow felt guilty.

"Look at all the problems you caused," Pete said to him. "Everyone's mad at you. Your mom's mad at you. I'm mad at you. Everyone is upset!"

Michael continued staring up at him in silence.

"What? What do you want from me? What do you want me to do?" Pete asked him.

"I don't want anything from you!" Michael said. "I just think…I just think that maybe you should go," Mikey suggested.

"What? You want me to leave," Pete said. He was shocked that the idea had come from the young boy. "Look, little boy! This is my fucking house! I'm not going anywhere," he said in anger. "I'm the one that pays the fucking bills around this place, not your mother! I'm the one who puts a roof over your head. I'm the one who puts food on your plate!" he shouted.

"And if anything happens to me, if I go to jail, then your mother goes to jail, too. You hear me, little boy! You need to realize who's really in charge here!" He stormed off into the house and slammed the door once again.

Over time he was able to convince Jacky that it was all a misunderstanding. He was able to convince her that things weren't the way the child had described. He told her that he wouldn't do such things, that he couldn't do such things. He told her everything she wanted to believe was true and she fell for it. He wrapped his beautiful web of lies around her and she believed him. She believed him because she had to believe him. For a while the molestation stopped. It was like Pete just waited long enough for the twins to think it was over. He waited just long enough for the storm to pass. He knew he had come close to the fire. He knew it was a close call. He knew he was one phone call away from going to prison. After a few months, after everything had blown over, it started up again. First it was inviting the kids to play video games, then it was a gradual touch. Soon he was right back at everything he'd sworn up and

down didn't happen and wouldn't happen. Pete was never one to keep his word about anything. The webs of deceit and the lies that he spun had bound his prey to fear and guilt. He'd poisoned and paralyzed those he called his family. Mikey had for a moment regained the voice that had been taken from him, but he'd then been silenced again. The phantoms that haunted their dreams continued to steal their voices. Mikey had stood up against this man. He had told the truth, and no one came. And the wolf continued to devour its prey.

Chapter 18 Porcelain Doll

Her hair so soft, maybe blonde, brunette, or fiery red. We tie her waist down to keep her thin and tight. We tape her mouth to keep her from being heard and out of sight. So easy to control and to possess. Those perfectly perky little breasts. An ass such as you cannot help but to caress. She has no blemish in a blemished mind. Her skin is like silk and not a wrinkle of time. In her tiny dress, she dances around. To have her, to hold her, to keep her bound. She's locked in contrived, coveted, salacious desire. She dances as a doll, a puppet of possession. She's locked away in the mind of her master's self-created disillusion.

Jacky threw herself into a great denial. She would not process the thoughts of what was happening. Instead, she ignored the problems and hoped that time would transform the situation. She believed what Pete had told her to believe,

because it was easier to believe that than the alternative. It was easier to believe that it was the misunderstanding of a young child than it was to believe that she slept next to a monster. It was easier to believe because it was everything she wanted to believe. She was afraid to start over alone with four kids. She was over forty years old now, and every decision she had made seemed to be falling apart. She felt the floor slipping from under her feet. She began to take the kids with her when they didn't have school. On the weekends she would make sure they always stayed at their friends' house if they weren't with her. For a while this had worked, and the molestation had stopped. But she soon let her guard down and felt that things had changed. No matter how much one tries to keep something like this from happening, it is impossible. Where there is a will there is a way, and people like Pete are only looking for the opportunity. She was living in denial, and her denial gave her a false sense of security. A leopard cannot change its spots. Maybe with the help of professionals who know how to treat people like Pete, he might have found help. But for him, counseling was not

something that he was willing to go through. It meant complete and open honesty. It meant facing his reflection in the mirror and seeing all that it reflected back on him. It meant taking responsibility for himself and owning up to the choices he made. It meant taking responsibility for the life that they all were living, a life that he created, a false semblance of a family. It meant facing his demon. Admittance always carries heavy consequence. But in the end, we much all face our own reflection and the shadow that it casts between the dark and the light. There is no avoiding this, and it serves as a warning to all of us. We must face our truth as well as the consequence that it carries.

Pete continued his charade as a law-abiding jailer. As he worked in a prison, so, too, did he begin to build his home to be like a prison. He locked away the truth from the world. The innocent beings that he transformed, that he disfigured, these broken dolls, became his prisoners. He would wait for moments of distraction. He would wait for Jacky to sleep or to come home late. He would wait for any moment he could find to exploit any

opportunity with the kids. The truth that Michael had revealed was swept back under the rug, and things became the way they once were.

One such opportunity came to Pete as Jacky was running late one evening. She had fallen behind and was trying to catch up with the tract homes she was cleaning. The holidays were coming, and she wanted to make and save as much money as she could before Christmas.

"Your mom called. She's going to be running late," he said to the kids. "She told me to make you some TV dinners. So, get something to drink and grab a fork. You kids can eat in the living room and watch TV if you want." The twins looked at each other and knew why he was being so nice. They knew he had an ulterior motive.

"Where's Faith?" Michelle asked.

"She went to the beach with some of her friends," Pete replied. "They went down there for the weekend."

"Well, when's Mom going to be home?" she asked.

"I told you, late!" he said. "She'll get home as soon as she can!" he said from the kitchen. He walked into the living room with the hot TV dinners in his hand. He sat next to Michelle and started eating his dinner. When he finished, he started playfully rubbing her shoulders.

"Hey, you want to play dress-up?" he asked her. "I'll let you wear Mommy's clothes and makeup."

"Um, okay." She said uneasily. She knew where he was going with this.

"Okay, but I get to pick out what you wear, and I'll take pictures of you," Pete said.

"So, I'll pretend to be a model, then?" she asked him.

"Yeah, we'll pretend you're a model," he said. He walked into the bedroom and pulled out all of Jacky's lingerie and put it on the bed. He got his camera out and went back into the living room. When he came back he said, "Okay. Go in there and pick something out to wear."

Michelle went into the bedroom and quickly returned in a red and black lace outfit. The women's clothing swam on her

small frame. Pete snapped up pictures quickly. "Michael, go model with your sister. Pretend you are underwear models."

"Does that mean I got to be in my underwear?" Mikey asked.

"Of course. Maybe we can send these in to your talent agent, Michelle. Maybe they will help you get into commercials?" Pete said, trying to make his reasoning sound convincing sound.

"Do I look like a model?" Michelle asked Pete as he took pictures.

"Absolutely!" he said in reassurance. Their naïveté made them gullible and easy targets. It wasn't long before Pete had his hands all over them and had them in the bedroom and on the bed. They wanted this to stop. They wanted this nightmare to be over. But they were afraid to say anything because of all the problems it had created before. They thought that when they had spoken the truth that all of it would come to an end, and now they found themselves here again in the clutches of their stepfather again. Pete got up from the bed and continued to take

photos of the kids. He suddenly heard the sound of gravel popping on the driveway.

"Shit. Your mother's home!" His heart raced at the thought of getting caught. "Go into the bathroom and jump in the bath, Michelle. Michael, you go to the other bathroom and wash up," he said to them. They all raced around. Pete cleaned up the bedroom as fast as he could and locked himself inside the bathroom with Michelle.

"If you say anything to your mom, I'll shoot her, then I'll shoot myself!" he told her. "Do you understand me?" he asked her in a threatening demeanor. She stared at him in fear and slowly nodded her head that she understood. He had many guns and would go target practicing often. The kids had seen him kill many stray cats, and they believed he would shoot them also.

"Hey, kids, I brought you some pizza home," Jacky yelled as she waked into the house. She put the pizza down on the counter. "Where are you guys?" she said loudly as she walked by the spare bathroom and heard the water running. "Mikey, are you in here?" she asked.

"Yeah, I'm taking a bath!" he said with anxiety.

"Well, where's Dad and Michelle?" she asked.

"I don't know. Maybe they're in the other bathroom," he answered. He was afraid. Jacky walked into the back and heard the water running in there. She turned the door handle, but the door was locked. She knocked on the door loudly. Her heart was racing as her thoughts ran rampant.

"Michelle? Pete? Are you in there?" No one answered. She used her fist to pound on the door and there was still no answer. She tried the knob again, but it was still locked. She rattled the door, but it would not open. "Pete, are you in there with her? You better fucking open this door right fucking now," she screamed out loud. No one answered her. She kicked at the door, but it didn't open. She kicked at it again and again. It started to crack and the frame around the door broke. Pete suddenly unlocked the door and opened it. He stood there in his robe, wet from the shower. Michelle stood beside him wrapped in a towel.

"What the hell is going on? What's your problem?" Pete asked her.

"What were you doing with my daughter?" she asked him.

"You almost put a hole in the fucking door. You cracked the whole frame!" he said.

"I asked you what you were doing with my daughter!" she screamed at him.

"Nothing. Nothing, she just needed a bath," he said to her.

"Why were you taking a bath with her? She's old enough to take a bath by herself," Jacky said.

"I wasn't. I took a shower earlier and she needed a bath, so I told her to take one!" he said. "Christ, Jacky what's wrong with you!"

Jacky grabbed Michelle by the arm and pulled her into the living room.

"Are you okay, honey? Did he do anything to you?" Jacky asked her. The girl thought about the threats Pete had

made to her and shook her head no. "Are you sure he didn't touch you or make you do anything?" Jacky asked again, and again the girl shook her head no. The thought of Pete shooting her mother was too much for her to think about. She thought about the stray cats. She didn't want anything bad to happen to her mom. There was no way she could tell her mom. "I want you and Michael to go and get into bed." Jacky walked back into the master bedroom.

"I told you never to touch my children ever again, didn't I?" Jacky screamed.

"Is that what you think is going on in here. I told you nothing happened! Nothing happened! How many times do I have to tell you? Those kids didn't know what they were talking about!" Pete implored her. She was crying hysterically. She walked to the nightstand.

"You're nothing but a fucking liar, like all fucking men, nothing but lying pigs!" she pulled a handgun out of the nightstand and pointed it at him.

"What are you going to do, shoot me?" Pete asked laughing at her. "You crazy bitch! Yeah, you know what? Go ahead and shoot me! You couldn't hit shit with that gun anyway!" he said. "Go ahead and shoot me, right here!" he said, pointing to the center of his chest. "Stupid bitch. You couldn't make it without me! How long do you think you would last without me?" Her hand was sweating, and the trigger became slippery. She held it tightly. The gun popped off like a firecracker. The bullet buzzed passed Pete's head and out the wall behind him. He turned his head and looked at the wall. The bullet had left a small, noticeable hole near the ceiling of the master bedroom. After Pete realized he wasn't shot, he lunged toward the stunned woman and tackled the gun out of her hands.

"I told you I didn't do anything!" he screamed at her. She started sobbing uncontrollably and she slid to the floor. "I can't trust you anymore!" she mumbled in between tears. She sat next to the bed in a fetal position, lost in confusion at what to make of her life.

They argued late into the night. He convinced her that it was yet again another misunderstanding, that she had made it all up in her paranoid mind. He told her that she couldn't make it without him. He convinced her that she was uneducated and that she couldn't afford to support the kids without him. That she would be nothing without him. He told her every reason why she should not do what she knew in her heart she should do. After a few hours of confrontation, she felt exhausted, exhausted mentally and emotionally. She grabbed a few blankets from the hallway closet and fell asleep on the couch. She didn't want to be anywhere near him at the moment. The thought of sleeping next to him irked her and sickened her. Pete rewound the film in the camera, placed it in the black little canister, and set it on the dresser top.

She cleaned the bedroom up a few weeks later and found the roll of film lying on the floor. She picked it up and put it in the drawer where Pete kept all the rolls of undeveloped film he had. Rolls from many family trips and vacations sat in this drawer still waiting to be developed. Undeveloped pictures of

trips to Disneyland, to Yellowstone, camping trips on the river. The rolls were undeveloped and unlabeled.

"Hey, did you find any film by chance in the bedroom recently?" Pete asked Jacky.

"Um, yeah, I found a roll this morning while picking up the house," she told him.

"Well, what did you do with it?" he asked.

"I put it in the drawer with the other rolls," she said.

"What?" he said as he stormed off into the back bedroom. Jacky followed him into the bedroom, where he was going through all the rolls of film in the drawer. "Now I can't tell it from the others," he said.

"What?" she asked.

"You put the roll of film in here before I could mark it, and now I can't tell it from any of the others," he said in a panic.

"Well, why is it so important? What's on it?" she asked him.

"They're just pictures I took!" he said in aggravation.

"Of what?" she asked again.

"Just pictures I took out at the range!" he said, lying to her.

"Well, why are they so important?" she asked.

"Because I told the guys I would get them developed!" he yelled.

"Okay! Well, I'll take them all down and get them all developed. I've been meaning to get around to it anyway," she said.

"No, no! It's okay!" he said. "I'll take care of it!"

She shook her head as she walked out of the bedroom and dismissed the situation. Pete went through roll after roll, repeatedly, but could not tell them apart. He never did find that particular roll of film, and he never got any of that undeveloped film developed. They purposely sat in one of his dresser drawers, undeveloped and untouched for years. Waiting and unnoticed.

Chapter 19 All Hallows Eve

The autumn wind came around once again. The sun had waned

away from that part of the earth, and the early morning frost had

begun to appear on the ground again. With the turning of the

season came the change of color upon the mountains. Oranges

came, then reds, and before too long the leaves fell from the

trees completely, leaving the barren ghosts of the trees behind.

Life was much more complicated for Michael and Michelle now

than it ever had been before. They were now grappling with the

events that were taking place in their home. As things began to

take shape they became much clearer in their young minds. They

had found their voice for a fraction of a moment, but no one was

hearing them. They were screaming into a vacuum and clinging

to the edges of an abyss. The holidays fell in line with the

changing of seasons and brought a temporary distraction from the true problems that were permeating their lives.

They both got up early on Halloween. It was their favorite holiday besides Christmas. They both dressed up every year. This year Michael decided he was going as Frankenstein. He went to his mother's pantry and found some green food coloring. He took it and applied it to his face, neck, arms, and hands. He used black hair spray, turning his fair hair to charcoal gray. He took his mom's eyeliner and drew in some fake scars across his forehead. He put on his black hiking boots and some black slacks he had grown out of a few years ago. He threw makeup powder all over himself, making it look like he had just crawled out of the grave. Finally, he took two old wine corks and superglued them to his neck. In his mind he rivaled the great Boris Karloff. The door rattled. *Boom! Boom! Boom!*

"Come on! I got to get ready," Michelle yelled from the other side of the door.

"Okay, I am almost done," Mikey said. He gave his hair a few more sprays and opened the door.

"God, you're taking forever!" she said overdramatically. They were in sixth grade now. They were so close to being teenagers, and yet it still seemed so far away. They were top of their classes and rulers over the scrubs. *Halloween is going to be off the hook!* Michelle thought, as she looked herself over in the bathroom mirror. Mikey sat at the dining room table eating cereal while she got ready. With every bite the milk in his cereal became greener. Soon there was a rattling on the back-sliding glass door. Mikey opened the blinds to find Kimmy on the other side of the glass. He opened the door.

"It's freezing out there!" she said. "Is your stepdad here?"

"No. He's at work! Thank God!" he said. "She's back there in the bathroom getting ready."

"Okay!" Kimmy said as she barged toward the bathroom. She always had this loud tomboyish personality, but she was fun-loving and high-spirited. When she got to the bathroom she could hear the blow dryer going full blast. She knocked on the

door. Michelle turned off the blow dryer and opened the door. She took one look at Kimmy.

"You're not ready!" she said, irritated.

"Yeah, I couldn't think of what to wear!" Kimmy said. "I thought you could help me!"

Michelle looked at her and shook her head.

"Well, hopefully we aren't late!" she said in irritation. "Okay, let's pick something out." They went into Jacky's room and grabbed some leg warmers, a few long sweaters, and some high heels. Michelle found a few pairs of her own leotards, some brightly colored belts that belonged to Faith, and they were set. It wasn't long before Michelle had her all decked out. They stood in the bathroom crimping and teasing their hair in the big fashion of the eighties. Michelle had a can of pink hair spray and sprayed florescent hues in their kinky crimped hair. They wanted to be Jem, the punk rock girls from the cartoon. They wanted to be "Truly Outrageous!"

"We got to go, or we'll miss the bus!" Michael said as he pounded on the door. The girls scurried and gathered up their things for school.

They walked down Water Canyon Road, heading toward the bus stop. The girls walked unsteadily toward the bus stop in their high heels. Along the way they ran into Frankie and Raul. They hadn't been able to come up with any costume ideas. Mikey had convinced them to put a few holes in some old bed sheets, and come as ghosts, which they did.

"Hey, Mikey, remind me later, I have something to show you!" Frankie said.

"Well, why can't you show me now?" Mikey asked.

"Um, okay!" he said. They were all standing at the stop, waiting for the bus. Frankie nudged Mikey with his elbow. He looked down and saw what looked like a little red bomb.

"What is that?" Mikey asked excitedly.

"Shhh. It's an M80. I got it in Mexico. I was saving it for something special. Don't tell no one!" he said. They got on the overly crowded bus. Everybody on the bus stared at them when

they got on. Half the kids weren't dressed up, and those who were wore kiddy costumes. They held their heads up high and walked toward the back of the bus where the older kids sat.

The bus made its rounds of picking up the kids, then dropped them off at school. All the kids congregated on the playground before the first bell rang. Those who'd dressed up showed off their costumes. When the bell rang, everybody lined up and waited for their teachers to come out of their break room. The three boys went to their separate classes, and the girls went to the class that they shared. School was now in session.

Michelle and Kimmy sat next to each other, they took their backpacks off, and started chatting before the final bell rang to signal class was in session. The teacher stared at them disapprovingly, and after the bell rang she gave roll call. After she was finished, she called the two girls to the front of the classroom.

"Oh no, this will not do!" she said.

"What, Mrs. Davis?" Michelle said. The girls looked at each other, wondering what was going on.

"The way you're dressed! Sorry but you'll have to go to Mr. Jenkins' office," the teacher told them.

"But!" Michelle objected.

"No buts, Michelle. Now go!" she said as she pointed toward the door. They walked out of the classroom and toward the principal's office.

"Into my office, girls," Mr. Jenkins said. The older kids in school called him Big Dick Jenkins. He walked around in these tight khaki pants, his bulge sticking out. Not only was he referred to as Big Dick Jenkins because of his protruding manhood, but also because he was a big dickhead.

"Please, have a seat!" he said. "So, what made you think you could come into school dressed like that?" he asked them.

"Like what?" Michelle said innocently. Kimmy just sat there in silence, wondering how much trouble she and Michelle had gotten themselves into.

"Does your mother know you came to school looking like that?" he asked.

"Looking like what, Mr. Jenkins?" she asked again.

"Like a prostitute!" the overweight secretary said from around the corner. Mr. Jenkins raised his hand to signal to the secretary to mind her own business. Michelle and Kimmy's mouths stood open. They were hurt, they were insulted.

"We are not dressed as prostitutes, Mr. Jenkins!" Michelle said in dismay. "We're punk rockers!"

"Well, whatever you are, you're dressed entirely inappropriate for school! I am going to have to call your mothers to bring you something else to wear!" He picked up the phone and dialed home. The phone rang but there was no answer. Then he tried Kimmy's number; again, no answer.

"Both of our parents are working, Mr. Jenkins!" Kimmy told him.

"Well, I guess you can go back to class, but I am going to keep trying until I hear from somebody!" he said. "We can't have you going around school looking like that!" They walked out of the office feeling like they were on top of the world. They felt, for some reason, that they had gotten away with something.

"I can't believe they thought we dressed up as prostitutes!" Michelle said.

"I know! I can't believe it, either!" Kimmy said. "Hey, Michelle. What is a prostitute anyway?"

"I don't know!" she said. "But I think we look hot! Who cares what they think?" When they returned to class still wearing the costumes, their teacher gave them a disgusted look. When she made eye contact with the girls throughout the rest of the day, she would give them a despised look, roll her eyes, and quickly look away while clutching the cross that hung from her neck.

The morning soon gave way to the afternoon and it was not long until the lunch bell rang. Michael, Frankie, Raul, and Doug quickly ate their lunches. The younger kids were having Halloween parties in class, and where there was Halloween parties, there was Halloween candy. The four boys stood guard at the back-hallway door. Anyone younger than them was required to pay a toll in order to pass. Anyone not willing to pay the toll was harassed until they ponied up the fee. This made for

a very lucrative arrangement. Not only did they score pockets full of candy, but they also scored quite a bit of milk money.

"So, when are we going to see that surprise you were talking about?" Mikey asked Frankie.

"Let's take a walk. I have something to show you!" he said. The boys walked into the bathroom and into the very last toilet stall. "See this stall here?" he said.

"Yeah!" Mikey responded. Frankie suddenly kicked open the stall, revealing a toilet full of toilet paper, piss, and shit. "That's fucking gross!" Mikey said.

"Yeah, I know, I plugged it this morning. We've had our treat," Frankie said, patting his pockets full of stolen candy. "Now we're going to have our trick!"

"What do you mean?" Mikey asked.

"When the final bell rings, you're going to run to the office and tell Jenkins that someone is smoking in the last stall of the guy's bathroom. When he runs down here, I'll light the cherry bomb and throw it in the toilet. And then, ka-splatter!" he

said, laughing. "All over his face! Ol' Big Dick won't even see it coming!"

"What if he sees you?" Mikey asked.

"He won't see me. All he'll see is a ghost!" he said as he pointed to his costume.

"This is going to be classic!" Doug said. "You know, Frankie, I'm proud of you! This is something I should have thought of!"

"Well, if you get caught, you're on your own," Raul said. "I don't want to be a part of this!"

They last bell finally rang. Mikey ran into the office just as planned, and just as planned Jenkins took the bait. Raul signaled to Frankie that Jenkins was on the approach. When he rounded the corner, Jenkins rushed up on him.

"What do you think you kids are doing in here?" he yelled. Frankie lit the cherry bomb and threw it in the toilet. He ran past Jenkins and out of the bathroom. Jenkins tried to grab him as he ran by, but he only managed to snag a little of his sheet. Jenkins looked in the stall, thinking he would find a lit

cigarette or a pack of smokes. Suddenly a shotgun blast went off, spraying him head to toe with shit and piss-soaked toilet paper.

The whole playground turned at the sound of the cherry bomb going off. They saw a ghost running out the back door of the hallway. Jenkins ran out soaking wet and covered in shitty debris. He slipped around, trying to chase after the ghost, but he fell, and the ghost vanished. Jenkins got up and kicked the hallway doors open. He stomped and cursed out loud as he trudged down the hallway, little bits of toilet paper and fecal matter splashed across his button-down shirt and his neatly pressed khakis.

Meanwhile Frankie rounded the back of the school. He tore off his costume and threw it into a Dumpster. He sat behind the sanitation bin, breathing heavily. When he caught his breath, he calmly walked to the line of kids waiting to get on the bus. He looked around and saw about half a dozen other kids dressed up as ghosts. He knew he was safe. The principal's voice rang out over the PA.

"Anyone with information about the firecracker incident is highly encouraged to come forth and report this information to the office immediately," he said in a loud and angry voice. Suddenly the entire student body erupted in laughter, and feeling it was safe to do so, Frankie erupted in laughter as well.

The kids were out of school to officially start celebrating Halloween. They congregated at Mikey and Michelle's house until right before the sun went down. "Oh my God! Look at you kids! You look amazing!" She said. "Let me a few pictures of you kids." Jacky said. She lined up the kids and took a few shots with the Polaroid camera. "Okay and just one more!"

"Okay mom!" Mikey said. "Daylights burning here!"

"Okay." She said. Jacky loaded all the kids up in her Buick, and they headed to town to start the trick-or-treating.

"So what street should we start on?" Mikey asked Michelle.

"What are you talking about? Kimmy and I are going to meet up with Jason and his friends by the park. And you're not

going to say anything to Mom, are you?" she said, trying to instill a bit of fear into him.

"All right, all right. I won't say a peep. Just don't expect me to be giving you any of my candy when she asks why your sack is empty!" he said.

"Whatever, Michael!" she said to him as she shrugged off what he had said.

"Yeah, whatever, Michael,'" Kimmy reiterated as they turned around with a swish of pink crimped hair.

"I guess that means more for us guys," Michael said to the boys.

Jacky dropped them off near the park as Michelle had asked her to do.

"Don't forget I'll meet you here at about eleven," Jacky told them.

"Okay, Mom!" the kids said in as they ran off in different directions. The boys ran up as fast as they could to every house they came across. They piled past the little kids, running up and ringing doorbells before their smaller counterparts could catch

up. They zigzagged up and down the neighborhoods. Up one side of the block and down the other. They blew past the unlit houses, and the houses with porch lights turned out. This was a telltale sign that either nobody was home or that those homes had already run out of candy. Some people were even stupid enough to leave their bowls of candy outside with little notes attached saying, "Please only take one!" The boys walked up to these gold mines, giggled with sinister laughter, and each poured a portion of the bowl into their sacks. Trusting kids with a sweet tooth with candy is like trusting a crackhead with your purse or wallet.

Meanwhile Michelle and Kimmy met up with Jason and a few of his friends. Jason had always been the tallest boy in class, giving him the illusion of being the oldest. He was always picked first for sports in PE class. He always made pitcher in Little League baseball, and quarterback on the youth football team.

"So, what are you girls up to tonight?" Jason asked them.

"Nothing?" the girls said in sync as they smacked on their gum.

"Ever TP'd a house?" Jason said, sounding so mature to the girls.

"No. What's that?" Michelle said as she blinked up at him in admiration.

"You know, rolled a house, toilet papered?" he said, shaking his head. She stared at him, not knowing what to say and not wanting to show her inexperience. "Come on, let's go," he said as they headed out. "There's a teacher that lives a few blocks over, Mr. Remming. He's my brother's teacher and I hear he's a real dick," Jason said.

They walked a few blocks over from the park. Jason held Michelle's hand, and Kimmy holding the hand of one of the other boys. All the boys were wearing backpacks filled with toilet paper and eggs. As they came upon the house, they noticed that it was dark.

"Looks likes nobody's home!" Jason said in excitement. He handed Michelle and Kimmy each a roll of toilet paper. "Just

382

unroll them a bit and throw them over the tree, like this," he said, hurling the roll he held. It sailed through the air, up and over the tree. The roll of paper dropped down to the ground and left a draping loop of paper in its trail. "When it drops to the ground, pick it up and throw it over again. Keep doing it until the roll runs out," he explained. Kimmy, Michelle, and the tall boy from class began throwing the toilet paper back and forth over the trees. Michelle looked around after a moment and was amazed. All the strands of toilet paper hung down off the nearly barren tree branches. Strands of paper were everywhere and swayed in the cool autumn breeze. It was mesmerizing and somehow beautiful. And to Michelle it was almost romantic. Jason came up to her and planted a kiss on her lips, completing her perfect Halloween night. It was her first real kiss. Blood rushed to her face and she blushed bashfully. They pulled the carton of eggs from the backpack and unloaded on the unsuspecting teacher's car and RV that were parked in the driveway. They unloaded on the front door as yellow yolk ran down the face of the door. The porch light suddenly flickered on,

illuminating the kids in the darkness. They scattered like cockroaches into the night.

"What the hell you kids think you're doing out here!" a voice erupted from the front porch of the home. The man raised a shotgun in the air and let out a blast. The kids hit the ground as their ear drums rang. "You get the fuck off my property or I'll put a hole in all your asses!" He walked out onto his lawn to see the tree in his front yard decorated in Quilted Northern extra-soft toilet paper. "You fucking little bastards! If I catch up to you, you're all dead! You hear me! I'm gonna bust your asses," he yelled at the silhouettes running down the street. He turned around to see his front door and vehicles covered in egg yolk. "God damn it!" He said raising the gun to the air and screaming.

The kids made their way down the block, laughing at the destructive beauty they had created.

"Man, old man Remming was pissed!" said one of the boys, laughing.

"Yeah, did you see the look on the old geezer's face!" Jason said. "We're lucky the old bastard didn't shoot our asses!"

"Dude, I totally thought we were done for!" one of the other boys chimed in. "I about shit when that light came on!"

"My brother's going to be so proud of me!" Jason said. "At least he'll have something to brag about on Monday!"

They walked until they got to the nearby park. They all sat there on the picnic tables out of breath. Michelle and Jason had never lost each other's grip as they ran down the street. He took out a little pocket knife, carved their initials into the soft pine wood, and scraped a heart around it. They sat at the top of the metal slide holding hands and kissing. They stared into the night sky that was littered with stars like diamonds. She wanted this moment to last forever. But young love is like a shooting star. It streams across the sky fast and bright, only to fizzle out in to a cinder on the horizon. Michelle looked down at the Swatches that were banded one after another up her wrist.

"Shoot. I've got to go; I'm supposed to meet my mom," she said suddenly. She pulled away from Jason, but he would not let her go.

"One more thing," he said as he pulled her close to him. He kissed her with passion. As he opened his mouth, she opened hers. Kimmy watched as they kissed. She felt left out. She suddenly turned to the boy whose hand she was holding, grabbed him by the face, and planted a wet one on him, forcing her tongue into his mouth. The boy seemed shocked and uncertain.

"So, I'll see you at school then?" Jason asked Michelle.

"Yeah!" she said as she felt a tingling sensation come over her. She felt almost dizzy. "I'll see you at school!" They stared at each other for a moment until she remembered the time. She grabbed Kimmy and tried to pull her off the other young boy.

"Come on, Kimmy. We're going to be late!"

When the girls got down the street, they soon realized they had no candy to prove that they had been trick-or-treating. As Michael had suspected, Michelle turned to him to get her out of her jam.

"Can I have some of your candy!"

"No way," he said. "Do you know how long I worked to get all this candy?"

"I don't want to keep it! I just don't want Mom to be suspicious and start asking questions," she pleaded with him. "Come on, just give me some. I promise when we get home I'll give it right back to you. I just don't want to show up with an empty pillowcase," she pleaded.

"Well, maybe, if you actually would have gone trick-or-treating, you wouldn't be asking for ours," Michael said. After some more begging and pleading, the boys shared the loot, but only on the condition that they would get it back after the car ride home.

After they got home, Michael told Michelle she could have some of his candy if she helped him sort it out and look for anything unusual. The kids sat up in Mikey's room past midnight going through the candy. Michelle and Kimmy shared with the boys the story of their first kiss and their first toilet-papering experience. The boys pretended not to listen.

Chapter 20 The Watchers

The night teetered on the brink of early morning. The darkness

of the sky was only lit by the scattered stars of the Milky Way.

The winter had caught hold of the air but had not yet produced

any storms. The night was cold like steel, but the sky was clear.

Pete stumbled into the house. He swayed back and forth barely

able to control his inebriated body and mind. He walked over to

the refrigerator, grabbed a beer, and cracked it open. He fumbled

around in his pocket for his cigarettes then lit one up. The wood

burning stove, sitting in the corner of the den, still burned hot.

He gazed into the flames barely able to keep his eyes open. He

stumbled back a few steps, then overcorrected himself, and

stumbled forward. He put out his hand to catch himself, burning

the palm of his hand. The pain only momentarily catching his

attention. He fell to the floor, dropping his cigarette, and

clutching his hand to his chest. He laid on his back cradling his hand. Before too long his eyes rolled into the back of his head and he fell asleep.

Michelle lay next to her sister Faith on the bed that they shared. The girls huddled under the thick winter blankets in deep sleep and lost in a world of their own imaginations. A glint of light caught the edge of Michelle's eyelids. Slowly she opened her eyes as she was awoken out of her slumber. She blinked as she caught her breath behind clenched teeth. Her body stiffened like a board. In front of her, floating a few feet above the bed, was a soft blue light the size of a tennis ball. She could not believe her eyes. The glowing ball of warmth sat over them in what seemed like observation. It hummed with a rhythm and pulsed in luminescence. It radiated as it seemed to be studying them. It seemed to be keenly aware of their presence. Suddenly the globe of light split up into three smaller orbs of light. The lights floated up and spread across the room. They floated towards pictures hanging on the wall. They floated along the tops of the dressers as if they were investigating the trinkets that lay there. They flew

with perfection, never knocking anything over. They came

hovering over the girls as they lay in their bed. Michelle closed

her eyes as one of the orbs came near to her face. She could feel

its pulsating presence near her skin. She pushed the back of her

head into her pillow, and squeezed her eyes tightly shut. She

could feel the warmth emanating from the globe. The glow

faded, and she opened her eyes to see the orb had backed away

from her. Something else had caught its attention. Suddenly the

globes of light collected over the bed into one large orb again.

Then it disappeared. She suddenly closed her eyes and fell back

to sleep as if she had never been disturbed in the first place.

Michael was lying in the other bedroom fast asleep.

Suddenly he was awoken by an intense white light that flooded

into his dream. He opened his sleepy eyes to see his room

become flooded with pale light. The light grew with such an

intensity that the corners of the room itself became

indistinguishable.

The objects hanging on the walls were unperceivable as

they were washed away in the light. The headboard of his bed

sat up against the window of his room. He lifted his head from his pillow and looked out the window. The entire end of the house where their bedrooms sat was engulfed in white light. It sat outside his window like a star hovering directly over that end of the house. It hummed, so as to ring in his eardrums. Suddenly the light backed away from the house and hovered over the ground for a second. It then shot out into the dark horizon and disappeared into space like a fading star. He lay in his bed for a moment, unsure of what had just taken place. He then laid his head down as he fell back into a peaceful sleep. It was almost as if the incident had not happened. It was almost as if it were a fiber woven into the fabric of his dreams.

Pete fell into a deep sleep. His leg leaning against the hot metal of the wood stove. Light danced around his eyes. He could feel himself falling back, sinking like a stone into an abyss, into a chasm he could not see the bottom of. As he fell deeper the warmer it became. He could feel himself become hotter and he began to sweat. He looked down noticing that he was nude and without clothing. He went to cover himself but could find no

stich of cloth. There was nowhere to hide. He was already

exposed. He felt vulnerable and afraid. He felt the sensation of

hands pulling him further into the abyss, and as hard as he tried

to pull himself free, the further they dragged him down. He

heard laughter that seemed to echo off into eternity. Memories of

his life flew before him like burning leaves. He reached out for

them, but they turned to cinders. He felt a panic and a sense of

dread the further he sank. He was trying to remember what he

was doing right before all is this had started. *"Where am I? What

was I doing? How did I get here?"* he thought to himself.

"You know how you got here?" a voice came to him.

"Who's that?" he asked as the air seemed to seep from

his lungs. The laughter came again, reverberating through the

chasm he found himself in. It was like that of a thousand voices

all laughing at once.

*"You don't know? Come on, do I really have to spell it

out for you?"*

"Spell what out?" he asked to the incorporeal voice.

"What it is you are doing here? Why it is that you are here?"

"I don't know! Really I don't know!" he said. He could feel the heat becoming intense. He squirmed like a worm on a hook, but he could not free himself. He looked down and saw that he was suspended over a sea of fire that spread out as far as he could see. His toes began to burn. Sweat poured from him profusely. He tried to pull his feet from the fire, but to no avail. He screamed out in pain. His voice echoed through the abyss above him. *"Please stop!"* he cried.

"You're doing it?" the disembodied voice came again as the heat receded for a moment. *"Things could have been so different."*

"What's that supposed to mean?" Pete asked. A flood of memories came to him. Memories of the kids and what he had done, memories of Jacky, memories of his own flesh and blood daughter. Memories of every child he had violated, every wrong he had committed came to him. Then images of another world came to him, images of all that could have been came to him.

Images of him standing tall and proud. Images of a loving family gazing upon a loving father.

"This could have been yours, but you gave it all away." the voice came. He could feel himself being lowered into the fire. The burning moved from his feet up his leg. He shook his head in pain. He squirmed back and forth screaming at the agony he found himself in. *"No!"* He screamed out. He opened his eyes holding his leg. He was once again in the den. A hole had burned straight through his denim jeans. The flesh of his leg was blistered and blackened. The muscle of his leg under the skin had been exposed. The wood stove had nearly caught his leg on fire. He pulled the burning denim from his body and hobbled into the master bedroom where Jacky was sleeping. "I need you to take me to the hospital. I burned the shit out of myself." he shouted out to her.

"How the hell did you manage to do that?" Jacky asked still trying to shake the sleep from her mind.

"I fell asleep in front of the fire place." He told her. She looked at his leg and could see that the burn was severe. She got

up, got dressed, and helped him to the car. She could smell alcohol coming from him and knew how he had managed the burn. A part of herself didn't want to feel any sympathy for him, which conflicted with her instincts to care for him and help heal his wounds. The burn was severe enough that it required a few days in the hospital and skin grafts to cover the burn area.

A few weeks had passed, and nothing was mentioned of the luminous display of lights in the children's bedrooms. In the wake of Pete's injury, the strange lights were almost forgotten. Jacky, Faith, and the twins were in the kitchen as Jacky was preparing dinner. Faith was at the stove stirring a pot of boiling greens beans. She seemed to be lost in a thought when memories began to flood her mind.

"Oh, I forgot to tell you!" Faith said suddenly. "I saw the strangest lights in my room the other night!" Michelle froze at what she said.

"What kind of lights?" Jacky asked.

"I don't know…they were just floating above my bed!" she said. "I just sat there frozen as they moved around my room!"

"Were there three of them and were they kind of bluish!" Michelle said, cutting in.

"Yeah, you saw them, too!" Faith said in disbelief. "I thought for a moment it was a dream!"

"Yeah, I saw it start as one light and then it split up into three lights," Michelle explained.

"Then it went back into one light," Faith said as she finished her sentence.

"Yeah!" Michelle said in confirmation.

"Well, what do you think it was?" Jacky asked.

"I don't know but it was creepy!" Faith said. "Maybe they were spirits."

"Maybe they were angels?" Michelle said.

Michael sat there listening to the story when his mind flashed to a bunch of his own recent memories.

"I saw a bright white light outside my room one night!" he said. "I wonder if it was on the same night?" he said.

"You saw a white light outside your room? What did it look like?" Jacky asked. She was amazed at what was coming out of her kids' mouths. Chills sent goose bumps across her skin.

"It was really bright, and it woke me up! It was so bright, I couldn't see anything in my room! It was just floating off the ground outside and was making a strange humming noise. Then it backed up and took off over the mountains," he said.

"Well, why didn't you come and wake me up?" Jacky asked.

"I don't know! It happened so fast! Then it was gone, and I fell back asleep. I thought I was dreaming!" he said. They all three sat there in amazement.

"Maybe it was a UFO?" Michael said in excitement.

"No, don't be silly!" Jacky said.

"Maybe it was an angel?" Michelle suggested again.

"Well, whatever it was, it is gone now. Besides, it doesn't seem like it was harmful, was it?" Jacky asked.

"No!" they all said.

"Maybe it was your grandma Bessie?" Jacky suggested.

They never did find out what the light was. Whether it was extraterrestrial or whether it was angelic could not be determined. Whatever it was, it was benevolent, and it was intelligent. After its appearance it brought a wave of changes in its wake. Kimmy and her family soon moved closer to town. Kimmy became enrolled in a different school, and she soon she fell out of communication with Michelle. Maybe it was the painful memories that drove them apart, maybe they just grew apart after some time. Soon after that Jacky and Pete put the house on Water Canyon up for sale. The old sign Pete had made to christen the property, "The Someday Ranch," had years ago fallen from its post. It now lay on the ground covered by dirt and overgrown grasses. Termites ate away at the soft pine wood. It was now a relic of a past that was trying to be forgotten.   They bought another home across the other side of the valley. They sold off all their livestock, including the horses. This made Mikey happy, for now he would no longer have to wake up early

to feed all the animals. Frankie and Raul's family stayed for a few years afterward, but they, too, put their house up for sale and eventually moved closer to town. They were the last to leave the old neighborhood. With that, the old neighborhood was never the same. Nothing was left of that place for them except the memories they carried with them. New people soon moved in to fill the vacancies they had left behind. The old neighborhood was reborn with new families, and with them new moments and new memories were created.

The molesting stopped not long after the move to the new home. The twins were getting older now and pretty much tried to steer clear of Pete. They began to create social lives outside of the house, and they made it so there was less contact between him and themselves. In its void Pete began sowing a new seed. A seed of possession and a seed of control. Anger grew inside of him. A loathing grew in him over the fact that he no longer had complete control over the twins. Because he could no longer touch them, he began trying to control them in other ways. To make up for the urges that lay unfulfilled inside his

body and mind, he found new ways to control them, and he

clamped down on anything he still had domination over. He

especially tried to exert his domination over Michelle. She was

growing into a young woman, and he hated that he couldn't

oppress her any longer. The more he tried to put her under his

thumb, the more she resisted him.

Around this time, he quit drinking and became a born-

again Christian. He convinced himself that he was now saved,

and that it was now up his duty to save everybody else. It was

now his responsibility to right all the wrongs he found in the

world, and to turn those who were lacking in Christ back to the

church. He had been saved, and now he wanted to be play

savior. He found his platform and his pedestal. He lifted himself

upon his soapbox and started preaching to the family of all the

ills of the world. He tried to implement a weekly Bible study and

forced the entire family into conversation about Christ. He

bought computerized versions of the Bible, and simultaneously

he downloaded software that alerted Jacky should he be tempted

to check out online pornography. It was as if he had no self-

control, and to keep himself from falling victim to the devil's grip, he used an automated system to keep himself in check. He preached about forgiveness, but what he really wanted was for everyone to forget. He wanted everyone to believe that he had changed and that he was a different man. He was no longer the child-molesting pedophile. He was Pete, the law-abiding, born-again correctional officer.

When his new religious order was met with skepticism, he became angry and defensive. What he failed to realize was that it was too late, that there would be no forgiveness, and that the twins could never forget what he had done to them. Quitting drinking brought to Pete a new focus. He soon forgot about his sins and moved on to pointing out the sins of others. Even as he found his new faith, he still molested. When he could no longer molest in touch, he would molest in mind. No matter how he might pray, he alone could never change the animal he was inside. And although the blackness inside his soul was buried, it still controlled and executed power over him. No matter how

hard he prayed, he could not bury his demons. No matter how

hard he tried, he could not bury the ghosts of the past.

Chapter 21 A Mother's Love

We are all born into this life with a set of conditions, a set of circumstances, a set of situations. We all take a chance with the roll of the dice, and we all must play the hand that we have been dealt. These situations and these circumstances exist because of the decisions our parents have made, and the decisions made by their parents before them. And so, it goes, back until the beginning of time. Some of these decisions are made by circumstances that are beyond our control, and some of the situations are created by the decisions we make of our own free will. When all these little, seemingly unrelated, variables add up, the equation of life is made. Some of us are born into a wealthy life, and some of us are born poor. Some of these lives are healthy and happy, while other lives involve sadness and instability. This truth crosses all social lines. Maybe somewhere

in a time before we are born, we make a pact with God, or the creator, or whatever you might call it. Maybe, before we are born, we agree to live the life we are getting ready to travel into. Maybe we accept the circumstances to a life yet unfolded. Or maybe there is no meaning or order to this chaos; we are born and then we die, and that is the end of the story. As we start to grow up, we start to grow into the circumstances that surround us. These circumstances start to take shape and mold the people that we will become. Somewhere down the line of time, we either allow these circumstances to continue to mold us, or we take what we have learned from these situations and decide to move beyond them. We begin to take control of our own lives. Somewhere we must decide to continue down the path that we have come into or choose a different path and break the molds we have been cast into. We must realize that there are things about our lives that we cannot change and cannot control, just as we must realize that we are the only ones in charge of our future and our destinies. We must come to terms with the fact that the past is set in stone and that it cannot be relived or retold. We

must realize that at some point it is up to us to shape and mold our own lives and the people that we will become. The only thing we have some control over is the future and the people we want to become. The future is wide-open, and this is where free will comes in.

Jacky worked long days in the valley down below. She cleaned the tract housing of new developments in Lancaster and Palmdale that were springing up all over the place. She took razor blades to the windows, scraping off stucco, plaster, and paint. She cleaned windows by hanging herself outside second story levels. She vacuumed out window tracks full of dirt and debris so that the new owners would be able to slide the windows back and forth with ease. She cleaned toilets with Comet until her hands were so dry they would crack and bleed. She removed construction debris from the bathtubs and the bedrooms, from the living rooms and the kitchens sinks. She would vacuum up tiny curled-up pieces from the freshly laid carpet that was strewn throughout the houses. She vacuumed out all the cabinets and drawers of debris. She wiped down all the

wood cabinetry and applied polish to make them shine. The owners of the new homes would walk into the freshly cleaned homes with the smell of household cleaners and freshly laid carpet in the air. And after they moved in, the houses would never be as clean as they were at that moment. And when Jacky finished with one house, she would walk outside, look down the street at all the newly built homes, and continue to the next.

After her grueling day of twelve hours, elbows deep in razor blades and cleaning products, she would come home to the excited faces of her children. The kids immediately dropped whatever it was that they were doing and rushed to meet her as her car pulled into the driveway. They ran toward her beat-up Buick with excitement in their hearts. She got out of the car, tired from her long day of cleaning cold houses with cold water. Her hands and her hair would smell of bleach, Ajax, and ammonia. Her hands and her feet were always dry and cracked. She seldom wore sneakers but instead preferred sandals and flip-flops, even in the cold of winter. She always greeted her kids with love and enthusiasm, even when she had no energy and she

wanted to fall down from fatigue. She always embraced them warmly even if it had been a rough day. If she had the energy, she would ask about their day at school and how things were going. Did they get their homework done? Were they keeping up with their grades? Did they clean up their rooms and finish their chores? Were the chickens, rabbits, and horses fed? How about the dogs and cats? Then she would go into the kitchen with her waning energy and get dinner started. She was an extremely good cook. She pulled things from the pantry and the freezer, and usually within a half an hour dinner would be on the table.

After dinner she would go into her bathroom and draw a bath full of steaming hot water. She added Epsom salts or Calgon if she could afford it. She lay in soothing hot water and let her tightened muscles soak until the tensions faded away, the day's work soothing its way out of her body. She would later emerge from the bathroom in her turquoise bathrobe with her hair wrapped up in a towel. She lay on the couch and unwrapped her hair, brushing the kinks and the tangles out of it. The twins ran up to her to fight over who got to sit in between the cushions

of the couch and the crook of her knees, like cubs sitting in the bodily warmth of their mother bear. Soon the twins got to be too big to fit in the small space of the crook of her knees. They didn't seem to realize this and felt rejected when she would no longer allow them to sit there as they had from the time they were old enough to crawl.

New babies are born to be doted over and coddled. They become the center of a mother's attention. With blinking eyes full of bewilderment and amazement, they stare into the faces of these women looking down at them. Women hold them and cradle them even if they are not their own. To enjoy her newborns' preciousness, their soft skin, and their blinking eyes, is one of the high points of a woman's existence. Those first three to four years are when a mother's love is of most importance. The feeding of the breast to supply nutrients, the cleansing and changing of the diapers, and the constant teaching of walking and talking are the fundamental building blocks of a baby's young life. Somewhere as time passes children's legs will grow. Their ability to walk and talk provides them with

independence from their mother. They learn to leave the nest and soon become their own persons. And as children grow, they no longer are their mother's babies, but instead become her children. This, to a child, is a rude awakening in life. Children realize this when a new child is born and soaks up their mother's attention. They know that they will never be coddled and doted over in that way again, and they yearn to be the focus of their mother's attention like they once were. This is where sibling rivalry is born. Even as adults, when things get tough and hard to handle, adults yearn to be held in the arms of their mother. They want her to wipe away the tears and for her to kiss away the pain. But those days fall by the wayside. Now they must learn to stand upon their own two feet. Such is the way of life, but if you were to ask almost anyone, they would give it all up for the chance to spend one more moment held close to her bosom and to become the center of her world once again.

Continue reading in The Land of Four Season Part 2.

Made in the USA
Lexington, KY
15 April 2018